The White Stuff

By the Same Author

FICTION

Little Green Man

NON-FICTION

All Points North

POETRY

Zoom!

Xanadu

Kid

Book of Matches

Moon Country

The Dead Sea Poems

CloudCuckooLand

Killing Time

Travelling Songs

Selected Poems

The Universal Home Doctor

The White Stuff

SIMON ARMITAGE

VIKING
an imprint of
PENGUIN BOOKS

VIKING

Published by the Penguin Group
Penguin Books Ltd, 80 Strand, London WC2R 0RL, England
Penguin Group (USA) Inc., 375 Hudson Street, New York, New York 10014, USA
Penguin Books Australia Ltd, 250 Camberwell Road, Camberwell, Victoria 3124, Australia
Penguin Books Canada Ltd, 10 Alcorn Avenue, Toronto, Ontario, Canada M4V 3B2
Penguin Books India (P) Ltd, 11 Community Centre, Panchsheel Park, New Delhi – 110 017, India
Penguin Books (NZ) Ltd, Cnr Rosedale and Airborne Roads, Albany, Auckland, New Zealand
Penguin Books (South Africa) (Pty) Ltd, 24 Sturdee Avenue, Rosebank 2196, South Africa

Penguin Books Ltd, Registered Offices: 80 Strand, London WC2R 0RL, England

www.penguin.com

First published 2004

I

Copyright © Simon Armitage, 2004

The moral right of the author has been asserted

Set in 12/14.75pt Monotype Dante
Typeset by Rowland Phototypesetting Ltd, Bury St Edmunds, Suffolk
Printed in Great Britain by Clays Ltd, St Ives plc

A CIP catalogue record for this book is available from the British Library

ISBN 0-670-91343-X

IN THE BEGINNING

The Sperm Test

It is not one test, but many. To begin with, the man must abstain from sexual activity for at least seventy-two hours but no longer than a week. It is a test of self-restraint.

At lunchtime on the chosen day he drives from his place of work to the peace, comfort and safety of his own home. But builders are at work. Builders are dry-lining the kitchen wall, listening to Radio 1, whistling, tramping in and out and up and down for electricity, water, coffee with sugar. At this point the man has second thoughts, but the idea of a further period of abstinence concentrates his mind. It is a test of time. With container in hand, he locks himself in the innermost room – a toilet without windows – and settles to the task. He is well practised, for sure, something of an expert even, though the pressure of wanting to do well cannot be ignored, and right now he will confess to ignorance and doubts. He has no memory of actually measuring his output and nothing but anecdotal evidence as to the productivity of others. A teaspoonful, didn't somebody once say? In which case, why the big brown pot? A soup spoon, perhaps? A fruit spoon? This mental calibration of domestic cutlery in no way helps him towards his objective, though it has, in fact, assisted in blanking out the noises of manly builders from down below.

Eventually, miraculously, it happens. The amount seems reasonable. Not too stingy, not too flash. It sits in the pot like mother-of-pearl in its fluid state. Steam clouds the container when the lid is replaced. Memories of insects caught in boxes and bottles come to mind, pricking holes in jam-jar lids so a beetle or snail might breathe. The container is blood-warm in the man's hand.

The next stage is a driving test. There's a twenty-minute time limit to reach the local infirmary. After washing his hands and making plausible

*small talk with the workmen ('When you've got to go you've got to go!'),
the man accelerates down the hill towards town and enters the ring road.
The traffic is heavy. Normally a reliable motorist, he makes mistakes. The
plastic container, now tucked in his left armpit, proves a hindrance to
driver-related manoeuvres, and the digital clock on the dashboard adds
on time penalties for violations. He has not been requested to transport
his sample in that particular cavity, but common logic and folklore inform
him that cold air might kill off a few million or so of the little critters,
whereas body temperature will keep them alive and active and make for
a respectable score. It is a case of lateral thinking. During a hill-start
involving use of the handbrake, the pot slides down inside his shirt, where
it has to stay until the long, straight urban clearway offers the opportunity
of one-handed steering and retrieval.*

*At the hospital the man double-parks in the ambulance bay before
entering the maze of corridors, the pot of liquid crystal cooling minute by
minute. It is a map-reading test, and a test of language. How to find the
way to the correct room without asking. How to ask without using the
S word. How to say 'sperm' without turning beetroot red. There's a bell
at the side of the hatch which must be rung. He rings it again, and then
again, before reading the handwritten note to the side, stating <u>The
Department of Urinary Medicine is open all day except on Tuesday, when
it will close at 2 p.m.</u> The man scans the week-to-view diary in his brain
for the day of the week. It is Tuesday. He looks down at his watch, where
the hour hand cowers behind the minute hand in the vicinity of ten past
two. He keeps his finger on the button, the button that makes the bell ring
in a faraway room, until nobody comes. Then he walks in a controlled
rage back to his car, and sits for a while, and burns.*

*Of course, he's tempted to hurl the container of cold and expired
substance from the vehicle window as he sweeps back along the urban
clearway. But this is sperm. <u>His</u> sperm. It is a test of pride. He returns to
his house, blusters past the workmen in their lumberjack shirts and
Timberland boots, and washes out the pot in the bathroom sink with hot
water and a finger. It will dry on the bathroom radiator. It will, as they
say, come in again.*

★

It is a month later. The man now looks on the previous episode as a dress-rehearsal. It is a memory test. It is a Monday or a Wednesday or a Thursday or a Friday when he rings the bell. The nurse who opens the hatch looks down at the brown plastic pot, a quarter full with the slow-moving balm of silver, mercury, graphite, latex, frog spawn, whatever, and asks, 'Is it urine or sperm?'

The man also looks down at the pot, then back at the nurse, then back at the pot, then back at the nurse, and replies, 'It's sperm.'

The deposit is made. He withdraws from the hospital, free to resume sexual intercourse and await his results by post.

Results, when they arrive, are meaningless to the layman, and easily mistaken for population statistics in the Third World or light-year distances to the nearest stars. But the man observes the word NORMAL stamped beneath the astronomical number and is satisfied. Content. Relieved.

That is not the end of the test. What follows is a test of courage, a test of spunk. It begins six months down the line, at seven in the morning, when the woman stands in the bedroom doorway holding a tissue between her legs, saying, 'I'm bleeding.' On a mobile phone, an emergency doctor explains how this can be quite normal, even at twelve weeks, but the test continues at midday, when the blood begins again, and this time it is not red but brown. Not red but brown. Pulling books out from under the bed and checking <u>The Fountain of Health</u> *for the meaning of brown blood is a test of understanding. A comprehension test.*

In the car, making the drive to the hospital, the woman says, 'I'm frightened,' and for the man this is a test of strength. The trick is to stay calm. To give reassurance. To say there is absolutely nothing to worry about. To drive carefully. To tolerate the pay-and-display machine in the hospital car park which demands money for the privilege of the visit. To be patient with the receptionist behind the slotted window who needs forms to be filled out in capital letters.

In a cubicle, a nurse with a pierced nose asks questions and takes notes. A junior doctor and his student enter the room to take measurements, either by inflating a blue hoop around the woman's biceps or by putting a thermometer in her ear, or by making other insertions. In their over-size white coats, the medics stand like two boys in their dressing gowns, ready for bed. They could be trailing teddy bears behind them, sucking their thumbs, except the words they use are adult words. For grown-ups only. Not for little ears.

It is not the end of the test. It is 'hard to tell'. It is 'too early to say'. More tests need to be done. The woman will stay overnight, the man will go home, come back with a nightie and toothbrush, go home again.

The twelve hours that follow are a test of stamina, patience and faith. Alone in the house, the man moves between rooms. Thinks between phone calls. Flits between chairs. He sleeps between dreams, dreams between sleep. If it is bad for him, it is worse for her. Between drinks he tells himself this. It is a waiting game, an endurance test, a test of nerve. Next morning when the alarm goes off it might as well talk to the wall, because the man is long gone: down the hill, on to the ring road, the underpass, the clearway, and into the car park. CLAMPERS AT WORK. THIS IS A TOW-AWAY ZONE.

In a glass-fronted room off the ward, behind a pink-grey curtain, a sonographer spoons a dollop of clear gel on to the woman's stomach and guides what looks like a computer mouse from side to side, up and down, sometimes pressing hard into the flesh, sometimes easing back. It is a screen test now. On the monitor, a vague, grainy picture comes and goes. The man smiles at the woman, who cannot see the screen, and reads the expression of the sonographer, a lady in her thirties, pregnant, who bites her lip as she stares at the image in front of her eyes but never blinks. There will have to be another type of scan, another insertion, another doctor, private discussions. Then a consultant to ask both the man and the woman to take a seat. Please. Screens are pulled back, equipment wheeled away. 'Please sit down.'

The next step is a multiple choice. Choice A: get rid now, because there is no pulse, no heartbeat, and it is very tiny indeed, and its bones are not bones at all but uncalcified strips of malformed cartilage. It probably died two weeks ago, and no baby ever came back from the dead. Choice B: wait for a week, during which time the pregnancy will abort naturally, possibly, but not necessarily at a convenient time. In other words, no choice at all. This is not the end of the test. Ten minutes later, in a private room, the woman turns to the man and says to him, 'You won't leave me now, will you?' It is a lie-detector test. A test of the truth.

Flowers pile up on the doorstep the next day. Neither the woman nor the man will answer the bell. The woman stares out of the window and says, 'I want my baby back.' Time will pass – that's what everyone says. The future is somewhere over the next hill, like the sky, but arrives every day full of clouds from the past. Night follows day. From the window, the woman stares and stares. The man waits. However it is for him, it is worse for her. It is a test of guts now, the acid test. It is a test of balls, a blood test, and a test of heart.

TAURUS *(20 April–20 May)*

I

The flat roof of Sconford and Tilden County Primary and Infant School was littered with pop bottles, Ribena cartons, sweet packets, half-bricks and several shoes. The roof itself was in need of repair. In three separate places the bitumen had bubbled and cracked, and from the water tank to the air vent a large fissure had opened up that reminded Felix of one of those mid-ocean trenches in a geography textbook. Not that any of this would have been apparent to the parents, teachers and former pupils beneath it in the glass-fronted reception area, lifting glasses of sherry to their mouths and circling around a huge platter of crisps and snacks. From his position on top of the slide, Felix had an unobstructed view of the whole school. Squeezing the record button with his thumb, he panned slowly from left to right, taking in the crowd of adults lining all four sides of the playground and the decorated podium with its row of empty chairs, then swung the camera high towards the school flag flapping in the breeze. From the flagpole, he followed a strip of lightning-conductor down the brick wall, then along a line of blue and white bunting tied to a handle inside the louvre window over the main entrance. Through the glass, the culminating moment of this long sequence should have been a face. Abbie's face, under her new lilac hat, smiling and chatting with some long-lost friend or raising her amber-coloured drink to the air, toasting the sunlight. But the image was fuzzy and blurred, and when it finally resolved, the subject of the auto-focus turned out to be a shockingly large pumpkin lanced with dozens of cocktail sticks loaded with either a cube of cheese or a silver-skin onion. Opening up the shot to take in the rest of the table, Felix was struck by the colour of the food, how it all seemed to come from the same part of the spectrum. Brown bread sandwiches, yellow crisps, Twiglets, corn footballs and other rusty-looking nibbles, a choice of cheeses, cocktail sausages, quarters of scotch egg (luminous yellow yolks encrusted with brown sausage meat and orange breadcrumbs), peanuts, pastries and an assortment of other more exotic footstuffs such as bhajis and goujons, all battered and tanned. Paul Corley, a boy in the church choir, had been allergic to all things orange. He could never eat anything at birthday parties and nearly died when Martin Piggot made him swallow a piece of tangerine peel after Evensong. Felix was still remembering the breathless and gurgling Paul Corley, flat on his back in the vestry with his lips swelling and his eyes bulging in their sockets, when the doors of the school flew open. By the time he'd pulled back with the zoom and readjusted his line of vision, the first half a dozen mini-astronauts in spray-painted silver wellies and crash helmets covered in tin foil had already entered the playground and were walking with slow, exaggerated strides around their cardboard rocket. Space, it emerged, was the theme for the whole display. No sooner had the first years departed to the sound of 'I Lost My Heart to a Starship Trooper' than out came a similar number of second years to the tune of David Bowie's 'Space Oddity'. And so it went on, until every year group in the school had enacted a scene from some distant corner of the universe to a soundtrack which included 'Rocket Man', 'Calling Occupants of Interplanetary Craft', Queen's 'Flash', the theme from *Star Trek* and Duran Duran's 'Planet Earth'. Felix filmed the performances but only a snippet from each. He knew from experience the tedium of the over-long home video, and in any case he was saving the battery for the main event.

It was getting towards midday, with the sun at its highest and brightest, when the last space cadets filed back into the school through the side door and Mr Fellows, in a tie and short-sleeved shirt, walked towards the hopscotch pattern painted in yellow on the grey concrete. Feedback howled between microphone and speakers, causing some of the children to stick their fingers in their ears and three pigeons to lift from the rungs of the monkey bars and head for a telegraph pole across the road. After the technical adjustments had been made, Mr Fellows cleared his throat and gave his opening address. Still at the top of the slide, but standing now with one leg hooked around the handrail, Felix had a privileged view of the whole proceedings, and even though the wind dragged at his amplified voice, the words of Sconford and Tilden's head teacher were audible and clear.

'Thank you so much for attending our celebrations here today, and as well as thanking all the children of the school for a display that really was *out of this world*, could we also show our appreciation to our music and drama teacher, Miss Swann, who has worked tirelessly on this project for several months.'

There was generous applause, then cheering and even a couple of wolf whistles, as a young woman in a pair of tight red trousers and a blouse that didn't quite reach her navel gave a theatrical curtsy and disappeared back into the crowd.

'And so on to what I can safely say is my favourite moment in the whole school year. The crowning of the May Queen has been an annual event at this school for over thirty years. In just a moment, our current Queen, Eliza Hardison, will be taking her throne. But this year is special. The powers that be insist that, at sixty-five, this will be my last year as headmaster of Sconford and Tilden, even if in my own mind I'm still the eager, energetic and, er . . . handsome young man that I was all those years ago.'

There was more applause, and another wolf whistle, this time from Miss Swann herself.

'To mark this occasion, we've looked high and low, far and wide, and are delighted to bring you a parade of all those darling buds that have blossomed and bloomed into true beauties since the year they were first crowned. So without further ado, from 1972, please welcome our very first May Queen, Christine Woodhouse, formerly Christine Tummings.'

Felix had already trained the camera on the main entrance in anticipation. Mrs Woodhouse, née Tummings, tall and elegant with her black hair screwed above her head and skewered with two small sticks, walked confidently across the yard and shook hands with Mr Fellows. Her two-piece pastel-green suit gave her the look of an air hostess with one of the better airlines. And there was something about the way she took her seat in the first empty chair – facing forwards, legs crossed, one hand on each thigh – that confirmed the impression.

'From 1973, Jeanette Tripp.'

This time, a smaller, rounder woman in a denim jacket and a white T-shirt printed with a big black question mark jogged into view. The bum of her jeans had been patched with a Carlsberg beer-towel, which Felix homed in on. And given the slur of words that poured from her mouth as she grabbed the microphone from a surprised Mr Fellows, his camerawork wasn't entirely inappropriate.

'Go for it, Jeannie,' shouted a boozy voice in the crowd, but when Jeannie did go for it with a throaty and drunken, 'Oggie, oggie, oggie,' there was little or no response. As she hopped up to the platform with a little hitch-kick in mid-air, then dropped into her chair, Felix would have liked to capture the expression of the immaculate Mrs Woodhouse sitting next to her. But to be pointing the camcorder at the wrong woman, at that precise moment, would have been more than his life was worth.

'And from 1974, now Abbie Fenton, but to us Abbie Lawrence,' boomed Mr Fellows, beckoning the next guest with his open hand. And as his wife pushed open the glass door, Felix was already rolling, his elbows and spine locked in a tripod, tracking Abbie as she walked smartly to the centre of the playground, removed her new lilac hat, allowed her old headmaster to peck her once on the left cheek, then climbed the two wooden stairs to the stage to take her seat. Got it. Only later, when Abbie was *in the can*, did Felix dare try a few tricks with his new toy. He scrolled through the function menu. Julie Hardacre, of 1979 vintage, was recorded using the time-lapse feature, and Paula Dewdeney, from 1983, in monochrome. The perfectly bald Kay Simmister, 1985, and 1986's Maureen Simmister, in a rather obvious wig, looked very weird in either half of the split screen. Fading up from black, he tried out the macro-zoom on Karine Moon, 1987, and the soft focus on 1989's Joyelle Bright, who was heavily pregnant and by Felix's calculation not a day older than fifteen. By the time ten-year-old Eliza Hardison had been lifted into her throne, arrayed with the purple robe, the gold sash and the glittering tiara, there wasn't a feature he hadn't tried and barely a minute's worth of power left in the battery. When the hem of Eliza's dress became trapped under the heel of her shoe, she was attended to by her mother, a woman of about Abbie's age, who ran to the stage and unhooked the dress before dabbing down a few stray locks of her daughter's hair with a wet finger. For his final shot, Felix tracked across the podium in sepia tone, capturing twenty-odd faces in various states of innocence, happiness, health, wisdom, maturity, failure and decay. Then the camera went dead. He waved at Abbie. She waved back and pointed him out to Mr Fellows, who was now surrounded by women and girls, and carried beautiful young Eliza, crowned and adored, in his arms. Felix made his way down the hot metal slide, tentatively at first, holding on to the side. Then halfway to the bottom he let go, and instantly saw the big Norfolk sky go flying backwards over his head, followed closely by the spotless, manmade uppers of his new trainers at the end of his upside-down legs. Followed by not much less than a thousand pounds' worth of digital camera, floating in mid-air.

2

She had forgotten her hat – the new one, bought specially for the occasion. But they'd gone too far now to turn back. The radio wasn't working, except for Holy Communion on long wave and even that kept going astray. In the passenger seat, Abbie had kicked off her shoes and curled up with her knees under her chin. The foetal position. Either she was staring out of the side window or she was asleep. At least that's what Felix had been happy to assume for the last hour and a half. But by fiddling with a button on his door, he tilted the near-side wing mirror to look back in the car, and when the image of Abbie's face finally swung into view he saw that she was crying. Meeting his eyes in the polished glass, she looked away. Another seven or eight fields went past, and a row of poplars, then a boarded-up petrol station with the pumps removed and two massive cubes of concrete blocking the entrance and exit. Then more fields.

'Someone told me that wherever you stand in Norfolk, you can see at least one church. Is that true?'

'No,' said Abbie, after a long pause.

'Maybe it was Suffolk,' he said.

'Is that what you do with them at work? Ask them about the distribution of places of worship in East Anglia?' said Abbie, sniffing and pulling the seat belt over her shoulder, as if it were something to comfort her, like a blanket or a shawl.

'Is that what I do with *who*?' asked Felix.

'The people who cry. The people like me.'

Felix gripped the steering wheel with both hands as a huge articulated lorry went past in the other direction. Sucked into its slipstream, the car swayed towards the centre line, and a dozen or so cat's-eyes thumped beneath the wheels before he brought it back to the left. The road was narrow and fast, and the grass verges to each side were ploughed with tyre tracks, some of which appeared to go right off the edge and didn't come back. Felix was a safe driver, his 60 per cent no-claims bonus said as much, although his mind did tend to wander. Only last week he had set off for work but ended up in the queue for the car wash. He'd been following a van with a big, oily tow bracket poking out from beneath the back bumper and had started daydreaming about a caravanning holiday with his parents in the Lakes. Who knows how far he would have followed it if there hadn't been a knock on the window and a man in a pair of blue nylon overalls asking if he wanted the foam wash or the turtle-wax finish. Too embarrassed to turn around and with three or four other cars behind him, he'd scooped a handful of loose change out of the ashtray, inched towards the entrance, then watched as the world disappeared in a white-out of jetted water and bubbling soap.

'Since you're asking, I keep a box of tissues in the drawer, and since you mention it, you're nothing like the people who come to cry in my office,' he said.

'Really? I thought I'd be a pretty good case, in the circumstances.'

'What circumstances?'

'Oh, well, off the top of my head, let's think. Like I'm totally screwed up because I want a baby and there is no baby, and I'm running out of time and fast. Like I haven't got a single relative in the world.'

'So your husband doesn't come into that category, right?'

'No, he doesn't,' she blurted out. 'Not when he doesn't care, not when he pretends everything's all right when it fucking well isn't.'

Abbie never swore, so now it was serious. Felix took his hand off the gear stick and put it on her thigh, but she swatted it away, catching the face of his watch with the bangle on her wrist. Solid Argentinian silver versus the miracle of sapphire glass. The watch had been a gift and he treasured it. The sapphire glass, so the guarantee promised, would shine for eternity and could be scratched only by diamond. Next time he lifted his hand to the wheel he saw there was no damage.

'Like the fact that I haven't a clue who my parents are.'

Felix said, 'We've been through this a thousand times already, Abbie,' but she was sobbing now, and he offered the comment to her as something she could dismiss, an invitation to get it out of her system, go on with her list.

'Like the fact that I'm a prostitute.'

'What?' he screamed. 'You're a market researcher!'

'I stand in the precinct propositioning men. What's the difference?'

They'd been gaining speed all the time and were now behind a white van with the usual comments written in the dust on the back doors, including, 'I wish my bird was as dirty as this.' Felix indicated and moved out to overtake, but there was a steady line of oncoming traffic. Rather than stare at the van for another ten miles, he pushed at the brake pedal, eased back and let the graffiti move gradually away. More of the sky opened up to the windscreen. More horizon as well and more light. Slowing down also seemed to make things calmer between them, as if they were hooked up to the engine.

'I'm ready for that tissue now,' said Abbie, after a few more miles.

'I've never been with a prostitute, but for fifty quid I'd expect more than a few questions about which aftershave I use or how often I cut my toenails,' said Felix.

'So how do you know it costs fifty?'

He put his hand on her leg and this time she let him, and put her hand on his, and curled her finger around his thumb. 'So with all those problems, would I qualify as one of your customers, then?' she asked.

'Clients.'

'Whatever.'

' 'Fraid not. You'd need to be stealing baby clothes or having a nervous breakdown outside Mothercare or hanging around outside the infant school before you landed on my desk.'

Abbie pulled down the sun visor and looked at her bloodshot eyes in the vanity mirror. Then she leaned back in the seat and put her feet on the dashboard.

'It's not work, it's the other stuff. Seeing all those women and their children today, all those families. It stirs it up.'

'I know. I'm sorry.'

'Not to mention being at the far end in that line-up. You know, I've always thought of myself as young. As being younger than most people. But today really brought it home. I've crossed the line.'

'Well, you weren't the oldest,' Felix pointed out.

'No, although Jeanette Tripp can't have long for this world, and that ice maiden Christine Tummings looks like she's practising for cold storage.'

'Well, I'm glad you said that and not me. Was she like that at school?'

'Tummings? No,' said Abbie. And, giving the impression that having crossed one line she might as well cross another, added, 'She was a right little scrubber.'

They talked about the parade. Abbie told him how it was every girl's dream to be Queen of the May. The winner was chosen by vote – every pupil at the school wrote down the name of their favourite girl, then Mr Fellows made a tour of the classrooms collecting the slips of paper in a biscuit barrel with a slot in the lid. Next morning in assembly he announced the result. On the day that Abbie triumphed she was off sick with chickenpox, and when the headmaster called round to the house that night to give her the news in person, she wept for hours, distraught at missing her moment of glory in front of her friends and enemies and mortified at the prospect of appearing with a big blotchy face under the bejewelled tiara and with two pimply arms dangling from either side of the purple robe. She also remembered going into Mr Fellows's office later in the year and seeing the outfit stuffed away in a cardboard box on top of a bookshelf. It took away some of the magic, she said, 'Like finding out about Father Christmas.' And then, a moment later, 'Or God.' She was also astonished that the May Queen thing still happened in this day and age, being thoroughly sexist, ultra-competitive and not exactly part of the national curriculum.

Felix shrugged his shoulders. 'Well, it's not as if there was a catwalk and a swimwear section. And anyway, I kept going back to the little girl's face with the camera. What was she called?'

'Eliza Hardison.'

'Yes, her, and she was totally spellbound, and as far as I could tell so was every other child in the playground, not to mention the mums and dads. So what harm can it do?'

'Anything like it at your school?' Abbie asked.

'Not really. They held a *Mastermind* competition one year, with the music and the lights and the chair and everything, but the boy who won it got his head stoved in for being a clever dick. They didn't bother doing it again.'

'It was you, was it?'

'It was.'

'Intelligence wasn't to be encouraged at your school, was it, sweetheart?' said Abbie, patting his hand.

'No, it was frowned upon. And if you were good-looking as well, you were dead.'

Abbie talked about growing up in Norfolk, and what it was like to live without hills, and how the wind made everyone deaf or mad or both, although she pointed out that small trees shaken by storms and gales grow up strong and true, whereas trees which are propped or tied as striplings become weak and sickly things. She'd read it in a magazine. She didn't miss the flatlands because, being adopted, she'd never really thought of it as home, just the place where she once lived. In fact she didn't think of anywhere as home. Like Maxine, their next-door neighbour, whose father had been in the air force. Not long after Abbie and Felix had moved house, in one of those conversations over the garden fence, she'd asked Maxine where she was from and Maxine had said, 'How do you mean?' That's why they got on so well. Because they didn't have roots.

They were like tumbleweed. Felix felt obliged to say that not more than thirty seconds ago she had been a tree in a storm. Ignoring him, she went on to conclude that women were more adaptable in any case. Women didn't need to support the nearest football team, or go drinking in a 'local', or get into fights with people from other parts of the country because they spoke differently, or have the name of their home town tattooed across their hearts. Men thought about their place of birth in the same way they thought about their mothers – with unquestioning affection. They were tied down and they were trapped. But women had grown out of all that crap. They were unattached to any part of the planet, which meant they were independent, both in body and in mind, which meant they were free.

They drove on. Past water towers on stilts. Past mounds of winter fodder left to sprout and rot. Past occasional road kill – patches of feather and fur outlined in dry blood. Past place names like characters from nursery rhymes and fairy tales. Over level crossings. Across quaint wooden bridges. Further north the roads got faster and wider. The tractors and harvesters had turned off into the fields, along with other assorted picking and planting machines and abnormal loads with their strange buckets and scoops and prongs, most of them taking the full width of both carriageways, many of them driven by nine- or ten-year-old boys. Blue motorway signs appeared, then the name of their town. They were making good time, until an amber light in the shape of a petrol pump flashed on the console, and Felix swung across two lanes and a set of chevrons before gearing down on the slip road and coasting into the service station. Abbie went to buy sandwiches and crisps and hot coffee in the mini-market while Felix filled up and paid for the fuel. She was gone a while, long enough for him to waste a couple of quid in the space-invader machine by the toilets and check for any traffic problems on the road-watch screen. In fact by the time she returned he'd also been on the weighing scales and tested his heart rate and his blood pressure, and, having been pronounced fit and healthy, had extracted a chocolate egg from the vending machine and eaten it. He was just contemplating the design-your-own-business-card gizmo when she came around the corner, balancing one polystyrene cup on top of another, and a minute later they were back in the outside lane.

'What did you get me?' asked Felix, having slotted the steaming coffee into the cup holder between the seats.

Abbie reached down into the blue carrier bag between her feet and passed him what felt like a glass or little pot of some kind. He was concentrating on the road ahead, keeping an eye on a car transporter on the inside. But when he did manage to look, he saw that the item he had been given was nothing less than a jar of pork-and-apple-flavoured baby-food. A toddler in a canary-yellow romper suit beamed at him from the label. And Abbie hadn't finished. From the bag she pulled out five more jars of the same food, followed by two towelling bibs, one in the shape of a horse's head, the other a cow, followed by a Noddy cassette, followed by four or five pocket-sized books featuring assorted cartoon characters. Lined up across the dashboard they looked like mascots or offerings at a shrine. Finally, she hooked out a tiny pair of baby's shoes – red satin slippers, no more than three inches long – and hung them by their laces from the rear-view mirror. They danced and jogged to the motion of the car. Felix stared hard at the surface of the road, and felt himself dipping the clutch and fishing for another gear, a sixth gear, an extra cog somewhere beyond the confines of the gearbox and the engine block, a gear that did not exist.

'I want something to happen and I want it to happen NOW,' said Abbie, and after a mile or so, even though it wasn't a question, Felix nodded his head and said, 'Yes.'

'And no more time-wasting, and no more sticking your head in the sand.'

'No.'

Abbie scooped the jars of food and other bric-à-brac into the bag, but left the shoes where they were, swinging and bouncing just a few inches in front of Felix's eyes.

*

The following Tuesday was her birthday. From the box of photographs in the back bedroom, Felix dug out the black and white snap of Abbie, ten years old, wearing the sash and tiara of the May Queen. Seated regally on the makeshift throne, in her right hand she held a posy of flowers. And with her head turned slightly to the left, sunlight revealed the pattern of tiny wrinkles – almost a sneer – which thirty years later still rippled around the corner of her lip when anyone pointed a camera in her direction. The photograph wasn't much of a gift, even in a silver frame, but for these past few years Abbie's birthdays were things to be overcome rather than celebrated, and not just because she was getting older, but because they were milestones on the road to childlessness. Especially this birthday, her fortieth.

3

Social work is not a joke. Social work is not inherently funny, unlike the work of doctors and nurses, for instance, which is full of comic possibilities. And social work has none of the humour, say, of the building site, or the police force, which is, by definition, hilarious. Nevertheless, every Monday morning as Felix took his seat at the team meeting and looked around the room, it did occur to him that he was among a group of people not appointed by the Department of Social Services and its various subcommittees and panels, but put together by a writer of sitcoms and gags. There were six other staff in the office, and while individually they were ordinary human beings, regular members of society and entirely plausible employees of the local authority, brought together in one room they were a sketch. Unlike Felix, of course, who was normal. A relative concept, admittedly. But normal in the sense that he did not suffer from multiple-hypersensitive syndrome, unlike Thelma, whose current and expanding list of allergies included nuts, bread, coffee, smoke, pollen, gold (but not platinum), denim (but not cotton), direct sunlight, most animals, furniture polish and dust (a particularly cruel combination), ink – especially the fumes given off by whiteboard markers and felt tips – and loud bangs. And that was just this week. Next week it would be something harder to avoid, like paper or air, and the office was bracing itself for the day when abstract concepts came on to the blacklist, such as time or love.

Felix was also normal in the sense that he was not 'reformed'. Unlike Roy. No one knew exactly what Roy had reformed from, but he bore all the hallmarks of someone with a 'past', including a number of misspelt tattoos on his arms and hands and one very nasty scar that ran from the corner of his right eye to the centre of his shaved head. Roy wore jeans, was the proud owner of a gold sovereign necklace and a gold sovereign ring. And he smoked. At team meetings he took the chair next to Thelma.

Felix was also normal in the sense that he was not cynical and foul-mouthed like Neville. Or posh and old like Marjorie. Or militant and right on like Mo. Normal in that he was not the boss, unlike Bernard, who was timid, useless and not far from retirement. Having been kicked upstairs to keep him away from the clients and the problems, then left at senior grade to keep him away from the policy decisions and the power, Bernard had sat for nearly twenty years in the same seat, putting his signature on unimportant documents, ordering stationery and drawing up rotas to ensure the smooth running of the lottery syndicate and the coffee fund. Bernard was the only person in the building who knew how to replace the toner in the photocopier, a knowledge he refused to share with anyone and a task he prioritized above all others, even if there were half a dozen seriously abused children in reception waiting for emergency accommodation. In the absence of Bernard as a leader (even when he was physically present), it was not unusual for the team to look to Felix for support, calmness and consent. But mainly they looked for normality. Twelve years ago, when he joined the office, this was a role he would have resisted, thinking himself far too young and enthusiastic to be relied upon for cool judgement and sound advice. But staff had come and gone – sacked, retired, transferred, retired ill, expired – and with the exception of Bernard, who didn't count, Felix was now the senior figure. Not the oldest; both Neville and Thelma could pip him on that front, and of course Marjorie, and maybe Roy as well, though his age was as much a mystery as his background. But the sanest, nevertheless. The steady one. The person capable of seeing an argument from both sides, taking a middle line, being rational in the face of extreme circumstances, exhibiting common sense. A safe, measured and practical man.

On this particular Monday morning, Felix was last to arrive

at the meeting. He'd been phoning the magistrates' court for information about a boy on his caseload arrested over the weekend, and had been on hold for more than ten minutes, staring out of the window. Social Services were located on the top floor of Prospect House, the highest point on the skyline, although the fact that the block in question was only five storeys high spoke volumes, as did the allocation of its penthouse suite to practitioners of one of the world's least glamorous professions. And if the building had failed as a landmark and a beacon of civic pride, it had also failed in its other function – as a roundabout. Planners had once intended it as the central hub of a traffic system through which all parts of the town would be connected. But residents objected to the proposed link road, and had gone as far as to pitch tents on the area of adjoining wasteland, a tatty, rubbish-strewn wilderness known locally as the Strawberry Field. Part of their campaign involved two monstrous lies. The first was a claim that the Strawberry Field was mentioned in the Domesday Book. It wasn't, but nobody had bothered to check. The second was to portray the field as a refuge for indigenous wild flowers and endangered wildlife, a kind of safe haven for flora and fauna, the last remnant of Eden holding out against rampant commercialism and urban sprawl. True, the odd dandelion had found a toehold there, and one summer Felix had watched a rotation of blowflies operating within the air space of a dead cat. But apart from that, it was tosh. Certainly no strawberry had ever been plucked there in a hundred years. And for the planning department, whose offices on the third floor of Prospect House overlooked the said nature reserve, it was very irritating tosh. The case went to appeal, but by this time the campaigners had attracted the free support of an environment-friendly public relations company whose slogan, 'Strawberry Field Forever', was the clincher. Peevish in defeat, the planners went ahead with the other three-quarters of the roundabout, 'the Horseshoe', which now acted as a kind of fortification to the main entrance of their building. Those approaching by car were repelled by a series of barriers and checkpoints and shunted into an overflow car park on the opposite side of the road. Those approaching on foot could either take their chances with the traffic or risk their life in the dark and piss-stained subway. Or they could tramp through the dust, dirt and dog shit of their beloved Strawberry Field and wait in reception until they were called. In winter, it was not an exaggeration to say the majority of Felix's clients would arrive looking like the losing finalists in a mud-wrestling competition. A carpet of broadsheet newspapers – newly laid by Bernard each morning – covered every inch of the floor.

Bernard wasn't present at the meeting.

'He's had to stay at home,' said Neville.

'Why? Is he ill?' asked Thelma, always keen to sympathize with a fellow sufferer.

'No, he's having some cushion covers fitted.'

There was a loud tutting noise from the direction of Mo. 'Is that true?'

'Well, at least you can't accuse him of malingering. I mean, if he'd phoned up with malaria or some other foreign-sounding disease, then he'd probably be lying. But soft furnishings – it's not exactly an excuse, is it?'

'What do you mean, *foreign?*' Mo wanted to know. 'Do you mean that in a pejorative sense?'

Neville, always one for throwing out the bait, was just about to start reeling in his catch when Roy walked in and sat down next to Thelma, who inched away from him. A waft of stale cigarettes had followed Roy across the room and, as it rejoined him, Thelma lifted the silk scarf from around her neck and tied it as a mask over her mouth and nose. Trying to help, Marjorie pulled back the zebra blind and slid open a window. Shrinking from the light, Thelma dived for her bag and slotted a pair of heavy, black sunglasses on to her head.

'Summat I said?' asked Roy.

Thelma waved her hand, silently absolving him from all blame, but at the same time pulled up the collar and lapels of her mac, raised the scarf and withdrew her hands into her sleeves.

'Did he ask me to chair?' asked Felix.

Neville nodded and passed him the agenda on a flimsy sheet of fax paper. In a previous meeting, again with Bernard absent, Felix had made the big mistake of asking for a volunteer to take the minutes. Roy, who could almost certainly read but in all probability couldn't write, had performed some well-rehearsed gesture with his face, implying that on this particular occasion he might give it a miss. Thelma had taken one look at the pen and, having correctly deduced that it contained what to her would have been a lethal dose of venom in the form of blue ink, not to mention trace elements of precious metals, declined. Marjorie suffered from carpal-tunnel problems and was awaiting surgery on her wrists. Neville said, 'No,' point blank, and, taking this as a challenge, Mo had also refused. This time, with a pained expression on his face, Felix began with Mo and offered her the pen. It was reverse psychology, of a sort. It implied she was his first choice, that she'd be doing him a great favour and that she was the only one remotely responsible enough for such a demanding task. It was also completely transparent. She tutted again but took the pen, and with that the working week had begun.

There were apologies from Bernard, given by Neville, in what was actually a passable imitation of his boss's voice. There were no matters arising, which meant that the main business of the meeting could take place, namely the doling out of new cases. A pile of eight or nine blue folders sat on top of the front table, some of them three or four inches thick, with the client's name written in black marker pen along the spine. The distribution of new files took place every Monday apart from bank holidays. Neville, like some self-appointed master of ceremonies, would begin the process by giving a brief synopsis of the case in a vocabulary not generally heard in a modern social work department. This was followed by a sort of arcane bidding procedure or secret auction, at which Roy was an expert, using a technique he could well have learned in some of the more notorious local boozers as a way of declaring his interest in a second-hand video recorder or a case of whisky. On this occasion, with two barely appreciable nods of the head, he accepted the case of a young mother whose husband had recently been sent to prison and an elderly man in the latter stages of Alzheimer's.

'And your next starter for ten,' announced Neville. 'Matthew Coyne. Who wants this little runt?'

'I wish you wouldn't use that word, Neville. Some of us find it offensive,' said Mo.

'Now let's see. History of self-harm, previous for theft, TWOC, arson. Glue-sniffer as well – a bit 1970s, that, wouldn't you say? Parents locked in custody dispute – can't bear to be without him. Mo, was that a bid from you? No? Thelma?'

'No, not solvents.'

'Marjorie?'

'What's the address?'

'Givens Lane.'

'Oh, just across the road from my bowling club. Yes, I'll take him.'

'I didn't know you played skittles?'

'Crown green. Ladies' vice-captain.'

'Super, Marjorie. Right, next up . . .'

And so it went on. Felix took the last blue folder with the name Moffat on the side, the case of an eleven-year-old girl, Ruby, excluded from school after exhibiting a range of peculiar habits and behaviour, including extreme arachnophobia. This left a single sheet of paper on the table, handwritten and folded in half.

'So, spider-woman goes to Felix. Oh, yes, and someone had pushed this through the letter box this morning. Some lost soul trying to trace her natural parents. Adopted at birth, blah de blah de blah. Any takers?'

Most people were already on their feet by now, picking up files and bags and getting ready to leave.

'Come on, who wants to tell her that her records will have been shredded by now and recycled as bog roll?'

'What's her name?' said Mo, still taking notes.

'Can't make it out. Lawton or Lawrence, I think. Abbie Lawrence.'

'What was that name again?' said Felix.

'Lawrence, it looks like. Abbie.'

'Er . . . I'll take it. Er, if no one else wants it. Her, I mean. Shouldn't be too much work and I'm not stretched at the moment. Thanks.'

He was still staring at the handwriting when Mo asked him if the meeting was officially closed.

'What? Oh, yes. Any other business?'

But everyone else had left the room. Mo drew a double line across the bottom of the writing pad and handed it back to him on the way out.

From the office he shared with Neville, Felix could look across the partial circuit of the roundabout and into the heart of the town. Holding the telephone receiver to his ear, he peered intently towards the pedestrianized precinct about a quarter of a mile away. Eventually a smallish woman with black shoulder-length hair, wearing a summer dress and carrying a clipboard, strolled into view between the Northern Building Society and the latest charity shop. Felix hit the speed-dial button on the phone, and even at that distance could see the woman reach into her pocket and lift the mobile to her ear.

'It's me,' said Felix.

Abbie raised her head towards the office block and waved with her free hand. 'Hi. Can you see me? I can see you.'

'Never mind hide-and-seek. What the hell do you think you're playing at?'

Abbie began to wander in a small, slow circle around a manhole cover in one of the paving stones, looking at the floor.

'Oh, got my note, did you? That was quick.'

'Of course I got your note. What do you think we do with things that come through the letter box – put them straight in the bin?'

'I'm sorry,' she said. 'It was a bit impulsive.'

'That's one word for it. Bloody stupid, more like. Why didn't you tell me what you were going to do? I could have . . .'

'Could have what?'

'I could have . . . It was just bloody stupid, that's all. Not to mention embarrassing.'

'Did they twig it was me?'

'No, thank God. But only because I dived in and . . .'

'So what's the problem, then?'

Now she turned around and faced him, staring directly up towards the window where he stood.

'It's just very irregular,' he said.

Suddenly he could visualize her expression, the narrowing of the eyes and the tightening of the mouth, and the way that her head, when she was annoyed, moved forward slightly on her neck, like a teacher talking to a child. Two men carrying a huge rectangle of glass passed in front of her but it didn't deflect her stare. Felix took a small step backwards, away from the light.

'Irregular, is it? And embarrassing? Well, I'm *so* sorry. How foolish of me, coming to Social Services with my personal problems and people finding out I'm adopted. What a scandal.'

With his finger, Felix pushed a thick notepad into the hole punch on his desk, and through the heel of his hand felt the hollow blade biting down into several layers of clean white paper.

'I thought you said you were going to help me with this,' she added, after a pause.

There was another silence as Felix straightened a metal paperclip into a single length of wire.

'I did. I mean, I will. But you've got to admit it's a bit . . . weird.'

'Why?'

'Well, for one thing, it's not every day that a social worker hears his wife's name being bandied about in a team meeting and for another it's probably illegal.'

'What's illegal about a woman wanting to find her parents?'

'No, I mean her husband taking the case.'

'So *you're* my social worker, are you?'

'Yes. No. Well, technically speaking . . .'

The door opened and Neville walked in carrying a roll of steaming newspaper.

31

'Wouldn't you know it? They were clean out of the fillets of poached sea bass with salmon mousseline and remoulade sauce, so it's jumbo haddock and chips again, with a buttered teacake to soak up the lard. Tell the ambulance to stand by.'

He pulled open a drawer in his filing cabinet and from it produced a handful of cutlery, a cruet set in the shape of a monk and a nun with holes in their halos, a small bottle of malt vinegar and two china plates, which he wiped with the sleeve of his jacket. Felix put his hand over the mouthpiece. 'Just talking to Abbie.'

'Who, that Lawrence woman? You're quick off the mark.'

'No, er, I mean my wife.'

'Oh, fine. Don't mind me, squire.'

Neville opened a Victim Support leaflet and spread it across his lap as a napkin, then unravelled the bundle of newspaper. Two enormous battered fish flopped from the greaseproof paper, followed by an avalanche of chips, which he guided with his finger on to the plates.

'So are you or aren't you?' said Abbie, in Felix's ear.

'Shall we talk about it later?'

'Just give me a yes or a no,' she said.

She was still looking up at him. For a moment, he imagined she could project herself through clouds and space, put an image of her face on the surface of a faraway planet. So that even as he stepped from the spaceship – the first man on Mars – she was right there, waiting for him in the red dust. And when he gazed back towards his home planet, it was her face that played on the visor of his helmet, her face in his eyes.

'Yes.'

'Fine. And there's nothing in the house for tea, so can you call at the chippy on the way home.'

'Yes.'

'And are you going to the crazy golf with Jed tonight?'

'The driving range. Yes.'

'OK. Well, see you later.'

She waved and walked out of sight. Neville pushed a plate of food in front of him.

'Marital disharmony?'

'Not really,' he said, and was just about to fork a chunk of fish into his mouth when the phone rang. He let his voice-mail pick up the message, and when he played it back after lunch, it was Abbie again, phoning to say thanks.

The Driving Range

Balls. Two pounds fifty for sixty-five or a hundred for three quid. The man inserts his token and places his wire basket under the vent near the base of the machine. The machine rumbles and churns and grinds. Balls are dispensed. Failure to position the wire basket correctly during the dispensing of balls results in an unstoppable outpouring of sixty-five or a hundred balls on to a wide section of the floor. The retrieval of runaway balls across a polished linoleum surface can be a time-consuming exercise, although the main expense is in terms of pride.

The man then enters the driving gallery, a curved row of booths or stalls or traps facing a seemingly endless and expanding area of mown grass. Advertising hoardings masquerading as distance markers are positioned at fifty-yard intervals all the way to infinity, carrying the brand names of golf-related products as well as the relevant number. And balls, hundreds, perhaps thousands of gleaming white balls, litter the grass. Under the floodlights they shine with the colour of polished teeth. The floodlights are on because it is dark, because it is night. It is like theatre. It is a performance. A show.

The man chooses his booth, leans his handful of clubs against the wall, then goes through a number of warming-up exercises, such as a prolonged but ultimately failed attempt to touch his toes and several long, slow intakes of breath with his eyes closed. It is a reminder of the importance of mental fitness. It is about concentration, focus, the whetting and sharpening of the most important club in any golfer's bag – the mind. It is art. It is Zen. He places the first of his balls on the raised rubber tee and hammers his first drive of the evening as hard as he possibly can, irrespective of loft, direction or even length. The first one is all about animal emotions and raw lust. All about release.

In their booths, every man is invisible from the waist down. Bobble hats can be seen, and shirts and sweaters are on display. A quick eye can make a momentary study of back-swings and follow-throughs as the silver clubs flash through their arcs. But below that line is a secret. Whatever takes place between a man and his ball at the moment of contact is a matter of privacy, and happens at such speed and in such a fraction of time it remains a mystery even to the man himself. It is religion and ballistics rolled into one. It is whiplash and prayer combined in a single act. From each booth comes the swish of carbon graphite through air, the cracking of heat-hardened metal against dimpled polymer resin. Then balls. Tiny white balls streaming upward and onwards, beyond the upper range of the floodlights and into the night sky.

Our man is no professional. Only a small percentage of his balls stream upward or even onwards, and in all his days as a driver of golf balls, those shots of his which have indeed raced like comets across the firmament of heaven can be counted on the fingers of one hand. Perhaps they were dreams. In the booths to either side of him, some men are worse. Some hit grubber shots or daisy-cutters that bobble along the surface of the grass and dribble to a halt well short of the first board. Some hit shots that are instantly overcome by lethargy and fatigue. Some hook to the right or slice to the left, and one man, near the fire escape, hits several balls that never appear at all but can be heard cannoning around the padded inside of the booth itself. But most men are better. Their swings make a more clinical sound. Their bodies cut a cleaner shape. Their shots are straight and true. And some men . . . some men are just special. Superhuman. Beyond belief. The back-spin imparted by their short irons can stop a golf ball dead in its tracks, as if its name had been called. Their long irons are nothing short of deadly weapons, bulleting balls across vast distances with fatal accuracy and machine-like regularity. And their woods. Their woods launch shots which are still on an upward trajectory as they escape not only the perimeter fence but the gravitational pull of the planet, and are never seen again, having disintegrated while re-entering the Earth's atmosphere. These men are not golfers – they are Drivers. They travel to Florida and hit balls as far as they can for large sums of money. Their clubs are made of special minerals found only in distant *galaxies. They cannot be spoken to. They can only be talked about and admired.*

Every couple of hours at the range the harvester emerges from its depot. Driven by two excitable and probably intoxicated youths earning a few pounds of drinking money, the harvester makes thirty or forty sweeps of the fairway, collecting its crop of ripe white balls in a converted sprout-picker towed by a vehicle which is one part stock car and two parts armoured tank. The windows are protected by wire mesh and the reinforced body panels to all sides have suffered a number of impacts. Among the more gentlemanly players, of whom there are very few, it is considered courteous to refrain from driving until the harvester completes its circuit, and also affords the opportunity of a cigarette and a drink. Among the regulars, however, its appearance is an opportunity not to be missed. Upon seeing it trundle into view, even the most casual golfer feels a new sense of urgency and purpose, and fires an increased frequency of shots in the direction of the vehicle. A direct hit brings about a cheer from the whole of the gallery (excepting the gentlemen golfers, with their cigarettes and hip flasks) and a pomp on the horn from the two pissed youths navigating and steering their way through the barrage of flak.

Normality descends. The evening progresses. Short and long, high and low, wonky and straight, glorious or utterly crap, men disseminate their stock of tiny white missiles into the night, each one a symbol of their worth, a particle of their essence and an object of hope.

4

Felix preferred to work in the office at the beginning of the week, making calls, sorting out paperwork and so on, and to save any home visits until Friday. If he set off on his rounds on Friday morning, no one really expected to see him again until Monday. If he made good time, he could be home by four at the latest, and mow the lawn or tinker around in the shed before Abbie came back.

The Moffats lived on the Lakeland Estate, a maze of yellow-brick three-storey houses built on the steep side of a north-facing hill above the town. Thrown together in the early 1980s by the same planners responsible for the Horseshoe roundabout, the estate had been advertised as an executive paradise, where the upwardly mobile could park their throaty sports cars in the downstairs garage and sip their aperitifs while enjoying the view from the upstairs lounge. For a split second in the middle of the night, behind the eyelids of a town planner flitting from one vision to the next, it must have seemed like a good idea. But as the sun came up over the horizon, it was doomed. Those in the town with even the slightest upward inclination had set their sights a little higher than the Lakeland Estate, despite its altitude, and those mobile enough to get to the train station had done so and had not come back. Pretty soon the Lakeland development had become a dumping ground for every dysfunctional family and malfunctioning individual within a ten-mile radius. There were two shops on the estate, one an off-licence, the other a bookmaker's, each being nothing more than a freight container of the type seen on the back of articulated lorries or cross-Channel ferries, and both operating through small hatches cut out of the corrugated metal. The only other commercial enterprise was a mobile shop known as the Big Blue One. Like a kind of military personnel carrier or something left over from the miners' strike, the Big Blue One was a thirty-year-old coach with grilles at the windows and thick rubber skirts protecting the tyres. The navy-blue bodywork was pockmarked with what could only have been bullet holes, including one spectacular pattern of shotgun spray just under the driver's window. The roof was painted with tar and rimmed with curls of barbed wire. The Big Blue One carried no number plate and avoided paying any kind of road tax or insurance by keeping off the actual road. It could often be seen churning up the grassy play area in the middle of the estate or crawling along the pavement. Not that the police visited the Lakeland Estate very often, and if they did they rarely got out of their cars, and certainly not to check the road-worthiness of an old coach. Besides, if people could get what they wanted on the estate, it meant they didn't have to come looking for it in town, and there were plenty of people within the strata of Prospect House who were happy with such an arrangement. Felix had never been inside the Big Blue One but nearly all of his clients had, and although he couldn't be certain what was on sale behind the reinforced doors and the painted-out glass, he presumed it was something more stimulating than Marmite and wet fish. As he turned down Grasmere Drive into Coleridge Avenue, the Big Blue One passed him in the other direction, trundling along a strip of dried mud and broken fence posts that had once been gardens.

Of all the forces at work against the Moffat family, gravity had affected them most. A stand-up fridge freezer outside on the lawn had tumbled over and strange liquids were oozing from underneath. Half a dozen daffodils in a milk bottle had wilted and slumped. With their brownish-yellow heads lying dry and inert against the peeling windowsill, they looked like a litter of kittens or rabbits born dead. In the porch, coats and jackets were strewn on the floor, and of the seven or eight wellies and leather boots left in a corner, not one had managed to stay upright. On the kitchen table, a full bag of cement had become a permanent fixture. The bottom half was glued to the Formica through various spillages. The top was solid, ringed with coffee stains and burn marks, and had become a convenient work surface as well as an impromptu telephone directory, judging by the names and numbers scrawled on the paper sack. From the kitchen ceiling, the plaster bellied downwards, stained with the brown tidemarks of several floods and other accidents in the bathroom above. Mrs Moffat, a tired-looking woman in her early fifties, offered Felix a drink, but he said no. And even though he was bursting, he decided not to ask for the loo, because, looking past the sink and the fridge, he could see the downstairs toilet, and not just the room often referred to as the toilet but the off-white pot itself with its cracked wooden seat. For reasons that were not obvious, the door to the smallest room in the house been removed and both partition walls as well. It was entirely open-plan and barely a yard from the oven.

'Sorry for the mess. It's a nightmare.'

'Don't worry, I understand.'

'With the gang and everything.'

'Are you . . . your boys . . . in a gang?'

'Oh, well, it depends who's asking, doesn't it? If you're from the dole, then they're all on the sick. Bad backs, the lot of 'em. Runs in the family. We've got X-rays to prove it. And it's being in the gang that's done 'em in. Years of it.'

'I see.'

'But you're not from the dole, are you?'

'No, I'm not.'

'Well, that's all right, then.'

'So they're in a gang?'

'Aye. A black gang.'

Felix looked blank. There were only a handful of black families on the estate and even if they'd formed a gang, it seemed unlikely the Moffats would be in it. The Moffats were not black.

'Gets everywhere,' she added.

'Does it?'

'And the white. They do some white as well. That comes off though, but not the black.'

'I see.'

'You don't know what the hell I'm on about, do you, love?'

Felix shook his head. Mrs Moffat pointed to a thick black smudge on the lino, then to another smear of blackness a couple of feet away, then to a dark-brown mark on the light switch, then to the white plastic kettle, which was covered in dirty fingerprints, as was the door of the fridge. Her hand invited him to continue looking around the kitchen. There wasn't a single object or square foot that wasn't daubed with the same kind of stain.

'Tar,' she explained.

'Oh, I see.'

'They do the tarmac. Filthy stuff it is, and sticks like shit to a blanket. I tell 'em to leave their gear in the porch, but when you've been grafting all day you don't want some woman going on at you, eh?'

'Do they work on the motorways?'

'Motorways, yards, driveways, anything. And bloody dangerous it is too. We've lost one, our Donny. Hit by a lorry on the A1. The white's more dangerous – painting lines down the middle of the road with those bloody great trucks thundering past. But at least the white comes off in the wash.'

Ruby was in the front room, watching television. Felix had asked Mrs Moffat to sit with them while they talked, but she had too much to do and said she'd listen from the kitchen. 'Walls are so bloody thin – you can't smile in this house without someone hearing you.' Felix asked Ruby why she thought she'd been excluded from school, but she didn't answer. In her short denim skirt and with her red hair tied in a bun, she looked older than eleven, but her body language was that of a child, and when Felix asked her another question she pulled the hood of her sweatshirt over her head.

'Ruby!' her mother shouted from next door.

'Don't you like school, Ruby?' asked Felix.

Inside her hood she shook her head.

'Why not?'

'Boring.'

'Mr Roderick said . . .'

'You mean Rubberdick?'

'Mr Roderick said that you were doing well up to a few months ago, then suddenly there was a problem.'

She switched the telly over with the remote, then started flicking through the satellite stations, moving from one programme to the next every few seconds. Felix asked about her friends, if she was in any kind of trouble, if there was anything she wanted to talk about, but from inside the sweatshirt there was no answer. He stood up and put a card down on the arm of the chair.

'Phone me whenever you want, if you want to. And I'll arrange for you and your mum to come and see me in the office, early next week. OK?'

He detected a nodding motion inside the hood and, taking this as a minor breakthrough, asked one last question. 'Do you want to say anything about the spiders?'

Again she said nothing, but held her thumb on one of the buttons on the remote so the programmes scrolled past in a rapid succession of adverts, cartoons, interviews, newsreaders, football, skydiving, doctors, soldiers, adverts, adverts – until interference filled the screen and a message popped up advising those subscribers having difficulty receiving a picture to call the helpline. Ruby ejected herself from the armchair and stormed out of the room. There couldn't have been any carpet on the stairs, because every footstep sounded wooden and hollow, like someone jumping on an empty box. Then a door slammed in a room above. Mrs Moffat stuck her head through the serving hatch.

'Said the magic word, did you?'

'Looks like it.'

'Don't worry, that's the third time today she's done her nut. This morning one of the lads put a plastic one in her cornflakes and she just went berserk. I've told 'em to stop teasing her. Speaking of which.'

A horn sounded outside on the road. Through the window, Felix watched as a flat-back van drew up carrying seven or eight men and what looked like a witch's cauldron, steaming and encrusted with shiny black tar. The last man was still climbing down through the tailgate as the first walked into the house. They filed past Felix, some of them nodding, others saying, 'How do' or 'All right', but none of them interested enough to ask who he was or what he was doing there. Felix thought he recognized a couple of the younger ones from juvenile court in days gone by, but he could have been wrong. Even though it had been a cool day they were all in T-shirts; their hands and faces were black with bitumen and smoke, and their arms were tanned and healthy from a life outside, under the sun.

'This is Teddy, my eldest,' said Mrs Moffat.

Teddy held up his right hand to show it was too dirty to shake, then stuck his head under the cold tap. From beneath the flow of water, he said, 'Tha's come to sort out our Ruby, an't yer?'

'Yes.'

'Well, if anyone's plaguing her I'll fucking nail 'em. We all will. What about Rubberdick down at the school? He were a right twat when I were there.'

'Actually it was Mr Roderick who referred her to us.'

'No smoke wi'out fire.'

'Do you know what's troubling her?'

'Nope. One minute she were fine, next news she's gone bananas. Mind you, she's female, in't she? That usually explains it.'

Mrs Moffat attempted to swipe him around the head with the tea towel, which he yanked from her hand to dry his head. A smaller, older man with a wild mane of grey hair threw a set of car keys on to the bag of cement on the table and pushed through the kitchen.

'Tony, this is the chap from Social Services, about our Ruby,' said Mrs Moffat.

But he didn't respond, and by the time Felix had turned around to introduce himself, Mr Moffat was already positioned above the toilet at the end of the kitchen and was undoing his trousers.

On the way back to his car, Felix heard a whistle and looked up to see James Spotland leaning out of his kitchen window, motioning him to come in. Felix had first met Jimmy in a custody case after his wife had run off to Blackpool with the kids, and still bumped into him two or three times a year. He waited while locks and chains were undone on the other side of the door, then followed Jimmy up through the garage, which was piled to the ceiling with boxes, crates, sacks of plaster, building equipment and over-stuffed bin bags bulging with mystery objects.

'Keeping yourself busy, then, Jimmy?'

'Oh, sure. You know me, never let the grass grow.'

'So what are you up to?'

'I'm in the distribution business. Product reassignment. You know how it is. What about yourself? Seeing the Moffats, were you?'

'Just a routine visit. Do you know them?'

'Everybody knows everybody on this estate. Unless the police come round. Then you don't know anyone.'

Felix moved a pile of *Loot* and *Auto-Trader* magazines from a leather swivel chair and sat down. Jimmy had gone behind the breakfast bar and pulled a pinny over his head – a glossy plastic one bearing the image of a topless woman wearing a black lace corset. 'I was just knocking up something to eat. Want anything?'

'No thanks.'

He turned the flame up under a frying pan. As a knob of butter began to sizzle, he reached into the fridge and lifted out a thick slab of red meat, which he lowered on to the bubbling fat. He pulled the cork from a half-drunk bottle of plonk with his teeth, poured a couple of glugs into the pan, then took a swig from the neck and replaced the cork, all in one seamless move while turning the meat over with a spatula in his other hand. He was a small man, not more than five and a half foot. When Felix had first met him he was scrawny and pale, with a nondescript haircut and a mouthful of rotten teeth like half-chewed toffees. These days he shaved his head, wore dentures and sported a thick gold earring in each lobe. His paunch made a comical bulge below the pair of bull's-eye breasts on his apron.

'Drink?'

'I won't, thanks. What is that, steak?'

'Venison.'

'Oh, very posh.'

'Well, venison family,' he said, turning the meat again and pressing down with the spatula, making it hiss. 'You remember the parade through town last Christmas Eve? Santa's grotto and the sleigh ride in the precinct?'

'Yes, we took some kids from the children's home.'

'Well, you remember that reindeer pulling the sleigh?'

Felix nodded and swallowed. Jimmy flipped the meat over one last time in the pan. It slapped against the Teflon and hissed. Then he slipped it on to a plate and parked himself at the table, reaching over to a drawer in the sideboard for a knife and fork.

'They said it had come all the way from Lapland, but it hadn't. It had come from a deer park near Wigan. Anyways, muggins here volunteers to take it back, Christmas spirit and all that. So I coaxed it into the van, right, but I'd had a few bevvies that night so thought I'd better wait till tomorrow. Anyways, next morning, when I looked in through the back doors, the thing was spark out on the floor.'

'Dead?'

'Dead as a dodo. I reckon it was the cold that killed it. Very parky that night. There was frost on the windscreen.'

He pinioned the meat with the fork and cut into the middle with the knife. Blood and melted butter oozed on to the white plate.

'A reindeer killed by the cold?'

'Yep. It's a different kind of cold we get here. Not like up there with the northern lights and all that. Anyways, I phoned up the deer park and they were going to charge me thirty notes just for them to chuck it in a hole. So . . .'

He lifted a chunk of it towards his mouth.

'Oh, almost forgot.'

Placing the cutlery to one side, he put his hands to his mouth, and when he stuck out his tongue Felix could see a small stud, like a silver rivet, countersunk in the flesh. Jimmy fiddled with the clasp, removed the stud, then clipped it back together and set it down on the rim of the plate.

'I wouldn't have bothered, but the girlfriend likes it. Know what I mean?' he said, raising his eyebrows and extending the tip of his tongue until it met with the point of his nose. Then he took up his knife and fork again and, through a mouthful of red meat, said, 'Don't worry, it's been in the freezer. Sure I can't tempt you?'

Abbie's car was in the driveway but there was no sign of her in the kitchen or the living room. As Felix was pouring himself a glass of water, he thought he heard music. And then the smell of perfume or flowers came to him as he stood in the hall calling her name. 'Up here,' he heard her say. As he climbed the stairs the music became louder and the smell stronger, something like pine or maybe lavender. Pushing open the bedroom door, he found Abbie sat up in bed with the pillows behind her head and the corner of the duvet pulled diagonally across her body. She was naked and she was smiling. Scented candles floated in a bowl of water on top of the chest of drawers, the little flames like bright yellow sails. Abbie leaned to one side and turned off the radio. On the bedside table Felix saw the silver end of a thermometer poking out from between the covers of her diary, like a bookmark.

'It's now, is it?' he asked.

She nodded. 'I thought you were never coming home. Get into bed.'

In the shower, Felix stood motionless under the jet of hot, fizzing water, as if work had formed a layer or film that had to be blasted away and rinsed from his skin. He let the water pound on his chest, then between his shoulder blades. By the time he slid into bed next to his wife, the upper part of his body glowed with a kind of raw heat.

'You shouldn't have it so hot, it kills them off,' said Abbie, sending her hand under the covers.

As she sank into the pillows and pulled him with her, Felix moved his head towards hers, then suddenly stopped and propped himself up on his elbow. 'What's that?'

'What?'

'That noise.'

They listened and heard a flapping sound coming from outside, like someone shaking a sheet or blanket.

'It's nothing,' said Abbie. 'Come here.'

Then the noise happened again, louder this time, like the cracking of a whip or a small clap of thunder, very near, and accompanied by a kind of creaking, and not just once but over and over again.

'Ignore it, Felix,' said Abbie. She gripped his waist with her arms and locked her fingers behind him. Then, looking beyond him, over his shoulder, she screamed, 'Oh, my God.'

Felix swivelled round just in time to see the flash of a hand as it disappeared below the sill of the open window. They heard the noise again, the flapping and the creaking, and watched as the hand appeared once more then vanished, then the noise again, then two hands, then two whole arms reaching for a moment towards the sky, and finally two outstretched arms and the top of a man's head. Felix pulled the duvet around him, padded over to the window and looked out. In the garden next door, there was something new. It had just arrived. Or it had just landed. It had big, circular feet and several poles jutting into the air. Padded plastic cushioning covered its metal frame. Across its base a shiny black membrane was held taut by thick, stern-looking springs, until Jed, all six foot four and fifteen stone of him, plunged into its centre, at which point it flexed and quivered and groaned, then flung him high into the air, above the garden fence and the bay window, way above the safety net

46

stretched around the poles, ten or a dozen feet clear of the ground. With his face suddenly level with Felix, he grinned like a mad person and just managed to shout, 'Trampoline. Got it for the kids,' before plummeting again.

5

It was a bright morning and almost ten o'clock when Felix went downstairs to make a drink and open the curtains. He'd already surfaced once, about an hour ago, but after Abbie's quick consultation with the thermometer had been called back to bed. Now she was lying on her back with her feet up on the wooden footboard. As he put a cup of tea down on the chest of drawers, she took his hand and put it against her tummy.

'It's all warm,' she said.

'Inside?'

'No, your hand.'

'From the cup,' he said.

'Tell your stuff to do its stuff.'

Felix bent forward and kissed the flat of her stomach. Abbie held his head against her. Sounds came from under her skin, sounds that reminded him of lying in the bath with his head under water, listening to the muffled echoes of the world beyond and the internal throbbing of his eardrum. His mother had told him never to stay under for too long because the pressure might damage his hearing, and had also given him the statutory warning about not putting anything smaller than his elbow in his ear. But the pleasure of a cotton bud wiggling about deep within that particular cavity had always proved irresistible and had led, in time, to several infections and one very nasty bout of labyrinthitis three years ago. Felix had never suffered from travel sickness and had been the only child in his class not to throw up on a pleasure-boat ride during a school trip to Lake Windermere. But the labyrinthitis was a killer. For almost a week he lay flat on his back, with just the slightest physical motion causing a violent whirling sensation at the very top of his head, like a weather vane in a windstorm. At its worst, anything travelling across his eyeline brought on the nausea, and on one occasion the sight of a blackbird flying past the window caused him to vomit. A course of antihistamine tablets did the trick, eventually. But even though the memory of the illness made his stomach turn, it hadn't stopped him meddling within his ear. Every once in a while he still caught himself with a toothpick or a spent match halfway to his brain, or fully submerged in a bath of cooling water.

'Your hair could do with a wash,' said Abbie, kneading his scalp with her fingers.

'I'll get a shower.'

'I'm just going to lie here for a while.'

Felix opened the French windows and took a cup of coffee and a slice of toast outside. He sat on the bench in a patch of sunlight at the far end of the garden, to the side of the greenhouse. A tile had slipped from the roof; he'd have to fix that, or borrow Jed's ladders from next door, or better still get Jed to fix it for him. Felix and Abbie had moved to the house five years ago, a red-brick semi on a close of twelve other identical properties. It was all they could afford at the time and had thought of it as a stop-gap. Abbie didn't see herself as someone who lived on a close and Felix would have liked an older house – something he could tinker with. But they'd spent money on it – a new bathroom and a new kitchen, including the dry-lining of the back wall, which was once part of the garage and partially below ground. More than that, they'd become comfortable, and a large part of that cosiness was to do with the neighbours, Jed and Maxine. Jed and Felix had gone to the same school, and although he'd never really had any contact with him, Felix had always thought of Jed as a bully, probably because of his size. Even at fourteen he was well over six foot and big with it. But a couple of days after they'd moved in, a football had sailed over the garden fence and straight through a roof-pane in the greenhouse, followed seconds later by Jed, offering an apology, a huge handshake and a four-pack of Stella. Maxine wasn't far behind him, a tiny woman with dyed black hair, telling Abbie and Felix what a clumsy oaf she was married to and if only his brains were as big as his feet. To which Abbie had responded, 'If only everything they had were that big,' a remark that made them instant friends. The cans of Stella had the same effect on Felix and Jed. The following month they'd put a gate in the fence. These days there was a well-worn path between the two lawns, scored in the grass by the coming and going of four adults, an ageing Rhodesian ridgeback called Smutty and two four-year-old girls, Molly and Alice, generally referred to as the twins. The twins were another reason for staying put. Maxine had once said that if Felix and Abbie moved away it would break their hearts, or their one, collective heart, as it sometimes seemed. Abbie had replied, 'Yes, and mine too.'

Thinking about Jed at the top of a ladder suddenly brought to mind an image of his face as it had appeared yesterday, in mid-air, with long wisps of his hair floating weightless above his head. Felix walked over to the garden fence to inspect the new trampoline. It looked even more impressive on the ground, very sturdy, with chocks under the feet and iron pegs driven into the turf to hold it in position. It was then that Felix caught sight of two training shoes poking out from under its base. One pair of very big training shoes connected to two hairy ankles.

'Morning,' said Felix.

One leg twitched. Felix scooped a handful of gravel from the rockery and showered it in the direction of the feet.

'I said, GOOD MORNING.'

There was a groan, then the clearing of a throat, then a low, rough-sounding voice. 'Time is it?'

'Half past ten. Sunday. AD 2004.'

'Which planet?'

It wasn't uncommon to find Jed asleep in the garden in the morning. In the hammock, in the shed, once in the kids' playhouse and once in the inflatable paddling pool. Sometimes it was because the twins had climbed into bed with their parents and wriggled and turned until Jed couldn't stand it any longer. But more commonly it was the result of a domestic dispute, and, judging by the noise coming through the wall yesterday evening, this latest episode had nothing to do with the children.

'Slight disagreement?' asked Felix.

'Difference of opinion about sex and violence in contemporary cinema,' said Jed, yawning.

'Meaning?'

'She wanted to watch *Pretty Woman* again and I wanted to watch *Terminator 2*.' There was a pause while he coughed, then added, 'Again.'

Jed half stood up, so the indentation of his head protruded through the trampoline. Then he crawled into the daylight. He was wearing a fleecy jacket zipped up around his neck and pulled down over his hands. He rubbed at the stubble on his face and leaned backwards against one of the metal posts.

'So I took Smutty down the park and when I got back the chain was on. I nearly called for you but there was no light on.'

'We had an early night. So where is he now?'

'Who?'

'The dog.'

'Oh, don't worry about him. He jumps on the garage roof, scratches at the landing window and she lets him in.'

Just then Maxine appeared in a dressing gown with a big mug of steaming tea and a plate of toast. As she came nearer, Felix noticed two white tablets on the rim of the plate. She put the tea and the toast on the lawn next to Jed, held his face in her hands while she kissed him on the top of his head, then gave a little wave to Felix before disappearing back inside. Jed folded a slice of toast in half, then in half again, and posted it into his mouth, followed by both paracetamol tablets washed down with a slurp of tea. The twins came into the garden, both wearing matching dungarees, and climbed on to the trampoline, using Jed's shoulders as a step. After bouncing up and down and into each other for five minutes, Molly said, 'Uncle Felix, can we go and see Auntie Abbie?'

'Oh, she's just resting at the moment. She'll be down in a minute.'

Then there was a voice from up above. It was Abbie, leaning out of an upstairs window, apparently naked apart from the two thin shoulder straps of her nightie.

'No, come on up, girls,' she was saying. 'I'm in the bedroom.'

Molly and Alice clambered down from the trampoline via Jed, ran through the gate and into the house. It had become something of a Saturday morning ritual. An hour later they'd emerge plastered with Abbie's make-up and hung with clip-on earrings and fake pearl necklaces, with Abbie, still not dressed, guiding her two little princesses into the garden for inspection.

Jed walked over to the fence and now Felix could see the intricate pattern of flattened grass imprinted on his left cheek. Jed finished off the tea and poured the dregs into a patch of raspberry canes.

'What you up to this aft?'

'I don't know. Nothing.'

'Let's have a barbie. Come on, we'll get down the garden centre before they run out of charcoal and grab a fry-up while we're in town.'

But Felix had taken off his shoes and was heading for the trampoline. 'Hang on a mo, I just want a go on this.'

'I thought you were scared of heights,' said Jed.

'Why, how high can you go?' said Felix, hauling himself over the frame and wobbling his way to the middle of the base.

'As high as your bedroom for a start, little Mr Pink Arse.' Then he laughed so loud Felix could feel the vibration through the soles of his feet.

The BBQ

The men will take care of the very hot things and the very cold things. They'll deal with the extremes. They'll go to the Arctic Circle and to the Gates of Hell, but they won't be long. An hour and a half later they return with the smell of bacon on their hands, a trace of egg yolk between their teeth and a rolled newspaper in their back pockets. Sustenance and stimulation were required during their expedition.

The mission was a success. Man number one opens the back door of the car and drags out a paper sack almost half as tall as himself. It is awkward and shapeless and fat, a lifeless weight he has to hoist from the boot and carry across his shoulders. He walks unsteadily to the garden, where he lowers it gently, like a dead friend fallen in battle. In front of him is the slab. The shrine. The sacrificial altar made from four concrete paving stones cemented on to four breeze-block legs. It is a fixed and permanent construction, crude but of solid build. It is 'on the large side', meaning a whole bison could be roasted here with room at each side for chicken or fish ('for the wives'). The triangular pile of cold, soggy ash is fettled out with a garden hoe, then cast among bushes and shrubs or dug into a flowerbed. The rusty iron grill is brushed with a leather glove, banged against a wall, held up to the light and declared clean.

Despite the flimsy appearance of the paper sack and empirical evidence as to the low tensile strength of paper in general, this particular paper sack refuses to be torn by bare hands alone. It even resists the strong teeth of man number one as he attempts to rip it open with a firm bite and a shake of his head. The garden shears are collected from the shed, but rather than trim the stitching from the top seam or cut along the perforated line in the right-hand corner, man number one prefers to tackle the problem bayonet-style, closing the shears to make a single blade, then lunging at his target. A small puff of black-grey dust issues from the puncture wound. Man number one then enlarges the hole and begins to excavate its dark, brittle contents lump by lump. However, on finding this a dirty, piecemeal and time-consuming chore, he finally wrestles the sack on to the barbecue station and shakes out an ample pile of charcoal briquettes on to the concrete plinth. One squirt with the fluid and one strike of a match and the heap ignites, burning with a hazy, invisible heat. To make sure, man number one lowers his hand over the transparent flame until something intensely hot forces him to snatch it away and nurse his wound in his armpit until the tingling stops. It is definitely lit.

Man number two, meanwhile, has carried his burden of eight plastic bags to the shade of a lean-to shed at the side of the house and is currently employed in the redistribution of waste products. He is to be found stuffing the contents of the green dustbin (recyclables) into the already full black dustbin (non-recyclables) by climbing into the black dustbin and jumping up and down. Cans and boxes rupture and pop under his feet, and when he looks down, a small quantity of baked-bean juice has spurted across the tongue and lace of his left shoe. Dismounting, he proceeds to line the inside of the empty green bin with a bin bag, partially burrowing inside it to squeeze out any pockets of air. His cargo is in many ways the opposite of the charcoal carried and ignited by man number one. His cargo is ice. Gouging one bag open with his nails, he swings it into the air and hundreds of bright, gleaming cubes are disgorged into the depth of the green bin, thundering and drum-rolling against the plastic base. Between each deposit, he adds in a consignment of lager or beer until the bin is two-thirds full with layers of alcohol and ice, topped with a litre-bottle of Frascati ('for the wives'). Then, delving into the coldness, man number two roots out two cans of Stella and carries one across to his friend by the fire, man number one, who touches the cool, wet metal to the parched and filthy blister forming in the slack, pudgy flesh just below his thumb.

Throughout the afternoon couples and families arrive. The kids pile on the trampoline, all of them jumping together, until one harmonious bounce – like a seventh wave – flings them into the side netting or dumps them in a heap. The women draw deck chairs and sun loungers towards the centre of the lawn. The men who congregate around the ice stand and drink. The men who congregate around the fire stand and stare. With the charcoal flaky and white and evenly spread across the slab, the burgers, chops, chicken wings and chipolatas are strategically arranged on the grill, sometimes with forks and serving tongs, sometimes with fingers and thumbs. Most of the men come to prod and point, or just to stand with their hands in their pockets and watch. The meat spits and cracks. Fat drips from the mesh and fizzes on the glowing, powdery coals.

After the food, the men disperse, but the women consolidate their position in the heart of the garden and they communicate. They communicate about the children and about the schools in the town – the good schools and the bad ones, the church school and the other one. They talk about parent governors. They talk about drugs and film stars. They talk about money. They talk about the European Union and the Middle East and breast-feeding. The women have come together, but the men have separated and spread out. They are elsewhere. The male diaspora extends as far as the road, where one man is checking his brake pads and has placed his bottle of Budweiser precariously on the wing mirror of the car. It also includes one man watching an international rugby fixture on a portable telly in the children's playroom, and a man in the kitchen loading the dishwasher for the second time, and a man asleep under the cherry tree, and a man on his mobile phone by the gate, and a man rehearsing the military-style execution of a garden gnome with a water pistol to the back of its head, and a man under a pile of children on the trampoline, and a man whose bleeper went off ten minutes after he'd arrived and hasn't been seen since. The children bounce and bounce and bounce and the dog barks.

At the end of the day the women stand and separate and go in search of their men, and the men come together to shake hands and seek out a task. Such as the pouring of a bin-load of slush and beer labels into an outside drain. Such as the extinguishing of embers and the scattering of ash.

6

'You're standing on a beach. It's lovely and warm. You can feel the sun on your face and the sand between your toes. The sea in front of you is calm and quiet and blue, like the sky. You lie down on the beach and close your eyes. There's no one else around – it's very peaceful, very safe. And as you lie there, feeling the gentleness of the sun on your skin, all your aches and pains seem to melt from your body, flow through you into the sand. The sand soaks it all from you, all the weariness, all the tension, any tightness in your muscles and joints – it's all absorbed by the sand. And the sound of the sea, the slow, easy rhythm of the tide, is soothing your mind, washing away all the frustration, all the anger, all the pressure and hurt. Listen to the tide on the shore. Let each swish of water wash another problem out of your mind, let each swell of the tide carry your troubles back to the sea. Back to the huge, blue, bottomless sea. Breathe the fresh sea air through your nose, fill your body with clean air, draw it deep into your lungs. Relax. Listen to the sea. Feel the sun on your face.'

There was a beeping noise outside in the street, a lorry reversing around a corner. Or possibly the noise of a pelican crossing, the traffic lights at red and the pulsing green image of a little robotic man in mid-stride.

'You stand up and just a few yards away there's a jetty with a boat tied to it, a little sailing boat with your name written on the side. You climb down into it and undo the rope. A warm breeze fills the white sails and pushes you out into open water. But you're not afraid, because the boat knows which way to go. You sit down and watch the water going past, and see tiny coloured fish down below, and shells on the sea bed, and beautiful coral, and the next time you look up you see you've come to land on a small island. It's a desert island with a few palm trees swaying in the breeze and a brilliant white beach. The boat has brought you here. It has brought you to meet someone. Someone you need to see. They're waiting for you in the middle of the island. And even though you're a little afraid, a little bit nervous, you walk to the top of the beach, feeling the warm sand under your feet and between your toes, and you push through the bushes and the grass and step out into a small clearing in the middle of the trees, and there in front of you, waiting for you, is the person you need to see.

'And now you talk to the person. You say the thing you've always wanted to say. You speak – words come out of your mouth.

'And now the person talks to you.

'And you listen.

'And you watch.

'And you stay with that person for as long as you need to, saying the things you need to say, listening to their voice, watching their face and their hands. And when you're ready to leave, you say goodbye.

'You say goodbye.

'And the boat with your name on it is waiting for you. You climb in and it carries you back across the water, and even though you watch the little island on the horizon until it disappears from view, you know you can return there whenever you want, that the little boat will always know the way. And now you look into the water again, seeing the coral and the shells and the tiny coloured fish, and when you look up you're back at the jetty, back at the beach. You lie down and let the warm sand and the sound of the tide soothe your body and your mind. Listen to the waves. Feel the sun on your face.

'Then, whenever you're ready, whenever you're calm enough and rested enough and ready to open your eyes, then you can open your eyes. Take all the time you need, then, when you're ready, open your eyes.'

After about five minutes, Abbie reached forwards and pulled a tissue out of the box. Both her cheeks were striped with the traces of dried tears. She wiped her face and dabbed at her eyes, and examined the tissue as if for some kind of explanation. Then she reached over for another tissue and blew her nose. The counsellor waited a few more moments as Abbie took a few deep breaths and reorganized herself in her seat.

'Sorry,' she said, shaking her head in disbelief.

'No need to apologize, no need to apologize at all.'

His voice was more matter-of-fact now that the boat journey had come to an end, but still measured and kind. 'How did it feel?'

'Sort of like being asleep but not asleep. A bit like a daydream, but more . . .'

'Focused?'

'Yes, very clear.'

'And did you sail to the island?'

'Yes.'

'Were you afraid?'

'Yes. A little.'

'Do you want to tell me what happened? You don't have to, if it's too much.'

'No, I want to.'

She'd pushed the tissues inside the cuff of her shirt. With her elbows on the arm of the chair, she locked her hands together and rested her chin on the saddle of her thumbs, partially obscuring her mouth. A few strands at a time, her hair fell from behind her ears in front of her face.

'I . . . I was nervous. I thought I knew what was coming, you see. So I walked up the beach, like you said, and into the grass and the trees . . .'

She swallowed and pulled the remains of the tissue from her sleeve.

'And pushed open the leaves and I thought it was going to be . . . I thought it was going to be . . .'

She was bent over now, with hunched shoulders, and tears

dripped from behind the screen of her hair on to her skirt, making small, dark patches on the denim. 'You know.'

'Who did you think it was going to be, Abbie?'

'My mum,' she sobbed.

'But it wasn't your mum?'

Without looking up, Abbie shook her head, and another tear fell on to her skirt, distinct and precise, almost black against the light blue cotton, like a small hole.

'Who was it, Abbie?'

Abbie straightened herself in the chair and lifted her face. As her hair fell backwards from her face, she took a huge, trembling breath, closed her eyes and, as she breathed out again, spoke two words that seemed to be made of air. She said, 'My baby.'

'The baby you lost?'

'Yes.'

'The last one, after the scan?'

She nodded. Then her head went down again and her shoulders shook, and a hand came out from underneath for another tissue, then another. The counsellor let her go on crying for a good few minutes, until the tears stopped, and when she reappeared it was with a creased and sodden face.

'Do you want to go on?'

'It was a little boy,' she whispered.

'And what did you say?'

'I said I was sorry.'

'Sorry for what?'

The beeping noise started again outside, definitely a pelican crossing, accompanied by the sound of a car screeching to a halt, then the revving of an engine, then the sound of squealing rubber and deep, sporty engine accelerating into the distance.

'For losing him, for not holding on.'

'And did he talk to you?'

Abbie nodded her head. 'He said . . . he said he was sorry too.'

'For what?'

'For letting go.'

'And did you touch him? Did you pick him up?'

'No, but he was smiling,' said Abbie, trying to make the same smile on her own face, and then, just before the tears flooded her eyes again, she said, 'He didn't cry.'

The counsellor handed over the entire box of tissues, put his hand on Abbie's shoulder for a moment, then went out through a sliding door. The room was actually his lounge; there had been no attempt to disguise it as an office or even a study, and while he was gone a cat suddenly appeared from under the piano and leapt into Abbie's lap. Not long afterwards the counsellor returned with two glasses of water. He handed one of them to Abbie, who took a few sips and put it down.

'Shall I?' he asked, offering to remove the cat.

'No, it's fine,' she said, running her hand from the back of its head to the tip of its tail, then flicking off the loose hairs that had clung to her fingers.

The counsellor held out the other glass of water.

'And what about you, how are you feeling, Felix? Felix?'

After successfully feigning invisibility up to this point in the proceedings, the repetition of his name made Felix not only conspicuous again but suddenly the centre of attention. Even the cat looked at him. And how was he feeling? Dry. More than anything he was dry. It was the thought of all that sun and sand. He downed the water in three or four gulps and croaked, 'I'm OK. I'm feeling OK.'

Abbie reached out across the armchair for his hand.

'Do you want to talk about anything?'

He didn't. But when Abbie squeezed his fingers and stroked his wedding ring with her thumb, he nodded his head.

'Do you want to tell us who was waiting for you?'

The beeping noise started up again outside. The cat rolled on its side and stared with its upside-down face and its bald, pink nose. Abbie gave Felix a reassuring smile and another squeeze of the hand. He nodded. The counsellor smiled and said, 'So you get out of the boat, walk up the beach through the warm sand, push through the foliage. Who's waiting for you, Felix?'

The counsellor went quiet, leaving a silence in the room that only Felix could break. The cat blinked at him, waiting for him to speak. The pressure from Abbie's hand began to increase. Felix closed his eyes.

'Oliver Cromwell,' he said.

7

Felix pressed the button, and when the beeping noise started they crossed the road and went into the café, which was really a greengrocer's with a few tables in the back and a percolator behind the counter. He was expecting the worst, but, after tasting her coffee, Abbie looked at him from behind a moustache of froth, grinned and asked him if there was something he wanted to tell her? Possibly about a famous character from British parliamentary history? Felix shook his head and said that he was sorry.

'I thought it was a different game.'

'Game?'

Technique, he had meant to say. Treatment. The point was this: a person can't practise social work on himself. It would be like trying to hypnotize yourself – you just can't. You can't play that kind of trick on your own mind.

'Trick?'

Whatever. She knew what he meant, and anyway he was just being honest. There was no point lying, was there? Abbie agreed that there was no point lying, especially not at 150 pounds an hour. Which led Felix to wonder, just for a moment, why the hell he was driving around the Lakeland Estate all year for not much more than the minimum wage, when he could just as easily stick a couple of comfy chairs in the living room, talk dreamily about sailing boats and sandy beaches and make a fortune. The pedestrian crossing beeped again. Abbie leaned over and squeezed his hand, the way she had done ten minutes ago, but with less intensity. His blood was free to circulate now. Her smile reminded him of the counsellor's cat with its upside-down face, like a bat. She didn't care if it was a trick or a game, she said, because already she felt a thousand times better. As if she'd done something she should have done ages ago.

'Like you've closed a door?'

'No, more like I've opened one. Opened a door and gone outside, and the sun's shining.'

'Good. That's . . . good.'

The sun was shining, and it was still shining when they got home. Abbie went next door to talk to Maxine, tell her everything that had happened. Felix dragged the Flymo out of the shed for the first time since last autumn, chipped the crust of dried cuttings from blade and mowed the lawn.

That was Monday. Tuesday was quiet. It wasn't an official holiday – the schools hadn't broken up – but a lot of people in the town still observed some archaic festival or feast day related to the cotton industry, even though not a single thread of cotton had been spun there for over fifty years. Felix saw it as a chance to clean out his filing cabinet and bring his records up to date. Neville saw it as an opportunity for arranging a trip to Australia next year to see his brother and for goofing around. When he wasn't sat behind a pile of brochures with the telephone to his ear, making calls to New South Wales, he was throwing darts at the dartboard hanging from the coat hook on the door, waiting for the travel agent to call back. At one point, Bernard stuck his head into the office to ask if anyone else could hear banging.

'Thud, thud, thud, then nothing, then three more, then nothing. Been going on all day.'

'Sounds like an airlock in the pipes, chief,' said Neville.

'Ah, could be, could be. Better get it checked out. Giving Thelma a migraine. Oh, while I'm here, anybody want to contribute to the coffee fund? We're down to the last few pence.'

'Can you break a twenty?'

'Er . . .'

'Tell you what, I'll pay double next week.'

'Felix?'

Felix dutifully stumped up a pound, then another for the lottery syndicate. As Bernard closed the door behind him, Neville reproduced the set of darts from his pocket, along with a fistful of change. 'Come on, then, Felix. Nearest the bull. Pound a game. Best of three.'

After lunch Felix called at the school to talk to Rubberdick. A prominent figure in the town, Captain Eric Roderick was often to be found in the pages of the local paper, expressing his opinion on crime, drugs, litter, skateboarding in the precinct, alcopops and other threats to society. An army man with medals for bravery, the Captain had reinvented himself in later life, putting his expertise in military manoeuvres and tactical warfare to good use in the classrooms and staffrooms of Britain's failing schools. A disciplinarian and a believer in old-fashioned values, he had single-handedly restored the reputation of a struggling comprehensive in a neighbouring borough and was high on the list of government 'superheads'. He was rumoured to be a close personal friend of the Home Secretary and had once appeared on *Question Time*. The nameplate on his door carried his full title and, after knocking twice, Felix was just about to turn away when he heard the instruction to enter. Inside, the Captain was sitting at his desk in front of a large, laminated sheet of card criss-crossed with red marker pen.

'Bit of a crisis – entire English department down with hay fever. Having to juggle the timetable.' Then, to himself, 'One bluebell and they fall like dominoes.' Then, to Felix, 'How can I help?'

He gestured to Felix to take the chair in front of his desk and Felix obliged.

'Er . . . do I call you Captain?'

'Mr Roderick will do. Unless you've come to present me with another of these, in which case I'll have my full title.'

Without turning around, he pointed to a photograph of himself in military uniform, receiving a handshake and some sort of decoration from the Queen.

'It's about Ruby Moffat. You wrote to us about her. I phoned last week but you were teaching at the time.'

'So I was. *Antony and Cleopatra* with Year 10. Pressed into action courtesy of the pollen count and the sensitive nasal passages of some of my junior staff. Do you have the reference?'

Felix pulled the blue folder from his briefcase and took out the only sheet of paper. The head teacher produced his own copy of the letter from his cabinet.

'Ah, yes, the Moffats. Are you familiar with the family?'

'We've had dealings with them over the years, on and off. And I called round last week to talk to Ruby.'

'And how would you describe them?'

'Er . . .'

'As a family?'

'Well, I . . .'

'In a word?'

'Busy?'

On not being supplied with the adjective he was looking for, the Captain went on to explain how a glance through the records confirmed that the Moffat 'brood' had presented the school with a succession of problems over the preceding decade. The boys, he said, of which there were a large but unspecified number, had completed their education last year, or rather they had ceased attending the school, and the school was happy to believe it had seen the last of them. Then came Ruby, 'their little afterthought', and although her first few months at secondary school had been largely uneventful, it now appeared she was determined to match the poor standards set by her brothers. In fact after recent incidents, it now looked as if she might exceed them, if he could put it that way, or descend below them, rather. After completing his appraisal of the situation, he sat back in his chair and waited for Felix's response.

'Could you describe these incidents?'

'They're logged on the computer. If you want the full *modus operandi* I could get Mrs Cousins to print you a copy.'

'Just a summary, for now.'

'Spitting, both between lessons and in class. Swearing – shouting expletives at the top of her voice. General lack of cooperation. Rudeness towards teachers and aggressive behaviour towards other pupils. Hasn't done a stroke of work for over a month now. And then there's all this silliness with the spiders.'

'Go on.'

'One minute she's drawing them all over her workbooks, despite being told not to. The next minute she's invented some kind of phobia. Won't go into the science lab because she saw one in the sink. Won't open her desk in case there's one inside. And then, the *pièce de résistance* – ran screaming from Mr Carrick's history lesson when he embarked on the story of Robert the Bruce.'

'Is she in school today?'

Mr Roderick eyed a large and complicated timetable on the whiteboard across the room. 'Double geography with Miss Maloney.'

'So, broadly speaking, you'd say that her recent behaviour is out of character. Yes?'

'She's a Moffat,' asserted Mr Roderick.

Felix said, 'I mean as an individual. As a person.'

Mr Roderick put his copy of the letter back in the drawer. 'Yes, you could put it that way, if you wanted. I might put it another way, but then we each have our different jobs to do, and we each have our different vocabulary. Now, Mr . . .'

'Fenton.'

'If you wouldn't mind, I'm sure you're very busy and I know I am.'

As Mr Roderick drummed his fingers on the leather writing pad, Felix noticed that his fingernails were not only immaculately manicured but shiny as well, and on looking closer at them he could see they were painted with transparent, glossy nail varnish. The two men exchanged a few more remarks about keeping an eye on the girl and staying in contact. Then, below the picture of Captain Roderick's investiture, Felix reached out and shook his hand.

★

Back at the office there was something of a drama taking place. Everyone was in the staffroom, looking out over the Strawberry Field. When Felix peered through the window, he could see that a large crowd had gathered in the far corner as if some kind of circus act were being staged. Or even a fight, like one of those illicit bare-knuckle boxing matches that once took place on the common. The crowd had formed a circle that couldn't quite keep its shape. At one moment people seemed hellbent on getting as far away from the action as possible, the next they were drawn back to it, shouting and waving at something in the middle. As the ring of spectators slewed towards the office, something huge and cream-coloured showed itself for a split second before disappearing again. The mob closed in, then panic broke out among a section closest to the building, and, as the bodies parted, Felix saw that the cream-coloured something in the middle was an animal. A cow, apparently. In fact a massive, thick-necked, prong-horned bull.

'Poor, dumb animal,' said Mo.

'Seen someone you know?' asked Neville.

For another five or ten minutes the crowd shrieked and ran whenever the bull made even the slightest movement in their direction. Then a loud cheer went up as a thin, gangly lad in a blue bomber jacket was pushed to the front. He staggered towards the bull, twisting and swaying in front of it, flapping his arms in a kind of mad dance. Then he went crashing to the ground as he attempted some kind of bicycle kick or cartwheel in mid-air.

'Oh, no,' said Marjorie. 'He's one of mine.'

'Who, the matador?' said Neville.

'It's Matthew Coyne, and it looks like he's glued up to the eyeballs.'

As she spoke, Coyne was climbing to his feet and wagging his finger at the bull, like a pantomime dame telling off a naughty puppy. The crowd loved it and whooped even louder as he stood no further than a couple of yards away from the bull's head and stripped off his jacket. Turned inside-out, the silky, crimson lining flared in the afternoon sun as he wafted it forwards, then held it to his side like a bullfighter's cape. The bull appeared unimpressed at first, puzzled as to why a daft-looking lad should be offering his bomber jacket, ignorant even of the appropriate response. But its state of idleness didn't last long. Suddenly, as if its memory had been triggered, the bull dipped its head, angled its horns in the direction of the jacket and snorted at the dust on the ground. A cheer went up as Coyne draped the jacket over the bull's face, then passed along its flank, drawing it slowly down its neck, then along the thick saddle of its back, then over its rump. Marjorie had just picked up the phone when a police car drove on to the field and parked about thirty yards away. She replaced the receiver. Coyne made a low, sweeping bow in front of his audience, much to their approval. And was just bending down for an encore when the bull jerked backwards – like the first reverse jumps of a shot-putter – then punched out with its hind legs, which in an instant were higher than its head.

From their position on the ground, the sight of a thin, contorted body suddenly rocketing skywards out of a crowd of onlookers must have been a puzzling sight to the two policemen in shirtsleeves putting on their helmets and ambling slowly towards the disturbance. From his aerial viewpoint, Felix couldn't tell what altitude young Coyne had achieved, but was reminded, momentarily, of the speed of sound relative to the speed of light. First came the sight of a body landing hard and flat on its spine, and fractionally later came the dull thud of a human being dropped from a decent height on to dried mud.

'That looks like one less on your caseload,' said Neville to Marjorie, who screamed.

What happened after that was complicated and hazy. The crowd ran. The police thought they were being chased so they ran too, but most of the crowd caught and overtook them. Then the police came back and so did the crowd. In the meantime, the bull had lumbered nonchalantly towards the edge of the roundabout, into the subway and out of sight. More police arrived, followed by an ambulance, followed by a bigger crowd. A human circle formed again with Matthew Coyne at the centre, only this time he wasn't moving. After the paramedics had loaded the stretcher into their vehicle and closed the back doors, the people closed in to fill the empty space. Then somebody looked up and pointed. Then somebody shouted something and then somebody shouted something else. Then everybody looked up. They looked to the top floor of Prospect House, at Felix, and at Neville, and Marjorie, Mo, Roy, Thelma and Bernard, who were looking down. They looked at the faces of social workers, and the faces of the town planners two floors below, and the faces of the housing officers on the floor below that. And what the people saw the people didn't like. The first stone lost energy and fell away. In fact at the top of the building the Department of Social Services was safely out of range. But from below came the sound of breaking glass. This continued as Bernard urged everyone to step away from the windows, shelter under a table maybe. Ignoring his advice, Neville and Felix and Mo watched until more police arrived, followed by a fire engine. From the top of a turntable ladder a couple of streets away a lone fireman showered the stone throwers with light but continuous rain for several minutes until the final twenty or thirty dropped their missiles and slithered off through the mud.

A bull and a riot, but it wasn't the end of the day. When Felix returned to his office the small red light on his telephone was flashing. There were three messages. The first was from Captain Roderick, saying there had been a further incident at the school involving Ruby Moffat. She had asked to leave early to go to the dentist's but had 'failed to produce the necessary proof of said appointment'. She had been sent to the head teacher's office, where there had been 'something of a scuffle', at which point Ruby had climbed out of his ground-floor window and was now missing. 'AWOL'. The second message was from a distressed-sounding Mrs Moffat. The school had phoned her. She'd told Captain Roderick that Ruby *was* expected at the dentist's, but this was a lie, to keep her out of trouble. Then Ruby hadn't come home, and now it was half past four and she'd left the school over two hours ago. The Moffat crew were out looking for her. The third voice was that of Police Constable Martin Nottingham, saying that Ruby had been found, or rather she'd arrived home at just after five o'clock. But there was something he needed to talk to Felix about, so could he phone back or call round at the nick on his way home.

At the police station, PC Nottingham took Felix into one of the interview rooms and closed the door. He was younger than Felix, in his late twenties at most, and when he spoke a small nugget of ivory-coloured chewing gum glinted in his mouth. 'Just need to have a quick word with you about the girl.'

'She's OK, is she?'

'Sort of. We were at the house when she got back. Any idea where she might have been?'

'Not really. Captain Roderick – at the school – said there had been some kind of altercation.'

'Yeah, we're looking into that. Thing is, when she gets home she's in a bit of a sulk and goes straight upstairs to her bedroom. Locks the door. Doesn't say where she's been. All the Moffat lads are there, giving it this.' He made his hand into the shape of a mouth, jabbering and pecking right in front of Felix's face.

'Anyways, she's thrown her coat on the kitchen floor, and when the mother picks it up, there's a pair of knickers stuffed in the pocket.'

'Ruby's knickers?'

'Exactly. Definitely hers. Dark blue with yellow sea-horses stitched on the side. And that's not all that's on 'em.'

He leaned closer and lowered his voice, pushing his chewing gum to one side of his mouth with his tongue.

'There's some very dodgy-looking silvery stains, front and back. So now they're in a plastic bag down in Manchester, waiting for the white-coats to run the tests.'

Felix said, 'That sounds worrying. Did she say anything about spiders?'

The policeman shook his head as he stood up. 'No. She didn't say nothing about nothing.'

'When will you have the results?'

'End of next week. But there's going to be an investigation anyway, so you should get the ball rolling at your end. Eleven-year-old girl comes home with her clouts in her pocket – that's dodgy, jizz or no jizz, yeah?'

Then he opened the door and walked Felix back towards the reception area, raising the hatch in the front desk for Felix to pass through.

'So I'll call next week, then,' said Felix. 'Should I ask for you?'

'No, I'll have passed it on to one of the brides.'

'One of the what?'

'One of the women. A WPC,' he said, spelling out the letters. 'Although we're all PCs now. Technically speaking.'

'Oh, OK. Thanks.'

It was nearly seven o'clock when Felix got home. He put his briefcase down in the hall, hauled off his jacket and tie and hung them on the newel post. He could hear music playing. Soft, atmospheric music, and as he made his way upstairs he was met by the smell of scented candles.

GEMINI *(21 May–21 June)*

8

The lift wasn't working. Felix waited at the top of the fire escape, watching the crown of her head and her hand on the banister rail as she made her way towards him up the tiled staircase. With his foot, he nudged a flattened cigarette butt over the ledge and watched it fall, then a sweet wrapper which parachuted slowly down to the ground floor. Abbie was slightly breathless by the time she reached the fifth floor, and as she leaned forward to kiss him on the cheek he felt the heat in her face.

'God, I couldn't do that every day. I'm knackered,' she said, pulling off her coat and throwing it over her shoulder.

'Keeps me fit,' said Felix, punching the code into the keypad and showing her through the heavy wooden doors. They walked slowly along the corridor, past the staffroom on the right-hand side, where Bernard was changing a fuse in the kettle, and into Felix's office. He closed the door behind them.

'Nice view,' said Abbie, staring out of the window.

'Haven't you been in here before?'

'No. It's a regular little lookout post, isn't it?'

'Well, I can keep an eye on you in the precinct, if that's what you mean.'

'So I see.'

She carried on looking out of the window while Felix made himself comfortable in his chair and began searching for a folder in the drawer in the desk. Then, still with her back to him, she said, 'Felix, what do men want?'

'How do you mean?'

'If I asked you what you wanted, as a man, what would you say to me?'

'I don't know,' he answered, after thinking about it for a minute or so. 'Depends on the context.'

Abbie turned around, and even though she'd had time to cool down he could see that her cheeks were still red, as if she were blushing.

'The context is that I come up to you on the street with my clipboard to ask you a few questions. And I'm a woman and you're a man, and I've never seen you before in my life, and I ask you, "What do men want?" What do you say?'

It sounded like a trick question. Maybe she was asking him what he wanted for his birthday. Or maybe he'd forgotten something, like Valentine's Day or their anniversary. Women were strict about things like that. If Jed didn't buy Maxine a Mother's Day present from the twins, he slept in the garden, frost or no frost, and Felix didn't imagine Abbie would be any more forgiving, should the opportunity arise. He pictured himself and Jed waking up under the trampoline, or sleeping top to toe in the hammock, Jed's giant feet in his face all night. There had been other times when Abbie had asked questions like this one, open-ended questions with an infinite number of answers, and one occasion in particular when she had asked Felix what he was thinking. 'Felix, what are you thinking?' They were sitting in the car at night, parked in a lay-by at the edge of the Peak District, watching chimney smoke from a farmhouse rising vertically into the cold, still air, silver in the moonlight. There was no baby that month. Like the month before that, and the month before. A full moon meant no baby. Trusting to his instincts, he had replied, 'That all good things come to those who wait.'

'Wrong,' she said.

He could still hear her saying it, final and definitive. Today he wanted to avoid his instincts. He wanted to get it right.

'How about . . .' he began, emphasizing that he was treating this as an exercise and that his answer should be taken as an example of what a man might say, in such circumstances, rather than a reflection of his own character. 'How about security?' he said. Then, on realizing this answer sounded too much like the response of a social worker, he appended, 'Or happiness?'

'Exactly,' Abbie agreed. 'Something abstract. Something vague but positive. Something apt. But oh, no, that isn't the case. Not in this town anyway. In this town that isn't what men want, not by a long chalk.'

'What do they want?' Felix asked.

'Blow jobs.'

'What?'

'Blow jobs.'

Felix didn't understand and shook his head, waiting for the explanation.

Abbie said, 'It's for a magazine, an article called *What Men Want*. So, I'm down in the precinct and a man comes out of the post office, and he fits the bill – between twenty and forty, professional-looking, in a suit – and I ask him if he can spare a moment of his time and he says he can, so I ask him what men want. And that's what he says.'

'Blow jobs?'

'Yes. Just like that.'

Felix hopped over to the window and looked out. 'Is he still there? Can you point him out?'

'No! This was twenty minutes ago. I had to go and sit in the park to cool down. Look at this – I'm still red.' She touched her hand to her face, then showed Felix her fingers, as if they might be stained with the colour of embarrassment.

'*You* wouldn't say that to a woman, would you, Felix?'

'No.'

'No, that's what I thought. Where's the loo?'

'Just on there to the left. Look, if anyone asks you why you're here . . .'

'Don't worry, I told your receptionist I've brought your sandwiches in.'

'What did she say?'

'Didn't hear her. Something about true love.'

When she came back she was shaking her hands in the air, saying there was no paper in the ladies' toilet and the hand-dryer wasn't working. He said he'd tell Bernard and made a note of it on a yellow Post-it. Then he asked her if she was nervous, and she said she was but wanted to get on with it, and sat down.

'Well, this is it,' he said, weighing a buff folder in his hands. The seams were worn through and the top flap had torn. Someone had tied a pink ribbon around its length and width to hold it together.

'It doesn't seem like much,' she said. 'For a whole life.'

Behind his desk with Abbie in front of him Felix felt more comfortable. This was a familiar situation, despite the fact that this was his wife in the chair. He could feel himself slipping into his routine, falling back on the little phrases and gestures that had become second nature. The words came easily, and Abbie listened, impressed and surprised by his confidence and manner, happy to let him talk.

'No, it doesn't look like much, but there will be things in here you're not expecting. Some things that puzzle or interest you. Excite you even. And things that come as a shock.'

She nodded and he went on.

'People are given up for adoption for all kinds of reasons, some of them pretty obvious, some of them more . . . dramatic. Have you given that any thought?'

'A little,' said Abbie.

'And what did you imagine?'

'Well, on the one hand there was, you know, stigma. Back then. If people weren't married. And sometimes they just couldn't afford to keep the baby, if money was tight. And on the other hand . . .' She swallowed, and looked at him to check she was taking the conversation in the right direction.

'Go on.'

'Well, rape. That would be the worst. Wouldn't it?'

He wanted to lean across and touch her. But on the day he'd

78

told her the file had arrived, she'd made him promise not to open it until she visited the office. She wanted what she called a 'proper' interview. No privileges or courtesies, no special services or lovey-dovey stuff. She wanted it done by the book, and when he asked why, she'd said, 'Because I don't want you to feel like you're doing me a favour.' He'd agreed, and he was good at keeping his word. Now he felt sorry for her. But maybe that was something she didn't want either – his pity.

'Before we go into things, I just want to tell you that adoption back then wasn't like it is now. These days everything is done in triplicate. There are procedures that have to be followed and it's all very formal, very standardized. In the past, it was a bit more . . . hit and miss, shall we say. Some of this information is going to be very haphazard. In fact the files are usually pulped after so many years. The clerk at the court in Norwich told me he found yours in a cupboard in the cellar, behind the boiler.'

'Charming.'

'I'm telling you that you've been really lucky, Abbie. There could have been nothing.'

Abbie nodded, as if she'd been told off. Then her eyes settled on the pink ribbon around the folder as Felix plucked at the knot until it began to loosen.

'And what about your mum and dad?'

'That's what I've come to find out, isn't it?'

'I mean your adoptive parents.'

'What about them?'

'Have you told them what you're doing?'

She shook her head.

'Why not?'

'You know why not.'

Felix raised his eyebrows. If he was going to keep to his side of the bargain then she had to as well. A proper interview – that's what she wanted and that's what she was going to get. It meant staying in character. Playing the game. He stopped tugging at the knot.

'All right, all right,' she said. 'I see Mum and Dad a couple of times a year. They're lovely people and I don't want to hurt them. When I was ten they told me I was adopted – they've never mentioned it since and I've never asked. They retired to the seaside three years ago and they're very happy and I'm very happy for them. I know this sounds like a daft thing to say, but it's none of their business. They've done their bit and they did it well. Now it's up to me. It's my turn.'

'You say they only mentioned it the once. Deep down, do you think you want to punish them, for not dealing with it properly?'

This time Abbie lifted *her* eyebrows. Yes, she wanted this doing by the book, but she hadn't come here to be analysed. She wanted information and facts. She wanted answers. She wanted Felix to stop teasing the pink ribbon and get on with it. He yanked a little harder, and as the knot sprang open the folder swelled slightly, a small but perceptible expansion, like a drawing of breath. He pulled out a dozen or so loose sheets of paper of various sizes and shapes, and shuffled them in his hand, unfolding a long-by-narrow document and placing it on top of the pile.

'Well, this is amazing. This shouldn't be in here really. Have you ever seen this before?' he said, holding a birth certificate towards her.

Abbie shook her head, staring at the paper with its red background and border and its bold, black calligraphy. 'No.'

'This is a real bonus.'

Felix laid it flat in front of her and pointed at the different boxes with the unprotruded tip of a ballpoint pen.

'Look. Maria.'

'Who's that? Was that my name when I was born?' said Abbie.

'No, Maria Rosales. That was your mother.'

'Rosales?' said Abbie, uncomprehendingly.

'Sounds Mexican or something. South American, maybe.'

'Rosales?' Her hair began to drift in front of her face as she studied the document and she put her hand to her forehead to hold it in place. 'Was that my . . . surname?'

'Sort of. In those days you could only take your father's surname. But look.'

Abbie's eyes followed the pen as it travelled to column number 4, entitled, 'Name, and surname of father'. The box was empty, except for a small, horizontal dash of black ink. In a low, quiet voice, Felix inquired, 'Am I going too fast? We could take a break here.'

Abbie's eyes were jumping from one part of the certificate to another. 'No. I'm OK,' she said, in a voice even quieter than his.

He carried on, thinking of the positives, taking his pen back to column number 6 and tapping at the name Rosales. 'It sounds Spanish to me. And look, the address she gave can't be far from where you were brought up.'

'Rosales,' she said to herself. Then again to Felix, as a question, 'Rosales?'

Felix scanned the next sheet of paper and put it down on the table facing away from him. It was typed but slightly fuzzy, as if it had been photocopied several times, and from his side of the desk Felix was only just able to decipher it. He read it out loud and guided Abbie's eyes with his pen again along each sentence. '"Adoption Act 1950. The infant was born on 9 May . . ."'

'The 6th,' she corrected him.

'"On 6 May 1964 at home and remained with her mother for three weeks only until being placed with the applicants, Mr and Mrs Lawrence, on a voluntary basis. The infant is not of an age to understand the adoption proceedings . . . The mother is Spanish and looking for work in this country . . . gives her consent freely and without pressure . . . satisfied that the adoption is in the best interest of the child . . . wants her to have a happy family life . . . states that as a young, unmarried woman at the beginning of her career she is not in a position to keep the child . . . is not prepared to reveal the identity of the father . . ."'

He broke off for a moment to ask again if Abbie was OK.

'Keep going,' she said plainly.

'"The adoptive parents, Mr and Mrs Lawrence, are not able to have children of their own . . . were actually recommended by the mother herself, which, although unusual, is not seen as inappropriate. The National Adoption Society therefore wishes to support the application."'

He pushed the paper closer to Abbie, implying that she should pick it up and read it for herself. There were several documents left to look at, but they were nothing more than admin really, court orders and the like. There would be no more bombshells, only aftershock.

Felix felt a kind of relief pass through him, remembering her enunciate the word 'rape'. This was the gist of it, right here in Abbie's hands. For a minute or so he watched her eyes travelling along each line of writing, and thought about how those sentences would be sounding now in her head as she read silently to herself. Maybe she heard the voice of the woman who had composed and signed that letter, a Mrs J. Campion, Moral Welfare Officer for the district. What would her voice be like? Disapproving and starchy, he imagined. A churchgoer, probably. A widow in horn-rimmed glasses and a woollen skirt with no offspring of her own, a dim view of sex before marriage and an active dislike of single mothers. A woman whose vocation it was to place illegitimate children firstly into the care of God and secondly into the charge of decent families, preferably C of E, with good table manners, a saloon car in the drive and a bit of money in the bank. He even pictured Mrs J. Campion sitting in his chair, doing his job, and thought of her in the staff meeting, arguing with Mo, telling her off for wearing jeans in the office. Social workers had changed. Once they were police court missionaries, do-gooders in cardigans, and there was still the odd one around, like Marjorie, who thought that most problems could be solved with common sense and a pot of fresh tea. But now they were people like Mo, with her short hair and Doc Martens. Or people like Roy, with his street talk and his contacts. Or people like Neville, who didn't give a toss one way or another, or like Bernard, who hadn't got a clue. Or damaged people like Thelma. And people like Felix. He thought for a while about what sort of social worker he was, but nothing definite came to mind. Abbie was still looking at the letter and at the certificate of her birth, but her expression was hard to read. Not just because she was silent and so utterly absorbed, but because she was someone else now. A foreigner. A woman whose mother came from Valencia or Salamanca or Madrid. Did he know anyone from Spain? Anyone from that background? No, he didn't, except for the woman in front of him. The woman he was married to. His wife.

Abbie put the papers down on the table. Normally at this point Felix would have asked if there were any questions, anything that wasn't clear. And he was just formulating a speech about the way ahead, the possible pitfalls of tracing birth parents and so on, when the door banged open and Neville walked in. He was carrying a huge stack of folders that hid his face.

'If they don't fix that fucking lift this week there's going to be a fucking lawsuit. Five floors and me with a dodgy spine. I'll get the bloody union on it, I swear.'

'Er, I've got someone with me,' said Felix.

He pointed at Abbie, who was very cool, and simply raised her hand and smiled. 'Hi.'

'Oh, sorry, Abbie. Didn't know you were here.'

Felix began to scoop the documents together into a pile. 'We, er, we were just booking a holiday, filling the forms in and all that.'

'So where are you going that needs a birth certificate. Albania?' He wiped the sweat from his forehead with the back of his hand, then began rummaging in his pockets for a hankie.

'On a cruise,' said Felix. 'Aren't we, Abbie?'

'Yes.'

'Yes. And it goes to lots of different countries, and they have to get all the passports and bureaucracy sorted out in advance, you see.'

He looked at Neville's expression to see if his story made sense, but Neville wasn't really listening.

'Pass me one of those tissues you keep for the weepies, will you? I'm in a right lather.'

Abbie stood up. 'Well, got to get back to work. Nice to see you, Neville.'

'Yeah, nice to see you too. Where does it go, then?'

'What?'

'This cruise? They must be paying him more than they pay me. Where does it sail to?'

'Oh, Felix will tell you. He's got all the details. Where does it go to, Felix?'

'Erm, Argentina,' said Felix, as he put the last of the paperwork back in the folder and threw it into the drawer.

'Argentina? How long does that take?'

'Oh, not long. It's a very fast boat. I'm just going to see Abbie out. Catch you later.'

But by the time he got to the end of the corridor and the top of the stairwell, Abbie was halfway down the fire escape, and even though he called to her she didn't stop or even look up. From the window he saw her disappear into the underpass, then reappear on the far side, walking quickly with her head down, towards the precinct and the shops, and even though he called her six or seven times that afternoon and left messages on her mobile she didn't phone back.

He drove home at about half-four, not knowing what he might find. When he walked into the kitchen Abbie was stood at the ironing board, pressing a crease along the leg of a pair of black trousers. Steam rose from the fabric as the iron glided from the waistband to the turn-up at the far end.

'How are you feeling?'

'I don't know,' she said. 'I just needed to do something. I've even mopped the floor.'

Felix looked down at the shining lino under his feet. 'You should come and see me more often. The house will be spotless.'

Abbie gave a quick smile, then stood the iron on its end. A big burst of steam hissed into the air and evaporated.

'I've brought you a present,' he said, opening his briefcase. She watched as he pulled out the length of pink ribbon, the one from the folder, and held it towards her. 'For your hair. To stop it falling over your lovely face.'

And with the ironing board still between them, he reached behind her, gathered her long black hair into a thick ponytail, looped the ribbon around it and tied it in a bow. When he tried to stand back to see how it looked she wouldn't let go, and pressed her face into his shirt. She was crying now. Her shoulders and head shook with the tears that bubbled up from deep in her body. He held her, and against his chest he sensed the warmth of her mouth as it opened and closed, and imagined he felt the words 'thank you' spoken into his ribs, even though he heard nothing but sobbing.

IKEA

As he makes the turn off the main road on to the trading estate, he still feels confident about what lies ahead. He can cope. But the moment the soles of his feet make contact with the metalled surface of the car park, a stiffness enters his body. It is a physical reluctance, beginning in his ankles. So in the main entrance he sits down on a pile of glossy catalogues and loosens the laces of his shoes. It's Saturday. The weekend. Children are playing in the ball pool, having a great time. It looks like a happy place, but even here by the front door three or four husbands have lost the will to go on. And they have to be husbands. Only the enforcement of a marriage vow could lead a man here against his will. They are standing with their hands in their pockets, without purpose or hope. They have declined to enter, or more likely they have been sent back. Beneath their flesh their spines are sinking under the weight of their shoulders and the heaviness of their thoughts, like the flagpoles of defeated armies sinking into mud. They are not even waiting, because waiting is an ambition. A cause. Waiting has an outcome. These husbands simply exist. Just. They will have to be collected or removed, or remain in the entrance of the store until they fossilize or die.

The settees are first. Arrows on the floor suggest the direction of travel. Short cuts are futile. A gap between two bookcases appears to offer a direct route to bedroom furniture, but via office equipment, futons and armchairs finally doubles back to settees. Better to keep to the channel, stay with the slowly flowing stream of humankind, stepping aside once in a while to avoid the flailing arms and thrashing head of some shipwrecked sailor swimming against the tide.

After settees come beds. The cruelty could only be strategic. Here are yielding mattresses. Malleable springs. Plump, inviting pillows leavened

86

with goosedown and candy floss. Duvets stuffed with fluffy white clouds and children's dreams. It is torture. The stiffness in the ankles has now risen through the shins and calves and is causing an arthritic discomfort in both knees. Only a deep, undisturbed sleep could help. Hibernation. Coma. Persistent vegetative state. Extinction of the species. No more than a hundred yards into the labyrinth and already his courage has deserted him. So much for inner strength. So much for focus and mission statements and self-control. He has toothache in his testicles. Breathing is difficult. In a zombified stupor he trudges on, and maybe he passes out, because his next conscious moment is an hour later, when he comes to with the smell of food in his nostrils and a knife and fork in his hands.

In the cafeteria, initially at least, there is an atmosphere of reprieve and respite. This is base camp. The husbands here are survivors. They have made it this far and are rewarded with cigarettes, meatballs, the relaxation of the prostate gland. They hunch over tables, their hands clamped around hot drinks. Their only task is to guard the trolley or trolleys piled with three-dimensional jigsaw puzzles sometimes referred to as shelves or desks. But their minds wander. Their thoughts turn to the trees and shrubs on the other side of the shatter-proof glass. To the fields on the far side of the motorway. Their eyes fall to their plates, to the confluence of thick brown gravy and jellied loganberry juice. Then a contemplative, philosophical mood descends. What are we but shit and blood? Lost souls a long way from home? What are we but pack mules and power tools? Travellers with many obstacles to overcome, many zones to be entered and passed through? Zones like Lighting or Fabrics. Or Kitchens, that hazardous interchange where a casual inquiry about a wine rack can lead to a formal interview with uniformed staff, where a wrong turn between breakfast bar and butcher's block results in accidental deportation to the starting grid in the main entrance. Zones like the Warehouse, that matrix of scaffolding and shadowy culs-de-sac. Zones like the Market Place, where unwanted material goods conceal themselves in shopping baskets like asylum seekers stowed away in the wheel hubs of intercontinental jets. It is with a deflated heart that the man drains the last of his refilled coffee and rejoins his shopping. His wife is a spectre disappearing into the distance. After three steps he has no feeling in his legs. Rheumatic pain assaults his knuckles as he grips the trolley. Like tree sickness, the inflammation in the root bole of his pelvis rises through his backbone and out along the boughs of his ribs. Neuralgia sets in, in both cheeks. The hospice of the café is already a distant memory. Cataracts are forming by the second, so the sunshine and fresh air through the doors beyond the checkouts are now just a dim and diminishing light.

9

Maxine had made a pot of chicken casserole and a big dish of white rice. The four of them had already gone through three bottles of wine by the time they sat down to eat. On the sideboard the monitor crackled every now and again with interference. If one of the twins coughed or cried out, a semicircular bank of lights lit up, green to begin with, becoming red as the volume increased.

'Ever been breathalysed, Felix?' asked Jed. He was spooning a second helping out of the pot. A line of juice trailed across the tablecloth and over the rim of his plate.

'Jed, you messy sod,' said Maxine. She reached over with a napkin.

'It's only gravy. Anyway, that's what these chuck-away table-cloths are for, in't it? For spilling on?'

'It's not gravy, it's sauce.'

Felix said he'd only been stopped by the police once, for a faulty brake light.

'Oh, Mr Dangerous,' said Abbie, but winked at him and squeezed his thigh under the table.

'I'd probably get the sack for drinking and driving,' he explained.

'It's not like that at our place. There's some of 'em with all kinds of criminal records, but nobody bothers. Most of 'em are still pissed in a morning from the night before, and go to the pub in the lunch hour for a top-up.'

'Isn't that dangerous, working with explosives?' asked Abbie.

'Suppose so. Anyhow, this cop car is following me home once, right up mi arse, he is, and I've had a couple so I'm sweating a bit. Then the flashing light starts, and he gives it a go with the siren, so

I pull over and sit there while he gets out and walks up alongside. And there's this packet of Juicy Fruit down by the handbrake, so quick as a flash I flick a piece into mi gob and start chewing like mad, to cover the smell of ale.'

'Bit of a giveaway, isn't it? If I were a policeman I'd breathalyse anyone who smelt remotely of chewing gum,' observed Felix.

'Anyhow, I winds the window down and he gives me the spiel, then pushes the bag in mi face and tells me to blow. But when I put mi lips to this breathalyser thing, the chuddie gets all over the mouthpiece and stuck in the end, and when I gives it back to him there's this big blob of Juicy Fruit stuck to it, all stringy and hot. So his machine's knackered and he hasn't got another, and for ten minutes he's trying to clean it with a packet of Wet Wipes I've found in the nappy sack. Bloody farce, it was. Then he takes mi name and address, like he's going to come and see me later, but he never does. Humiliated, probably. Snookered by a lump of chuddie. You can just hear the other coppers down at the nick ripping the piss out of him. Useless, they are.'

'So when was this?' Maxine wanted to know.

'I don't know, three or four years ago.'

'You never told me. Where were the kids while you were drinking and driving? Not in the back of the car, I hope.'

'Were they hell. I'd been at a darts match. I don't take the kids to a darts match, do I?'

Maxine had started collecting the plates. Jed had to shovel the last lump of chicken from his before she stole it away and put a dish down in its place.

'Only apple crumble, I'm afraid. Keep your forks. I'd wanted to do a *mille feuille* but the kids were round my ankles all day.'

'I'm amazed you've even managed to bake a crumble. It's more than I ever manage,' said Abbie helpfully.

'Don't be too amazed. Jed got it from the garage on his way back from work. It's probably still frozen in the middle.' She went to the fridge for another bottle of white wine and handed it to Felix. 'Open this, will you, while I dollop the pudding out.'

Felix scraped away the foil with his thumb, inserted the corkscrew and pulled, but the cork remained where it was. Eventually he stood up to give himself more elbow room, but it wouldn't budge.

'Give it to Jed,' said Abbie.

'No, honestly, I think it's coming,' said Felix, bent double now, with the bottle between his thighs and a napkin wound around the handle to stop the metal biting into his hands.

'Pass it here, man,' said Jed, 'before you give birth to yourself.'

Felix handed it over and without too much effort Jed eased out the cork, then began filling the four empty glasses. 'Don't tell me, you'd loosened it for me, yeah?'

Red-faced with effort and embarrassment, Felix sat down and held out his right hand to show Abbie the pressure mark where the corkscrew had dug into the fleshy part of his thumb. Abbie nodded and asked him to pass the custard.

After the meal, they sat at the table for another hour or so with the dirty dishes in front of them, talking about houses, about holidays and eventually about work. Maxine had opened a designer clothes shop in another town about eight miles away and wasn't sure if it was going to be a success or not. Every second Tuesday in the month she drove into Manchester to load up with cut-price stock from the warehouses and outlets along Newton Street. Some of the clothes were genuine, or genuine seconds at least, but most of them were cheap copies and came supplied with a roll of designer labels which Maxine stitched on by hand. Most evenings after the twins had gone to bed she sat in front of the telly with a needle and thread, and said she'd be ten times quicker if only Jed would buy her something called an over-locker, which not only made the job easier but gave a more professional finish. The people who bought the clothes knew they weren't the real thing, but as long as they looked right and carried the proper logo they didn't care. 'Some-times they're better quality than the originals.'

'What kind of stuff is it?' asked Felix.

'Oh, just crap really. Like that shirt Jed's wearing.'

'Thank you, my angel.'

'You'd pay 400 for that in London and I bought it for twenty-five.'

'You shouldn't have, sweetheart, you really shouldn't have.'

She ignored him, and carried on ignoring him as she undid the front of his shirt to demonstrate the stitchwork around the inside of the buttonhole, then dragged the collar to one side to show off the label.

'Have you finished with me now?' asked Jed, after Maxine had taken her seat again.

'Yes. And fasten yourself up, will you? We don't want to sit here looking at your hairy chest all night.'

Abbie said, 'Sounds like you're on to a real winner.'

'Maybe, maybe not. The rent's pretty high, even though I'm not in the middle of town, and I could do with more stock, so there's always a bit of a cash-flow situation. I'm thinking of borrowing more from the bank but Mr Skinflint here thinks it's a bad idea.'

'Don't look at *me*,' said Jed. 'I'm just a tailor's dummy.'

'Anyway, I want to design my own stuff really. Buying and selling is OK, but my heart's not in it.'

'Tell me about it,' said Abbie sourly, and went on to talk about market research and the blow-job incident in the precinct. Maxine was disgusted and said she should have slapped his face. Turning to Felix, she said, 'So did you run after this guy and give him what for?'

'Oh, you know me, I can't even get the cork out of a bottle.'

'Maybe he was married,' said Jed, filling his glass and reaching towards the mantelpiece for a packet of cigarettes.

'What's that got to do with it?' asked Abbie.

'You know, like in the joke. What's the connection between chicken Kiev and a blow job? Go on, ask me, Felix.'

'Don't humour him,' said Maxine.

'Let him speak. Go on, Felix, ask me.'

'All right, Jed, what *is* the connection between chicken Kiev and a blow job?'

'You don't get either of 'em at home.' He exhaled a stream of smoke towards the lightshade – a white paper globe suspended from the ceiling – then roared at his own joke. It was the kind of laugh that made everyone else laugh, everyone except Maxine, who slapped him hard on the shoulder and said, 'Do you know what the saddest thing about that is?'

'Go on, tell me,' he said. The lightshade was swinging from side to side, as if from the reverberation of his laughter.

'That you couldn't think of anything more exotic than chicken Kiev. How pathetic is that? You'd got the whole of Delia to choose from and all you could think of was chicken Kiev. Two ninety-nine for a pack of four from Safeway. Pathetic. I think we've even got one in the freezer.'

'Yeah, right at the bottom. Frozen solid. Next to the blow jobs,' he said.

'Well, pardon me,' said Maxine, standing up and piling the four pudding bowls on top of each other and throwing the spoons into the custard jug. 'It's just with a business to manage, two girls to look after and a house to run, I've got better things to do than . . .'

With her voice trailing off, she picked up the bowls and the jug and walked towards the kitchen.

'Than what? Stick a meal in the oven?'

She turned around. 'Better things to do than suck your dick.'

'Hurray!' shouted Abbie, and applauded the comment.

Then from inside the kitchen Maxine shouted, 'Anyway, it's more like fast food with you. It's all over in five minutes and I'm still hungry. Know what I'm saying, Abbie?'

Abbie found this so hilarious she had to spit a mouthful of wine back into her glass to stop herself choking with laughter. Felix laughed as well, but it wasn't convincing. In fact it was so unrealistic that both Jed and Abbie turned towards him, and if the sound of crying hadn't come crackling through the monitor he might well have found himself having to explain just what sort of meal his own sexual performance amounted to.

'Now see what you've done, stupid,' bawled Maxine.

But Jed was already on his way out of the room, ducking under the doorframe and clomping up the stairs, then crossing the landing above them, the floorboards squeaking under his weight. Through the monitor, they could hear him whispering and shushing one of the girls, saying, 'All right, my little button. Sleepy time now. That's the way. You cuddle up and close your eyes,' and a tiny, drowsy voice saying, 'Daddy, my daddy.'

'Does he always go up?' Abbie asked Maxine as she came back in with a teetering pile of coffee cups balanced on a stack of saucers.

'Mostly. If I go they want another story, or they want a drink or the toilet. But they see Jed and they nod off again. In fact he usually nods off with them. I went in at three in the morning last week and there he was, sprawled all over Alice's bed, dead to the world. She'd fallen out and got in with her sister.'

'I don't suppose there's much room for Jed and another person in a single bed?'

'There isn't much room in a double and I'm only tiny. When we got married I kept thinking he might roll over in the middle of the night and squash me, like one of those big fat pigs crushing its litter.'

'Don't tell me you never went to bed with him before you got married?'

'Course I did. But not to sleep.'

'Can you tell them apart?' Felix asked.

The women looked sideways at him.

'The twins, I mean. When they're crying.'

'When we had them, we wrote their names on ankle-bands so we wouldn't get them mixed up. But after a while you just know. I can't say how, exactly. It's not like one of them has got blue eyes and the other's got brown. But you just know. Even without looking, I can tell. It's natural.'

Abbie held her wine glass with her fingertips and looked down into the last inch or so of swirling, pale-yellow liquid. 'That must be nice,' she muttered.

'Sorry,' said Maxine, and rested her head on Abbie's shoulder.

Abbie kissed her hair and carried on looking into her glass.

When Jed came back into the room he was holding a bottle of brandy by the neck. From the way he carried it in his big hand it looked more like a small bell. 'If you girls want to get it on, it's fine, so long as me and Felix can watch, eh, Felix?'

'You're pissed, Jed,' said Maxine. 'And you know what brandy does to you.'

'It's Friday, in't it? I'm just unwinding.'

'Well, unwind with your mouth shut. Felix was just telling us about work.'

'Er, yes, well, it's fine. Busy, but fine.'

'Got any juicy cases on the go?'

'Yes. One or two interesting things. One in particular that's keeping me occupied.'

He was thinking of Ruby Moffat, but when Abbie looked up from under her fringe and smiled, he was happy to let her think he was talking about her.

'I read about that bull in the Strawberry Field. That's right under your office, isn't it?' said Maxine.

'Yes, we saw it happen.'

'Kicked a boy, didn't it? Is he all right?'

'They took him in the ambulance but he died in hospital.'

'Oh, no. That's terrible.'

'Do you get a car allowance, Felix, or does it come out of your own pocket?' said Jed, pushing what looked to Felix like a goldfish bowl of brandy under his nose.

'Jed! I was just asking about a boy who died, for pity's sake,' said Maxine, shaking her head in disbelief.

'Yeah, well, I got a bollocking for talking about funny stuff, so now I'm talking about cars.'

'It's a fleet car,' said Felix, comfortable with this change in the conversation. 'I get it on a lease arrangement. They pay for the servicing and the insurance, all I do is put petrol in the tank and air in the tyres. Then at the end of two years they buy it back at the going rate, so long as I haven't trashed it.'

'Well, then, you're lucky you haven't got kids.'

'I wouldn't say that,' whispered Abbie.

'Because if there's one thing guaranteed to turn a car into a worthless pile of junk, it's a kid.'

'Here we go,' said Maxine. 'Light the blue touch and stand well back.'

Jed was pouring himself another glass of brandy and reaching over to top Felix up, even though Felix hadn't tasted his yet.

'They put adverts in car magazines saying one careful owner, non-smoker, no dogs. But the one question you want to be asking when you buy a second-hand car is this: how many kids? I'm telling you, we got that Espace three years ago and it's not worth tuppence now. There's feet marks on the ceiling. There's half-eaten sweets in the door pockets. There's gunge all over the windows. The rear de-mist is buggered from piling toys on the parcel shelf. There's a five-foot gash all down the near side from one of the girls dragging her bike out of the garage . . .'

'Actually that was me,' said Maxine, standing up, but Jed wasn't listening.

'And I found a tomato growing under the back seat. A bloody tomato, with leaves and everything. Three years old and it's not worth tuppence. I'm too ashamed to try and sell it. I might as well just dump it on the allotments and let some old codger keep his pigeons in it.'

Maxine had left the dining room and was now in the hall, reaching into the broom cupboard. Abbie folded her arms across her chest and leaned back in her seat, saying, 'But you love them really, don't you, Jed? I've seen you with them. You'd do anything for those kids.'

'Don't encourage him,' shouted Maxine. 'It's his favourite subject.'

'Course I love 'em. I love 'em to bits. But what about me? I'm practically crippled with carting them here, there and everywhere, one on each arm. I'm telling you, they've got it all wrong, those social scientists, about why women live longer than men. It isn't bacon butties and booze that's killing us blokes, it's fatherhood.

Arthritis in this knee, dodgy back, permanent fatigue. I've been to casualty five times with a grazed cornea, and when you get up the 'ossie it isn't drunks and junkies and people with broken arms waiting to see a doctor, it's dads, all done in by their kids, all knackered. It's the front fucking line. Look at these bags under mi eyes – I ought to be in London Zoo, eating bamboo shoots. I haven't had a full night's sleep for four years, and don't talk to me about having a holiday – that's a joke. The car's solid with luggage, not to mention the roof rack and the trailer, and all I've got is a spare pair of undies and a toothbrush. I go to work when I want a break. Gunpowder – it's less dangerous. I don't own one jacket that hasn't been spewed on or ripped, and what's worse, I don't care. Why bother – I'm nobody. I'm just a bloody pit pony and a dishcloth.'

It was a speech from the heart, Felix thought, but a well-practised one. Otherwise, how could somebody who was so pissed connect such a sequence of thoughts and get the words to come out of his mouth in the right order? Jed was like the drunken man stumbling home from the pub: his body remembered the way even if his brain didn't, and it was only muscle-memory and years of practice that stopped him lurching into some side alley and falling flat on his face. During his monologue, Maxine had come to stand behind him. By inserting her index fingers into his armpits, she had made him rise from his seat. As he continued his rant, she slipped one arm into the sleeve of his coat, then the other, then stood on a chair to pull a bobble hat on to his head and wrapped a scarf so tightly around his neck he had to yank it forward to finish what he was saying.

'I'm buggered and I'm skint. So you want kids, Abbie? Well, you can have mine, 'cos they're doing mi bloody 'ed in.'

Abbie said, 'I don't want your children, Jed. I just want one of my own and I haven't got one.'

Then she started to cry. Maxine, invisible behind Jed's great bulk except for the occasional glimpse of her hands, had almost finished dressing him. It was an act that seemed as well rehearsed as Jed's outburst, the finishing touch being the application of the dog leash, which she wound tightly around his wrist before whistling for Smutty, who came scrambling across the hardwood floor and dutifully slipped his neck through the chain-link noose at the other end. Jed said he was sorry to Abbie, he hadn't meant to upset her, 'But I'm telling you this for your own good.'

Smutty dragged him towards the outside door, which Maxine held open. She had very nearly closed it behind him when his foot reappeared through the gap. 'Wait a minute, I'm still in mi bloody slippers.'

'Tough.'

'Come off it, Max.'

'Get some wellies out of the shed.'

'What about Felix, why isn't he coming?'

'He is,' said Abbie.

'Why? What did I do?' protested Felix.

'Just go.'

Smutty started to bark, then the monitor began to squawk with the sound of a howling child, then the red light at the top end of the spectrum throbbed as a second voice joined in. Felix sighed and lifted himself out of the dining chair and past Abbie.

'And bring the brandy bottle,' said Jed, his eyes peering in through the letter box and his protruding finger pointing to the half-empty bottle of Martell on the sideboard.

Maxine slammed the door.

'Bloody hell, Max. You could have broken mi nose,' said the voice on the other side.

It was five to one in the morning – they could see the illuminated church clock from the top of the slide. Jed put a ten-pence piece on its side and let it roll away down the polished aluminium, its milled edge making a hollow, tinny noise that reverberated in the empty playground in front of them. With his back to him, Felix sat on the top rung, looking down the ladder to where Smutty peered up. The dog's ears twitched at the sound of the money. The coin launched itself into the silence beyond the end of its descent; Smutty bolted after it, sniffing and scratching in the bark chippings on the ground. Jed passed the brandy bottle over his shoulder and Felix took a big gulp. All the heat of the day had disappeared into the wide-open, cloudless night, and the iron handrail and the cast-iron steps under his feet felt abnormally cold, brittle almost, as if one tap with a hammer might shatter the whole structure into smithereens.

'Why do you call him Smutty?' Felix asked, handing the bottle back.

'When he was a pup he used to put his head up Max's skirt.'

The dog had unearthed a lollipop wrapper or a crisp packet and was holding it down with his front paws, trying to get his head inside.

'Sorry,' mumbled Jed.

'For what?'

'Talking about kids.'

'Don't worry.'

'You still trying?'

'Trying too hard if you ask me.'

'Can't you go for one of those test-tube babies, then?'

'No. Costs thousands. But we can try something similar.'

'A right good fuck – that's still the best way. Always was.'

'Tell me about it. Ever do a sperm test?'

'Nah.'

'Well, it's no fun, I can promise you. Don't know how I managed it. When you're under all that pressure you don't feel very . . . you know.'

'What?'

'You know.'

'What?'

'Aroused.'

'Oh, right,' said Jed. It wasn't an entirely unsympathetic response, but its main purpose was to dispel the image of Felix's semi-erect penis and to bring the subject to a close.

'Who started all this stuff about children anyway? What were we talking about?'

Felix's memory was beginning to blur with the drink. 'Don't know. Cars, wasn't it? Or was it work?'

'I hate my job. I wouldn't mind if it was genuine explosives. Semtex or nitro-glycerine, something with a bit of glamour. But fireworks? Bangers that wouldn't blow your hat off. Fucking sparklers, for fuck's sake. They're so gay. I'd pack it in tomorrow if it wasn't for . . .'

He paused and must have heard himself about to launch into his diatribe again. So even though Maxine was at least a mile out of earshot and things were about as bad as they could possibly get, he restricted himself to 'the family'.

'What would you rather do?'

He swigged the drink and studied the question for a moment or so, as if it was an actual job that Felix had offered him. 'Celebrity handyman. Like on those home-improvement programmes.'

'You hate DIY.'

'Only because I'm too knackered when I get home from work. But on telly all I'd have to do is swan around with a drill in mi hand and crack a joke every now and again in mi regional accent. Doddle.' The bottle came back over his shoulder. 'What about you?'

It was a question Felix had asked himself only the other week after a particularly uncooperative team meeting, so he knew the answer. 'Well, you know at the airport they have those little buggies for taking people from one gate to another, like golf carts that run up and down the corridors with old fogies and their luggage?'

'Yeah.'

'I'd like to drive one of them.'

'What?'

'They're really quiet – electric engines – and it's carpet or lino on the floor. Very smooth. Just press down on the pedal and you're away. And then sometimes, like when there's a strike, or in the middle of the night when the place is deserted, I'd just whiz around between the terminals. There'd be five or six of us whizzing around all night, racing and banging into each other. Like the dodgems but very, very smooth. Fantastic.'

The two men had been sitting spine to spine, resting against each other, and Felix suddenly felt the cold on his back as Jed hitched forward and turned around to look at him.

'I think you'd better give me that bottle back,' he said.

'What's wrong with driving a buggy?'

Jed drained the brandy. 'You're a pervert,' he concluded. He'd lit a cigarette and, with his lips pursed like a trumpeter's, blew thick grey smoke into the empty bottle and screwed the lid on. Then he said, 'Hey, if I roll this down the slide, do you think it'll smash and let the genie out? Smutty, come out of the way, you daft mutt.'

10

'Chalk?'

'Apparently.'

'Nothing else?'

'No.'

'Thanks for calling.'

'I've passed it over to PC Lily. She's your contact now.'

Felix had taken the call downstairs on one of the secretaries' telephones. Coming out of the lift, he bumped into Marjorie, who was dressed in a dark-blue skirt and jacket with white shoes and a white leather handbag under her arm.

'You're looking very smart. Going to Crown Court?'

'Yes, giving evidence in a trial. Does this outfit look all right? I've got a committee meeting at the bowling club later on and won't have time to get changed.'

Felix said she looked fine and helped her on with her mac before she disappeared into the lift. In the office Neville was looking out of the window. He was stooping slightly, with his hands by his face, and it wasn't until he turned around to say hello that Felix saw what he was doing.

'What's that?'

'It's a telescope. A refractor, to be precise.'

'I know it's a telescope, Neville. But what are you doing with it?'

'Looking.'

Felix decided to ignore him. One of the techniques he'd learned during his social work diploma was that of extinction. Basically, many forms of antisocial behaviour are ways of seeking attention. To acknowledge the behaviour only rewards the perpetrator and therefore reinforces the problem. At least that was the theory, although with Neville naughtiness was a congenital disease that would never be addressed by psychology. So after ten minutes of watching his colleague peering silently through the long, white tube, Felix's curiosity finally got the better of him.

'All right, Neville, why have you got a telescope?'

Without breaking off from his observations, Neville explained that a couple of months ago he'd heard a story on the radio about the popularity of telescopes in Manhattan. But it wasn't anything to do with astronomy, because the glow of the streetlights made it impossible to see the stars. 'It's all about people-watching,' he explained.

'I heard that story too. It was about snoopers and Peeping Toms. People in high-rise buildings looking through their neighbours' windows. It was about spying.'

'Yeah, that was the one,' said Neville. 'Hey, did that copper get in touch? He phoned earlier about Little Miss Muffet.'

'I've just spoken to him downstairs.'

'And?'

Neville left the telescope positioned on its stand and folded his arms, waiting for Felix to tell him the story.

'Did I tell you they were running tests?'

'Yes, on the knickers.'

'Well, it wasn't what they thought it was. It was chalk.'

'What kind of chalk?'

'Don't know. But you know what the family business is, don't you?'

'Shoplifting?'

'They do road-marking. Painting white lines on the road. And guess what they do it with?'

'Paint?'

'Yes. White paint mixed with chalk. Makes it go further.'

Neville was impressed. 'You're a proper little sleuth, aren't you? Remind me not to play you at Cluedo.'

★

The disclosure meeting wasn't for another hour and a half. Felix caught up with his paperwork and made a few phone calls. Bernard called in to remind him that he still had nine and a half days to take before the end of the leave year. Then Mo stuck her head around the door to ask if he'd be attending the union meeting at the town hall later in the week. Felix said he'd like to but unfortunately he was too busy, and Mo said that was highly ironic because the main item on the agenda was overtime. She also asked him about the annual conference in Bournemouth in the autumn, but he told her he couldn't make it because of a holiday he'd already booked.

'Going on a cruise, aren't you?' she said. 'All right for some.'

'Who told you that?'

'Neville.'

'I thought you didn't speak to Neville?'

She mumbled something under her breath as she turned away but Felix didn't catch it. Before leaving the office he took a closer look at the telescope, a cheap thing from Dixons or Comet probably, perched on a plastic tripod. He put his eye to the lens, thinking he might see Abbie in the precinct. Of course, as soon as he got home he'd tell her, because it wouldn't be fair not to. On the other hand he didn't want her to think he was snooping on her, so maybe it would be better to keep quiet . . . But the telescope was actually locked in position, pointing at what looked like an ordinary field on the far hill, under the monument to those killed in the Crimean War. When Felix lengthened the focus, a small graveyard above a fairly remote church came into view. It was raining lightly. He watched a small party of mourners at a graveside and, further off, a man under a large yellow and blue golfing brolly. When the man swung the umbrella across his shoulders, Felix thought he recognized him. Not by his face, which was blurred and ill-defined, but by his clothes and his stance, and his general demeanour – his relationship with the world and the space he occupied within it. By fiddling again with the lens he confirmed the sighting. It was someone he didn't expect to see.

Disclosure

The man watches through the mirror.

In the room, the girl sits on the floor with her hands over her eyes. The woman sits cross-legged about five feet away from her. They have been silent for some time now. Then the woman says, 'Tell me if you want to stop, Ruby.' Although muffled, through the glass her voice is audible to the man behind the mirror. But words aren't so important here. It has less to do with language, more to do with action. To do with fingers, and legs, and limbs.

'Shall we try again with the doll?' asks the woman.

The girl doesn't take her hands away from her face but appears to be nodding ever so slightly behind them. The woman gets to her feet and walks slowly and calmly towards a trunk, like a toybox, in the far corner of the room. Opening the lid, she reaches in and lifts out a doll. Except it is not a baby doll with a cute face and bald head, but a scaled-down little girl dressed in jeans and a T-shirt. It has hair made from wool. The wool is red. The woman sits the doll on the floor, where it leans against a chair leg. The woman and the girl are very still and quiet, like the doll. After more silence, the woman asks the girl, 'What happens next?' Her voice is very soothing. Very kind.

The girl's voice has a scratchy, raw edge. 'The thing,' she mutters, through her fingers.

'What thing?'

'The thing.'

'Do you know what the thing is called?'

The girl nods.

'Do you want to say it?'

The girl shakes her head.

'Do you want me to say it?'

The girl pauses. Then the girl nods.

'Is it a spider?'

The girl waits. The girl nods.

'There are no spiders in this room, Ruby. But could you show me how the spider climbs the waterspout? Could you pretend that your fingers are the spider?'

'NO.'

The girl has said NO before. She shouted NO and the woman put the woolly-haired doll back in the box. But this time she leaves the doll leaning against the chair and asks, 'Could I pretend? How about if I pretend with my fingers?'

None of the girl's face is visible through the mask of her hands. Her head doesn't move and she remains silent. It isn't a yes. But it isn't a no either. It isn't NO. The woman lifts the doll and lays it down, gently, on its back.

'Does the spider . . . does it touch you?'

The girl nods.

'Where?'

No response.

'Here?' inquires the woman, pointing to the doll's tiny, moulded hand.

The girl shakes her head.

'What about here?' she asks, pointing at the blue plastic shoe at the bottom of the doll's leg.

The girl shakes her head.

'Show me what happens. Where does it touch you?'

The girl curls the little finger of her right hand into her mouth.

Behind the mirror, the man clicks his pen and makes a note.

'What happens next?'

'Climbs the waterspout.'

'The spider?'

The girl nods.

The woman thinks. Then, hooking her thumbs together, she walks her eight fingers across the cheeks of the doll and along its shoulder. 'This way?'

The girl shakes her head. Her face is still covered but she is watching. Through the gaps between her fingers she stares at the pink, fleshy spider as it makes its way back to the doll's mouth, then sets off slowly towards the opposite shoulder.

'This way?'

The girl shakes her head.

The spider abseils the chin of the doll and crosses the border between the smooth plastic neck and the stitched collar of the T-shirt. 'This way?'

The girl nods.

'Further?'

She nods again.

The spider stops at the press-stud that fastens the dark-blue jeans around the doll's waist. But this time the word 'Further' comes from the scratchy voice of the girl, followed by the word, 'Inside.'

'Down here?'

The girl nods.

Under the denim, the spider crawls along, downwards. Then stops.

The woman asks, 'What happens next?'

The girl, after a while, answers. 'Down comes the rain.'

'And washes the spider out?'

The girl nods.

'Back to where?'

The girl curls her little finger inside her mouth again.

'To here?'

The girl nods.

'And then what happens?'

Silence. Stillness. The girl. The woman. The doll.

'Ruby, what happens next?'

From behind her hands. Mumbled. 'Out comes the sunshine, dries up all the rain. Then . . .'

'He climbs the spout again?'

'Yes.'

'Like this?'

The eight-fingered spider makes its way down the doll's T-shirt and towards the top of the jeans again.

'Stop now,' says the girl.

'I just want to ask . . .'

'STOP NOW, I SAID.'

The red-haired girl jumps to her feet, drags the red-haired doll across the room, throws it into the trunk, slams the lid and sits on it.

The woman unlocks her thumbs and the spider disappears in her hands. She looks towards the mirror.

Behind the mirror the man clicks his pen and makes a note.

11

Rosales. Meaning what? Derived from rose? From red?

Before Felix sat his O Levels he constructed an elaborate revision timetable from an A2 sheet of graph paper and magic markers in several vivid colours, one for each subject. It took him at least two days to put together. The wording couldn't just be written with any old biro, it had to be stencilled using a fine-tip cartography pen. A professional draughtsman would have been happy with the hatching and shading which indicated rest breaks and lunch hours. It was, of course, a displacement activity, something to keep him from the actual task, just like the diagram in front of him now, with its arrows and vectors and curvy lines. He'd started it at half past nine, as soon as he'd arrived at the office. It was now twelve forty-five. Three and a quarter hours. He had also made several raids on the stationery cupboard on the ground floor for various writing implements and other useful items, such as a pencil sharpener, a protractor and a sheet of self-adhesive green dots. He blew the pencil shavings from the paper and then let his eyes follow several different routes from the top of the page to the bottom.

It reminded him of something else from his past, a game called bagatelle. It had belonged to his father, a kind of Stone Age pinball machine consisting of a green wooden board with dozens of nails sticking out. A ball-bearing was fired from a spring-loaded handle in the bottom corner which made its way up then back down the board, pinging from one nail to another. Sometimes it found its way into a pocket or slot worth fifty or a hundred points, and deft use of the firing mechanism could result in a score of a thousand points or more. But usually the ball-bearing trundled from nail to nail, then plopped into the trough at the bottom, which indicated failure.

Felix looked again at his diagram. It began with the heading 'Mother's maiden name', then traced various lines of inquiry and avenues of investigation as they criss-crossed down the page. Several routes terminated at the word 'Deceased'. When he'd finally satisfied himself that every possibility had been taken into account, he picked up the phone. Neville was right – Felix would have made a good detective. A 'sleuth', hadn't he said? He had an analytical mind. But thoroughness was one thing and time-wasting was another.

'Which name, please?' asked the voice on the other end of the line.

'Rosales.'

'Is that business or residential?'

'It's a private number.'

'And which town, please?'

Felix thought for a few seconds. 'I've no idea.'

It was a long shot. Maria Rosales might no longer live in Britain. Or she might be ex-directory. Or she could well be married and go under a different name, although Felix had a vague recollection of someone once telling him that Spanish couples took the woman's surname. There were three listings under the name M. Rosales. The first was very helpful and lived in Brighton, but was called Michael. Michael told Felix that Rosales was a common name in the Spanish-speaking world. The second M. Rosales was also very helpful, and the right sex, but two years younger than Abbie, and as systematic and painstaking as Felix's flow chart was, it did not allow for the possibility of time travel. M. Rosales number three was not at home. The area code was Derby. Felix rang five or six more times throughout the afternoon. On the last occasion, the phone was answered by a man and Felix hung up. He needed to be careful. There were enough broken marriages in the world without adding to the tally, and it was a distinct possibility that Abbie's mother had gone on to have a new family without ever letting on about her first-born. Felix was a social worker. He was in the healing game, the business of bringing people together, not lobbing hand-grenades into their living rooms. And yet despite his mis-givings, by Thursday he had descended into further subterfuge and was drifting further away from the protocol that governed his working life. Speaking to PC Lily about the Moffat case and police procedure in general, he had made a casual-sounding inquiry about the possibility of tracing an address from a phone number, rather than the other way round. It was an innocent enough question, asked, apparently, out of curiosity. So he was amazed when she produced a pen from her pocket and asked him to write the number on her hand. They were in the police station, at the front desk. PC Lily had asked him to call in and make contact. She was older than PC Nottingham, thirty-five maybe, with sandy-coloured hair pulled back off her face. She had freckles and a nice smile, more like somebody playing the role in an Australian soap opera than an actual police constable. As he clicked the top of the pen and pressed the inky blue ballpoint into the tanned flesh on the back of her hand, he looked around sheepishly and saw a security camera pointing directly at them.

'Don't worry, there's no film in it,' she said.

Then PC Nottingham came into the reception area through a side door and, seeing the two of them almost hand in hand across the counter, emitted a peculiar noise that seemed to originate from the back of his nose and managed to be both disapproving and lecherous at the same time. He looked as if he was on the point of following it up with an actual piece of language but was brilliantly disarmed by PC Lily's comment. She said, 'This hunky young social worker is just giving me his phone number so we can meet up later and have some hot sex.'

'Yeah, right,' said Nottingham, and squeezed his head into his helmet before leaving the station through the main entrance.

After the door had swung closed she said to Felix, 'He thinks I'm joking.'

Then, seeing the redness beginning to gather in Felix's cheeks and the way his eyes had become fixed on some neutral and insignificant place on the desk, she added, 'Don't worry, love. I'm spoken for.'

She held up the back of her left hand. A small, single diamond on a thin ring of gold shone on her finger.

'Mind you,' she said, turning towards the door behind her, 'when did that ever stop anyone?'

Felix had never been to Derby, although he remembered his father going there to watch a football match, the second leg of some obscure knockout competition, and coming home with a black eye. Or was that Chesterfield? The address PC Lily had given him was about two miles outside the city centre. For some reason he had imagined tree-lined suburbs, semi-detached houses with bay windows and herbaceous borders. He had even imagined gnomes. But navigating with the *A–Z* propped on his lap he eventually found himself among shabby, terraced streets. On a piece of wasteland to his left four or five kids were spinning a burnt-out car on its roof. Every telephone kiosk he passed stood in a pool of shattered glass. Felix was familiar with poverty and deprivation. He encountered it every day of his working life; he understood its causes and was sympathetic towards its victims. But somehow the people he worked with were not real. They were clients, cases, 'punters', according to Neville, and when Felix drove home at night they disappeared. Whereas a very real person could be living here, behind one of those grubby windows and tatty doors. A woman called Maria Rosales. His mother-in-law. He had pictured himself parked under a horse chestnut tree or copper beech, watching a middle-aged lady pottering among her roses and lavender, then sitting for a moment with a cup of tea to one side and a pair of gardening gloves to the other. Which would have been his cue to lift the hasp of the gate, walk quietly towards her and say, 'Is it Maria? Maria Rosales?' She would nod, and Felix would explain, gently and carefully, who he was, why he was here. There would be confusion, denial maybe. But then tears. Tears of guilt. Tears of relief. He even had a packet of Kleenex in his pocket. Then would come thanks, an embrace, a pot of Earl Grey. Felix realized he had even visualized this woman in the passenger seat of his car in a kind of mercy dash as he drove her north at high speed for an ecstatic reunion with her daughter. Abbie had wanted to come with him, but he had flatly refused. Now he half-wished she was sitting next to him, seeing what he was seeing. That way he wouldn't have to explain, and that way she would be able to tell him what to do next.

About a third of the houses on the street were boarded up. Only two houses had numbers, number 29 written in yellow spray-paint on the door and further along number 33 written in black marker pen on the stone lintel. From that, Felix worked out that 51, the address he was looking for, was a habitable property with net curtains at the downstairs window and a cobalt-blue Ford Orion parked outside. He passed by a couple of times, then pulled up thirty or forty yards away. The tiny pair of red satin slippers still hung from the rear-view mirror, rocking back and forth after the car had come to a halt. It was eleven o'clock in the morning and the street was quiet. Felix let the back of his seat down a couple of notches, opened a large packet of Hula Hoops and waited. At midday two men in their thirties came out of the house and drove away in the Orion. Ten minutes later they came back up the street from the other direction, parked and went into the house. They didn't look English, but they didn't look Spanish either. They looked Greek, maybe, although Felix was notoriously bad at guessing people's ethnic background. He was even worse at detecting accents. He had once asked a man on a training course which part of Scandinavia he originated from and the man had replied, 'Wolverhampton.'

There were more comings and goings over the next hour. At quarter past one Abbie phoned to ask what was happening. She said, 'Have you seen anyone yet?'

Felix told her that he wasn't very optimistic and that in all probability this was the wrong address.

'What makes you say that?'

'Just a feeling.'

'What kind of area is it?'

'Very . . . working class. A bit of a tip, to be honest.'

It was a minor detail, but in the absence of a family history, details were everything, no matter how insignificant. Since Abbie had found out about her mother's surname, she'd started buying Rioja instead of the Australian stuff they usually drank, and on two occasions in the last three weeks had made paella. The knowledge that her mother could be living below the breadline somewhere in Derby was another scrap of information that had to be factored in and acted upon. He could well return home tonight to find her pursuing a sudden interest in fine porcelain and worrying about the economic prospects for the East Midlands since the sale of Rolls-Royce to overseas investors.

'Have you been to the house yet?'

'No, I'm outside in the car. Just trust me on this, Abbie. I know what I'm doing.'

'All right,' she said after a while.

She didn't sound particularly convinced, but at the same time she didn't have any other choice. Felix wasn't convinced either. But his state of inaction was brought to an abrupt end about ten minutes later when the same two men plus another, taller man came out of the house and walked towards his car. As they passed, one of them tapped on the glass next to Felix's head with his ring. As Felix wound the window down, the door of the passenger seat was yanked open and the tall man jumped into the car beside him. The other two climbed in the back, one from each side, and slammed the doors. Instantly, the smell of stale tobacco filled the vehicle. The legs of the man sitting next to him were so long his knees wouldn't tuck beneath the glove compartment. Like a stick insect in a matchbox. He had to hitch sideways, with his back against the doorpost, and as he shuffled in the chair he reached for the gear stick and knocked it into neutral. At any moment Felix expected an arm to come sliding around his neck or even a knife at his throat, but the man directly behind him sat with his hands by his side and the other stared out of the window, apparently uninterested.

'So what's going on, feller?' asked the man in the passenger seat. He had a very thin, almost pencil-line moustache, and what Felix thought was a local accent, although going on previous experience that placed him anywhere from Bromsgrove to Oslo.

'I'm not the police,' blurted Felix.

It was a spontaneous remark. Something in his nervous system told him that appearing weak and ineffectual was the right strategy when cornered in a dodgy part of a strange town by three men who probably had little regard for the law. All three men sniggered at Felix's response.

'We know you're not a copper. The coppers don't come round here. Not on their own, like. So either you're being very smart or very stupid. Which is it, like?'

'I'm being very stupid,' said Felix emphatically.

'Good answer. Now go and be stupid somewhere else.'

Again it was a gut reaction, an instinct rather than a reasoned decision, but before the man had fully extricated himself from the confines of the front seat, Felix said, 'I'm looking for Maria Rosales.'

Later, he found it interesting to consider that the man who had burst into his car and threatened him was marginally less frightening than the prospect of returning home to Abbie empty-handed. But in the second or so that it took for the words to leave his mouth and in the pause that followed, Felix was simply amazed at himself. These roughnecks were on the point of leaving his vehicle and exiting his life, and by opening his gob he had stopped them.

'She's my mother-in-law,' he added, like an apology, or like a plea.

The tall man hesitated, then eased back into the car.

'Your mother, yeah?'

'Mother-in-law.'

'Hey, fellers. Maria Rosales is his mother-in-law. Get that!'

They sniggered again, all three of them, louder and with more feeling. The one who had been gazing absent-mindedly out of the window now seemed interested, almost excited. He leaned forward and in a foreign accent said, 'Son of a bitch.'

After that remark they all rocked with laughter for a good few minutes, until the stick insect wiped his nose along the top of his index finger and sniffed.

'Explain.'

It took a while to go through the details but the men listened, with only the occasional giggle. Felix even got out his identity card at one point to prove who he was. Stick insect nodded every now and again and helped himself to the remaining Hula Hoops, inserting his tongue into the potato rings before crushing them between his front teeth. When Felix had finished, he licked his lips and said, 'Come with us. There's someone you should meet.'

Inside the long, narrow hallway of number 51 the whiff of roll-up tobacco eventually gave way to the smell of cooking – a fatty, meaty smell, strong but not unpleasant. It was lamb, probably. Abbie didn't like lamb. In a room to the left, eight or nine men sat on white, plastic garden furniture watching a portable telly. One of them stood and pushed the door closed as Felix glanced in. At the end of the hall they entered what would have been referred to by an estate agent as a dining room, which had nothing in it other than two moth-eaten armchairs, an office table and a cassette player on the floor. Several mobile phones of different shapes and sizes were thrown on the mantelpiece. The room beyond, where the steam and the cooking smells were coming from, was a lean-to kitchen.

'You sure about this, like?'

'Yes,' said Felix.

The man clapped his hands together. 'Maria. Get in here. Maria!'

From inside the kitchen there was a shuffling, stirring sound, then the sound of quick, light feet on bare wood as well as a peculiar squeaking noise, and in the next moment Felix found himself staring into the rich brown eyes of one Maria Rosales.

12

Abbie wasn't upset at all. In fact she thought it was hilarious, and now that Felix had permission, he found it hilarious as well. Hysterical. And when they had finished laughing, which was the most laughing they'd done for as long as Felix could remember, Abbie sat down in the big wicker chair hanging from the ceiling and said, 'What kind of dog exactly?'

'I don't know. Old and smelly. Like an Alsatian but with long hair. And it only had two legs.'

'Oh, give up, Felix. I'm going to wet myself in a minute,' she said, crossing her legs and holding a cushion to her stomach. Her face was alive, lit up, as if she'd suddenly been plugged in and switched on.

'Honestly. It only had legs at the front, and a pair of pram wheels at the back. And it needed oiling.'

'Felix, stop it,' she squealed.

She hurled the cushion at him and an arrangement of dried flowers on top of the bookcase went flying. As he gathered them up, one straw at a time, he told her as much as he knew about the dog in the house in Derby. That it had been christened Mario, after the video-game character, but renamed during her first pregnancy. And that because of her lameness she was now entitled to invalidity benefit as well as jobseeker's allowance and a whole range of other Giros that arrived at the address every week courtesy of the welfare state. And that Felix wouldn't breathe a word of this to a living soul, because if he did the stick insect with the pencil tash would send a few of the Kurdish or Albanian men from his 'employment bureau' up the M6 to 'do a job for me, like'.

'Not that I was in a position to argue. I shouldn't even have been there, officially.'

'Why Rosales, though? Did you ask him?'

'Yes. He just held up his hands and said, "Why not?"'

'And why put a dog's name in the phone book?'

'Don't know. Authenticating detail?'

Before he went to bed Felix wondered about his next move and glanced at the carefully constructed flow chart, which was now folded in half and inserted into the back of his Filofax, between the pull-out map of the London Underground and a table for converting imperial measurements into metric. He didn't want Abbie to see it, in case she accused him of reducing her emotional turmoil to something that resembled an intelligence test or, worse, a game. He remembered the look she'd given him on discovering he'd filed a leaflet on artificial insemination on the bookshelf between *The Larousse Field Guide to British Birds* and an operating manual for *Windows 98*.

'I didn't want to lose it,' he'd said.

'But why there?'

'Well, where would *you* have put it?'

'In my handbag. Somewhere close.'

He'd taken to keeping the Filofax in his briefcase and clicking the lock. It was ridiculous, because this was his way of lending a hand, his way of helping her find the thing she most wanted in life, except for a baby, perhaps, and even the mystery of childbirth could probably be reduced to a troubleshooting guide, given the right level of expertise. Why couldn't it be like science and facts? When he took the car into the garage last month because it kept stalling in low gear, a man in blue overalls simply wired it up to a computer, looked at the numbers on the screen and told him what the problem was. Half an hour later he was back on the road with the engine purring like a kitten. Felix flicked through the pages of his diary, looking at the week to come. Each day came printed with a small, round icon, shaded in part, becoming a solid dark circle by Friday. The phases of the moon. The lunar cycle. There would be hope for a few more days, then blackness and despair, and a silver light through the window in the small hours as they lay awake. There would be no baby again.

The team meeting on Monday took its usual course. Thelma wondered if the air-conditioning might be switched off because she felt sure that a number of harmful air-borne bacteria were being circulated throughout the building. Neville and Mo ignored each other. Roy was attending a Neighbourhood Watch meeting on the estate where he had grown up. They had asked for him by name, describing him as someone with the 'inside track'. Roy was exactly the right choice, given that he had spent time in many of the estate's residential properties, albeit fleetingly, in the dead of night, with a balaclava over his head and a holdall over his shoulder. As boss, Bernard chaired the meeting and took the minutes, which spared him having to make any meaningful or sensible contribution to the conversation, and he concerned himself primarily with the dismantling and reassembling of a fountain pen. Thelma watched in horror as he squeezed a droplet of ink through the nib like someone about to administer a lethal dose from a syringe. There were only two files to hand out. Felix took the case of a nine-year-old boy in foster care being advertised for adoption. And Marjorie pointed out that she had a 'gap' in her caseload, following the sad death of Matthew Coyne.

'Olé,' said Neville, which brought the meeting to a close.

As they walked back to the staffroom together, Felix said to Neville, 'I just don't understand you sometimes.'

'Who, me? I'm just a callous bastard, that's all. Nothing too complicated about that.'

'So why did you go to the funeral?'

'Which funeral?'

'Matthew Coyne's.'

'Don't be daft.'

'I saw you, Nev. Through the telescope.'

Neville veered off towards the toilets on the left. When he

returned, it was to say, 'So maybe I'm going soft. Keep your trap shut.'

On Tuesday James Spotland was waiting for him in reception. The last time he'd seen Jimmy he'd been forking lumps of pan-fried reindeer into his mouth, an image Felix had struggled to forget. He caught sight of Jimmy's pierced tongue and couldn't help gawping at the tiny silver stud as it flashed between his teeth.

'Thing is, Felix, I've got a shed-load of toys in the back of the van. I had a buyer lined up but he's been called away on business. Thing is, they're cluttering up my garage and it's costing me just to keep them, so you can have them, all right?'

'Why would I want them?'

'For those deprived kids you work with, down at the children's home.'

'That's a nice thing to do. Are you sure they're not knock-off?'

'Don't insult me. I'm trying to do a kindness here. I'm not saying that everything I touch comes with a receipt, but if something's a bit warm I've got more wit than to pass it on to Social Services. Anyway, the knock-off stuff is usually top quality, and I've got a living to make.'

He scratched his potbelly with both hands. It looked almost detachable, a whoopee cushion strapped around his middle or a phantom pregnancy.

'Thanks again,' said Felix. 'It's really good of you.'

Jimmy hitched up his trousers and spun his fob of keys around his middle finger.

'I must be going soft in my old age. Don't tell anyone.'

Felix called after him, 'You're the second person to say that this week.' Then smiled, thinking that maybe the world wasn't such a crummy place to live in after all.

On Wednesday it rained. A light drizzle in the morning cleared up about eleven, then after lunch the air became heavy and thick, and dense black clouds began to mount over the hills to the east. Just after two o'clock there was a terrific bang, like a bomb going off, and a minute or so of hail that drummed on the roofs of the cars down below was followed by torrential rain. Within seconds the gutters and fall-pipes were swamped, and water sheeted down the windows of Prospect House. The light outside turned from dark blue, to brown, to almost bottle green. Felix and Neville watched from the staffroom as the Strawberry Field became saturated, then waterlogged, until finally a fast-flowing stream was coursing through the underpass and out towards the precinct on the other side. The fire service turned up with the vague ambition of staunching the flow or pumping out the floodwater, but after taking one look at the scale of the problem decided to sit it out. They parked on the inside lane of the roundabout, laid out a line of traffic cones to steer oncoming traffic away from the tender, and passed an hour in the rain by dropping Coke cans and other items of litter into the deluge below, then running to the other side of the road to watch them reappear. Another fireman, the driver, sat in the cab and appeared to be smoking. Every once in a while, electricity ripped across the sky or earthed out somewhere on the horizon, forking down into the outlying estates, with the heavy artillery of thunder not far behind.

It was the same day that Captain Roderick had been spoken to by PC Nottingham and PC Lily as part of their inquiries into the temporary disappearance of Ruby Moffat a few weeks ago. Roderick had told them that as far as he was concerned the girl was a 'fabulist' whose weird behaviour was an elaborate hoax designed to excuse her poor performance in class and her bouts of truancy. PC Lily, relating the discussion to Felix over the phone, went on to say how much she would have liked to slap the pompous bastard across the head.

'Did you see his nails?' Felix asked.

'Sure did. I was going to ask him for the name of his manicurist. What's the betting he paints his toes as well?'

On Thursday Felix made a home visit to the Moffats. He took the first entrance to the Lakeland Estate, but halfway up Keswick Lane the Big Blue One pulled out into the middle of the road, blocking the way ahead. After waiting a minute or so, thinking the coach had stalled or even broken down, Felix pomped his horn. There was no response. He got out of his car, locking it behind him, and walked towards the coach. The door handle had been removed, but at eye level there was a small spyhole and to one side of it an old-fashioned button with the word PRESS written on it. A few weeks ago he wouldn't have even approached the Big Blue One, let alone rung the bell, but his encounter in Derby had given him new confidence, or even courage, perhaps. If he could talk the talk with illegal immigrants and labour pimps in a strange city, why couldn't he chat amiably to the driver of a mobile shop in his own backyard? Not only that, in the space of twenty-four hours he'd heard admissions of compassion from two people he'd previously thought of as irredeemably insensitive or pathologically selfish. Not miracles, exactly, but little incidents that were full of humanity and hope.

'Fuck off,' said a voice. It came from inside the bus but was amplified by a small loudspeaker mounted above the wing mirror.

'I just want to get past in my car,' said Felix.

Felix waited for more dialogue with the person or persons inside, or another instruction from the speaker. But nothing happened. The coach sat there, monumental and silent. Alongside it, Felix was insignificant and small. He had a job to do, guidelines to meet, responsibilities to carry out. The coach had all the time in the world and nothing to care about. One day it might meet its match in the form of a bulldozer or an armoured tank. Its comeuppance would come. But not like this, with a social worker of medium build politely ringing its doorbell and asking to be let through. Another three or four minutes went past, not in fear but in embarrassment, before Felix did exactly as he had been told, executing a three-point turn and heading for Coleridge Avenue via Grasmere Drive.

The fridge freezer was still on the lawn in front of the house but had been converted into a pretend car, with tyres propped against each corner, two car seats installed – one in the freezer and one in the fridge – and an actual steering column rammed through the thin metal base. Whatever shortages the people of the Lakeland Estate had to cope with, spare parts for motor vehicles were not one of them. Two little boys were playing at driving the car. 'Hey, mister, will you shut the door while we're inside? Go on, mister. Why not, yer mean twat?'

Mrs Moffat said that Ruby had been quiet since the disclosure interview. No outbursts or incidents, although she had heard her crying in bed on a couple of occasions, once in the middle of the night and once in the morning, just before it came light.

'But she hasn't said anything?'

'Not to me.'

'Does she speak to Mr Moffat?'

'No. But he's not really the talkative kind.'

'What about her brothers?'

Mrs Moffat shook her head. 'Teddy, a little bit, the eldest. They all look out for her, but I wouldn't say they talk. We're not like that. We're never going to be on *Family Fortunes*.'

Ruby was watching television, just like the last time. She mumbled a hello but other than that only nodded when Felix asked her if she was OK and shook her head when he asked if there was anything she wanted to tell him. Maybe Captain Roderick was right. Maybe this was nothing more than an old-fashioned case of attention-seeking behaviour. Who could blame her, a young girl in a family of seven or eight older brothers and a mute father?

The Big Blue One was still straddling Keswick Lane with its wheels on the pavement at each side of the road. Felix went the long way round.

On Friday he went home early to mow the lawn and stopped at the garage at the side of the ring road. The gauge on the petrol tank was pointing to full, but he needed a bottle of wine – two, probably, Spanish if possible – and a bunch of flowers.

13

Some cases stayed around for years, lifetimes even, the blue folders becoming tatty, faded and torn, swollen with documents, letters and notes. A baby might be taken into the care of the local authority or put on the at-risk register. The same child would be well known to Social Services by the time it made its first appearance at juvenile court, charged with its first offence. Then came further court appearances and more complicated problems, often involving illegal substances. Then parenthood, divorce, custody, poverty, insanity, infirmity, meals on wheels, the local hospice and even burial. Obviously not everybody who came into contact with the department stayed on the books for ever, and Felix could point to any number of clients who had gone on to live happy and normal lives, people he could think of as his success stories. But for those who wanted it, or needed it, or were told that, like it or not, they were going to have it, social work offered the complete service, from cradle to grave.

Then, once in a while, a case would last no more than a few days or a week, and disappear as quickly as it had come to light. An issue would be resolved, or a person would move on, and with them the blue folder. They were now, in the unofficial language of the profession, SEP. Someone else's problem. The case file labelled John Valentine had been someone else's problem, but now it was Felix's. He had arrived at the children's home having been transferred in from another district. He'd been passed from one foster parent to another, and two attempts at adoption had broken down in the early stages. He was now nine and three-quarters, and in the opinion of his previous social worker time was running out.

A suitable family needed to be found as quickly as possible, before he lost his boyish grin and what was left of his innocence. When those had gone, no one would want him. Then the problems would really start. Felix read through the file in the office and went over the relevant facts in his mind as he drove to the home. Inside, a handful of kids of various ages were sat around a television eating toast. They all looked as he walked in, then turned back to the screen. Off to one side a couple of industrial spin-dryers rumbled through their cycle. The air was clogged with the smell of washing powder and margarine. Carlos, the officer in charge, was behind his desk. Felix didn't know his full name. Whenever he came to the home he always felt sad for the kids, but sorry as well for the people who worked there. They got the least training, the lowest pay, the most flak. If there was a front line, this was it. At least Felix could retreat to his office on the top floor of Prospect House, or show someone the door when he'd had enough. But this was wall-to-wall, twenty-four-hours-a-day, 360-degrees, four-dimensional, full-blown, in-your-face social work. Carlos had been expecting him.

'He's in the games room. Want a coffee?'

'I wouldn't mind.'

'Spuggy,' he shouted in the direction of the television, 'two coffees.'

A thin boy in a blue football shirt peeled himself out of his chair and ambled off towards the kitchen.

'You've got them well trained,' said Felix.

'Reward system, we call it. They call it slave of the day. They get a fiver for doing jobs. It's Spuggy's turn today.'

Felix could hear the clack of pool balls as he walked towards the door. Inside, a small boy with a mop of brown, unbrushed hair was bending over the table to take a shot. There was no one else in the room.

'Hello. My name's Felix.'

The boy grunted, then drilled the white ball towards a red close to where Felix had rested his hand on the cushion.

'Do you want a drink? Some juice, or . . .'

'No.'

'Fancy a game?'

John Valentine shrugged his shoulders. Spuggy delivered the coffee. Felix picked up a cue that was resting in the corner and put his coffee on the windowsill. The window was made of toughened glass. The pool cue had no tip, just a black plastic cap.

'Are you any good?'

'Not bad,' the boy said.

'Well, I'm fantastic,' said Felix. 'You can break.'

The boy grinned and gathered the balls into the triangle. Then he walked to the other end of the table, chalked his cue with a stick of white chalk from the tray under the scoreboard and fired the cue ball as hard as he could into the pack.

Later on, in McDonald's, Felix explained about the advert.

The boy said, 'I know. They did it last time.'

'So you know you have to think of a name. We can't use your proper name.'

'I know.'

A blob of red sauce dripped from his burger on to the tray. He wiped it up with a chip and ate it.

'That good, is it?'

The boy couldn't speak because his mouth was full of food, but he nodded enthusiastically, chewing and swallowing, then opening wide for the next bite.

'Any ideas? About the name?'

It was an odd business, trawling for prospective parents in the classified section of the local paper, next to planning applications, notices of bankruptcy and advertisements for happy hour at Cinderella's nightclub. It had to be done anonymously for legal and moral reasons, and it was considered good practice to let the child choose the name he or she would be advertised under. Mostly they went for the names of their idols and heroes: pop stars who had everything; footballers with their faces all over the telly; cartoon characters

126

who could put the world to rights with a single punch. It showed the power of their imagination and the size of their dreams. But more than anything it proved they were children, or spoke of a childhood that had never happened, or had to be kept a secret. And there was always a secret. One thing that all of these kids had in common – they were all on guard.

'Lee,' he said.

'Not Beckham, then? Or Eminem?'

'No. Lee.'

Felix helped himself to a chip. 'Lee. Fine. Any reason?'

'It's real. Like what proper people are called.'

'How do you mean?'

'I don't want another stupid name.'

'John isn't stupid. John's a real name, isn't it?'

The boy swallowed a mouthful of food. 'My name's Valentine.'

'What's stupid about John Valentine?'

'I'm not John Valentine. I'm Valentine John.'

'But I've been calling you John all day. Why didn't you say something?'

'I just thought you were being . . . you know . . . the boss.'

Valentine had a milk shake and a cherry pie, then another milk shake to go. Felix drove him back to the home. That afternoon he drafted out the advert on a word processor in the clerical office. He'd missed the deadline for tonight but if he dropped the copy in tomorrow it would appear in the paper the following evening.

Lee is nine. He's a bright, fun-loving boy with a gleam in his eye. He likes football, riding his bike, playing pool – all the things that boys enjoy. But Lee needs a home and a new family to take care of him and support him. If you've ever thought about adoption, and think Lee is the kind of boy you could love and help, please phone Social Services at Prospect House and ask for Felix.

That night, Abbie came out of the utility room and into the lounge holding a piece of paper.

'I found this,' she said.

Felix was reading a magazine. 'Oh, the ad,' he said.

'Is this what happens? Adverts in the papers?'

'Sometimes.'

'Does it work?'

'Sometimes.'

'What's he like, this Lee?'

'He's a great kid. A bit troubled, but a good lad, basically.'

Abbie went back into the kitchen with the piece of paper. He could hear her stacking the dishwasher, slotting the plates into the rack on the bottom shelf, then the cutlery in the little plastic basket with its eight separate sections for knives, forks, spoons. Then the metallic clunk of the pans that were really supposed to be washed by hand, the ones with the pine handles which had been through the machine so often they now looked like lengths of driftwood or old bones. Then he heard the kettle boiling, its vibration on the worktop on the other side of the wall, just behind his head. Then a teaspoon clinking against the inside of a cup. Then the fridge door. Then the silence of milk being poured, then the ker-thunk of the pedal bin. Finally she came into the lounge with the drinks, set them down on coasters on the coffee table and curled up against his shoulder. He lifted his arm and put it around her, holding the magazine in his other hand. After a while she said, 'We could have him.'

'Who?'

'Lee.'

Felix lowered the magazine and rested it on the arm of the sofa, and as quietly and with as little movement as possible took a deep breath.

'No.'

'Why not?'

'A million reasons.'

'Give me one.'

'He's got problems.'

'I thought you said he was a great kid.'

'He is. But . . .'

Felix reached for his drink and put the hot tea to his lips. They'd never actually discussed taking on one of his clients before, although the subject of adopting a baby had come up several times, speculatively at first, then with more conviction. On each occasion Abbie had pointed out that if some kind souls hadn't found it in their hearts to welcome her into their midst . . . Felix took another sip of tea. Then, because he couldn't think of anything useful or different to say, he said, 'He's not called Lee, he's called Valentine.'

He hadn't meant it as the concluding remark, but for whatever reason it struck home.

'Valentine?'

'Yes.'

It was some time afterwards when Abbie spoke again, because her tea had gone cold and Felix actually thought she had fallen asleep.

'Valentine?'

'Valentine John.'

She stood up and yawned, ready to go to bed.

'Somebody's love child. Poor kid,' she said.

Three days later Felix had a phone call from Valentine's previous social worker in Keighley saying that his great-auntie had agreed the boy could go and live with her. He'd stayed with her before and things hadn't worked out, but she was prepared to give him another chance on the condition that he was more helpful around the house and promised not to go to the slot-machine arcade in town. The advert had gone in the paper, but apart from the forty-pound fee that would come out of the office budget there was no harm done, because nobody replied.

That night he began telling Abbie that Valentine John had gone back to his family, but she wasn't interested. A letter had come from the hospital with an appointment. At the fertility clinic. She pushed the letter across the kitchen table and tapped the date with her fingernail. A leaflet, 'Explaining IUI', was stapled to it. Felix opened the leaflet and looked down the list of 'frequently asked questions'. 'What does IUI mean?' 'If IUI fails can we try it again?' 'Does IUI hurt?' 'How much does it cost?' On the reverse was a line drawing of a thin, plastic tube inserted into a womb, with a quantity of sperm being injected through the tube via a syringe at the other end. Abbie walked around the table, put her arm across Felix's shoulder and whispered in his ear.

'A month from now, we could be pregnant.'

Her breath was warm and loud. Felix looked again at the letter and at the highlighted number in the box at the bottom.

'Why does it cost so much?'

'It's the drugs. To make sure I ovulate.'

'It's just about everything we've got.'

Abbie pulled back and snatched the letter away from him.

'You mean bastard. Our one and only chance for a baby and you start moaning about the price. Unbelievable.'

'I wasn't moaning, I was just saying . . .'

'Forget it,' she snapped, and slammed the door.

Later, before he turned out the lights, Felix retrieved the screwed-up letter and the leaflet from the bin and flattened them out against the arm of the chair. He wrote the date of the appointment in his Filofax and shaded out the three days leading up to it – the period of sexual abstinence – with a blue pencil. He looked again at the drawing. It was more like something from a car-maintenance manual or the instructions for a new dishwasher than anything likely to produce a baby. And even though Felix was a man who often put his faith in such mechanical descriptions, there was something about this particular diagram that didn't ring true. Something was missing – the man. The man who comes up with the goods. The man who has to do well under pressure. The man charged with the responsibility of delivering a feasible amount of quality sperm on the one occasion – on the one and only occasion – when it truly matters. In other words, him. He was missing. And it was at that moment, as he visualized himself locked in the bathroom with a specimen bottle in his hand and Abbie pacing to and fro on the landing outside, that Felix sensed something in his groin. Or rather he sensed a lack of something. A kind of absence. A numbness or an unwillingness between his legs, and the more he tried to concentrate, the more remote and disconnected that region of his body began to feel. As if to test himself, he closed his eyes for several intensely pornographic minutes.

But there was no response.

14

The trail hadn't gone cold exactly but there was nothing else Felix
could do from the end of a telephone. Neither did he want to waste
any more time staking out refugee hostels where German shepherd
dogs were given fictitious identities and received generous support
from the state. Every once in a while, daydreaming, he still came
face to face with the sad, watery eyes of that dog and could hear
the squeaking of its solid rubber wheels as the back end of its body
trundled around the corner.

During his training, he'd spent a two-week placement with the
Department of Social Security and accompanied one of the officers
on a number of 'unannounced' visits. This involved turning up on
the doorstep of a council house – always a council house – usually
in the early hours of the morning. Then flashing an identity card in
the face of some puzzled and sleepy occupier and touring the
property for evidence of fraud. A loophole in the system meant
that two people living in the same house could claim a higher rate
of benefit as individuals than they could as a couple. The purpose
of the unannounced visit was to rumble any man and a woman
'living as husband and wife', but rather than taking the bedsheets
away for forensic testing, the wily officers of the DSS were on the
lookout for more subtle indicators of cohabitation. For instance, a
shared tube of toothpaste was considered to be proof that two
claimants were more than just good friends. Likewise, the existence
of a single bath towel was confirmation of sexual congress, as was
a communal pint of milk in the fridge or joint use of a frying pan.
In the living room, assumptions could be made from photographs
or birthday cards on the mantelpiece, and from more mysterious

sources such as the particular arrangement of chairs or the contents of an ashtray. If access could be gained, his-and-her slippers or dressing gowns in the same bedroom were a dead giveaway, and a condom packet, full or empty, was the ultimate signifier: the couple in question might as well have been writhing naked on top of the duvet.

It was a humiliating experience for those under investigation, and sinister as well, in that no object or item was touched or moved throughout the whole search and few words were spoken. Afterwards, in the car, the officer would go through his checklist, ticking boxes with his pencil and making thick black crosses in others. He'd also record a few minutes of legalistic babble into his Dictaphone, then drive off to the next unsuspecting household where the curtains were still drawn, where human beings were sleeping either in one bed or alone. Four or five visits could be made before breakfast. After that it wasn't worth it.

'The jungle drums will be banging by now, and besides, everyone claiming the dole will have gone to work.'

Felix didn't hate the man with the clipboard and the Dictaphone. He was just a person doing a job, someone carrying out instructions, someone at the business end of a bad idea. When the suits in Whitehall drew up a plan for clamping down on the spongers and the cheats, they probably didn't project as far as an actual person having to scrutinize the pubic hairs in the plughole of a bath on a poverty-ridden housing estate in a godforsaken town somewhere over yonder, sometime before dawn. Or maybe they did, but what did they care? It was miles away. Someone else's problem. Those *other* people, with their different, distant lives. Felix sniggered to himself, wondering what the DSS super-snooper would have made of Maria Rosales. Wondering if there was a special box on his checklist for large dogs with Spanish-sounding names, and whether its mechanical undercarriage gave any clue as to its marital status or affected its entitlement to single benefit supplement.

'What's so funny?' Abbie asked him.

They were nearing the outskirts of London after three hours in the car. Abbie had slept most of the way, which was fine by Felix, because it allowed him to think his thoughts as well as concentrate on the road ahead. Mo, at work, had once explained to him that, contrary to popular opinion, men were not incapable of multitasking – they were just lazy. Felix had never heard of multi-tasking, but as soon as the concept was explained to him he instinctively felt that popular opinion was correct. He couldn't even unload the dishwasher if the radio was on, and one morning had nicked a sizeable chunk out of his ear with his razor when the telephone rang. Daydreaming and driving were two activities he had just about managed to combine, but driving and talking – that was more complicated. After a long journey with Abbie he'd often think of things he should have said, little phrases he could have used instead of what actually came out of his mouth. Or he'd wonder about his performance at the wheel – whether he should have dropped into third at the roundabout at the top of the slip road, or how much time he'd spent dawdling in the middle lane when by rights he should have moved over to let faster vehicles go past.

The traffic got heavier as they neared the end of the motorway. Roadworks forced them into a contraflow, then back to the other side of the road into single file along the hard shoulder. It was stop/start, stop/start, pushing down, then easing back with the clutch. Brake lights were invisible in the glare of the sun. Three or four cars had pulled over, bonnets in the air, steam rising from the engine, or black smoke in the case of an old Dormobile painted with lime-green gloss. After the bottleneck of the final junction, they entered busy streets where pedestrians stepped from the kerb without notice and without looking. Cars were parked in the bus lane, clogging the system, making a burst of thirty or forty yards in second gear seem like some kind of progress. Abbie, wearing her sunglasses, glanced at the *A–Z* every now and again and at one point suggested turning off and trying a different way. But Felix had memorized the route. He could visualize the road patterns in his head. He corrected Abbie on several occasions for saying left when she obviously meant right, and vice versa, and for failing to notice the small arrows, printed in black, indicating a one-way street. Finally they arrived, with all four windows open and the sun roof closed to keep out the heat from directly overhead.

Inside the Family Records Centre the air was cool and the atmosphere more peaceful. Neither of them had known what to expect, but the building struck Felix as being somewhere between a library and a post office. There was a measured quietness, a controlled hush. Row upon row of huge ledgers were shelved in metal cabinets with wide, wooden tables between each stack. Things were businesslike and formal. There were no chairs; no one was being encouraged to linger or take longer than they needed to. At one end of the room was a counter and a small file of people waiting to be served. They were probably on the verge of some life-changing moment, on the brink of some cataclysmic revelation which would alter their self-image or entirely question their identity. But they looked like people queuing to buy stamps or pay the gas bill. They looked like citizens. Customers. The lady behind the desk asked Felix and Abbie if they had been to the Centre before, then gave a brief explanation of how the ledgers were arranged and how best to tackle them. They had intended to search the volumes together, because two pairs of eyes were better than one, and Felix wanted to be with her if anything important came to light, and Abbie wanted to be with him. But after locating then throwing open the first half a dozen volumes and trawling through the endless lists of names, it became obvious they would have to split up. Either that, or they'd be at it for weeks, and Felix had only paid for two hours' parking.

'Which do you want to take?' Felix asked.

'I don't know,' she said. Her voice was faint, almost drowsy.

'You do the marriages, then, and I'll do . . .'

'No. It's OK. I'll do it.'

'Are you sure?'

Abbie nodded. Felix squeezed her hand, then watched her turn towards the section of shelves that ran diagonally to the other rows.

To the registers of deaths. To the lists of the deceased, whose ranks outnumbered the living, whose lives, however long and fascinating, were reduced here to a name and a date. Millions of them, all piled up. Think of all the bodies, all the bones and possessions of the dead. Where did everything go? How could it fit? Abbie turned behind one of the shelves and vanished. Felix slotted a ledger back into the empty space on the shelf and walked his fingers along the alphabetically ordered spines to the next.

He figured it like this: Maria Rosales was either alive or dead. That was a fact, an incontrovertible truth, and a starting place. If she was alive she was no longer known by the same name, or at least there was nobody listed under that name with either directory inquiries or the electoral roll, and in all likelihood she was married. By scouring the register of marriages, Felix could discover her new surname, although he would need to follow that name all the way through to the present day in case she had married a second or third time. It wasn't a flawless progression of logic – it was a case of playing the odds. But the little diagram tucked in the back of his Filofax told him the odds were good. Of course, there were other possibilities, variables that were hard to control. For instance, Maria might not be living in Britain any longer. She was Spanish, after all, and could have returned to her homeland. In a more extreme scenario, Maria might have entered a convent. Or she might be living in a witness protection programme somewhere in Utah. But those thoughts took him beyond the boundary of probability. They were things that happened to people in films or books, and Felix was trying to concentrate on real life. He was a social worker. He had an instinct for this kind of thing, and his instincts told him that the name of Maria Rosales was printed on one of these pages, between the covers of one of these great books. It was just a case of which one. A book from his shelf or a book from the other side, where Abbie was looking. The books of the dead.

After half an hour or so Felix had become quite adept at tracking down the right volume, levering it from the cabinet, laying it down on the table and flipping back the cover. Quickly he'd got the hang of riffling through the pages, like a bank teller counting a wad of notes, and homing in on Maria's surname via the coordinates of similar-looking words. Ross – that meant he'd gone too far. Rooney, Roper, getting close. Rosier – too far again, then working back through Rosendale, Rosen, Rose – thousands of Roses, in fact, page after page after page. He went out to feed the meter and came back and carried on. He saw Abbie going to the toilet, then returning. He watched other people in the building checking the records. Some seemed like experts, crashing the books down on the table, slamming them closed. They could only be prying into someone else's business, delving into the life of a stranger. It wouldn't be possible to be so slick, so proficient, with one of your own. After three hours, neither of them with anything to report, they sat on a low wall across the road and ate the sandwiches Abbie had packed at home. Slow traffic grumbled along the road. People strolled past, men in their shirtsleeves with their jackets over their shoulders, women in flip-flops and flowery skirts. Abbie was still quiet. She hadn't spoken more than a handful of sentences all day. She pulled two pieces of fruit out of a plastic box, an apple for herself and a banana for Felix. More people went by. Someone on rollerskates. A couple of lads in school uniform kicked an empty can along the pavement. It wasn't as bright now, but the air was still humid and slow. They went back inside, back to their shelves and tables, and it wasn't more than ten minutes later when Felix looked up and saw Abbie walking towards him. She was looking into his eyes, but in her hands one of the big books lay open. She could have been bringing him a small animal, something broken or hurt, like the owl that flew into the windscreen last autumn. The way she'd lifted it, carried it to the side of the road, kneeling as she placed it in the grass.

'What is it?'

'She's dead,' said Abbie, still looking at him.

Felix took the register of deaths out of her hands and lowered it to the table. Abbie's finger pointed at the name. Maria Rosales. Then at the date of birth. It was her. No question.

'I found it an hour ago.'

'Before lunch?'

She nodded her head. 'I just needed to think about it for a while.'

Then her face began to crumple, and as she breathed in she moaned, a noise that was involuntary, beyond her control, and she lifted her hand to her mouth. She reached out for him and held on. A man next to them, one of the experts, closed the volume he was studying and tactfully disappeared. He'd seen this before. Every day, probably. Felix told Abbie it was OK to cry. She did for a while, inaudibly, until she regained her breathing. Then she backed out of his arms and took a tissue from her sleeve.

'I'm OK.'

'Honestly?'

'Yes. I'm going to the loo. Will you get the certificate?'

After she'd gone, Felix looked again at the entry. Maria Rosales. Born 1939. Died 1988. He scribbled a note on a piece of paper, then closed the cover. Then he carried the book solemnly and with respect back to the gap in the shelf and eased it gently in.

There was a longish queue for the counter. A dozen or so people. Felix got chatting with the man in front of him, a guy in his mid-thirties, a northerner, looking for a birth certificate for a friend of his.

'Didn't take long. His surname's Pompus. There aren't many of them around.'

'Have you been here before?'

'No. But if you ask me it's a scandal that any old Freeman, Hardy or Willis can walk in off the street and order up a copy of someone's birth certificate just for six and a half quid and no questions asked. But I didn't make the law. I'm just an interested party exercising a democratic right. And anyway I was in the area.'

He said all this over his shoulder, without really looking at Felix, so probably didn't notice whether Felix had nodded in agreement or not. Then he said, 'It's like shopping at that place . . .'

'Index?'

'Yeah. Or Argos. Everyone waiting with their little order form.'

They chatted a bit more until they reached the front of the queue.

'Barney,' the man said, holding out his arm.

'Felix.'

They shook on it, and went in different directions to hand in their requests and pay the appropriate fee.

The grave wasn't so hard to find, despite the Japanese knotweed that had colonized the top half of the graveyard and the best efforts of many other weeds and shrubs to overrun the paths and walkways which ran parallel to every second row of headstones. Abbie walked a little further up the track, then returned with a small metal vase taken from another plot. She slotted the lilies she had bought into the vase, one at a time, placing it on a flat stone disc in the middle of the grave above the scattering of green stone chippings. Then she stood back and looked. Felix had scraped the moss from the lower part of the headstone, but there was nothing else to see. Nothing beyond the simple inscription which read 'Maria Rosales 1939–1988'. There was a small piece of red card on the ground attached to a withered length of grey string, a gift tag presumably from a bunch of flowers, with the words 'From B' written in faded ink. But it could have blown over from the next grave or the one behind it, or from anywhere really. There was nothing else to go on, no other clues. Later in the car, on the way home, Abbie would lift her hands to her face and weep until the tears ran through her fingers and on to her rings and her watch, saying her mother mustn't have married, saying she must have died alone. It was shock. Delayed reaction. Felix had been expecting it, and stopped the car to hold her and tell her how sorry he was. But here in the churchyard Abbie was blank and impassive.

'You seem OK,' he commented.

'Well, I didn't know her, did I?' she replied. 'Hard to feel something for someone you've never met.'

She pushed a few fingers of grass away from the masonry with her foot, but they sprang back into position. At some time during the summer the undergrowth had been strimmed, but beneath the weeds another order of vegetation was at work on the grave. These plants were smaller but more tenacious, like some form of sea plant or fungus, with suckers and roots that spidered out across the stonework in search of a fracture or fissure. Other graves had completely disappeared below stands of rose-bay willowherb and saplings of sycamore and lime. The knotweed on this side of the church had been battered and clubbed so all that remained of it were thousands of hollow tubes, like so many blow holes in the earth. Carpet and underlay had been draped across two patches to cut out the light. But it was unkillable stuff. Next year it would be back, four, five, six foot high. And on the opposite slope, behind the steeple, not one gravestone could be seen through the rust-coloured stems and the thick, flourishing leaves. Beyond it, in the very top corner, trees had risen to maturity, and the area within the green metal railings that formed the top boundary of the church was no longer a graveyard but a wood.

The rain poured and the sun shone and everything grew. A grave needed to be tended. It needed to be watched over and cared for. Otherwise what was it but a flowerbed, an oblong of rich earth in a quiet, undisturbed corner of the world? Maria Rosales had only one grave-keeper, the daughter she'd never met, and Abbie stood wordlessly and unmoved with her hands in her pockets, nudging at a dandelion clock with her shoe. At this point in time she didn't look like a woman about to make any promises or commitments to this rectangle of holy ground. If you want a person to take care of you when you're dead, you should look after that person while you're alive. That's what Abbie's silence meant, that's what her foot was saying to the dandelion clock.

But later, in the car, that all changed. And Felix was a social worker, so he knew what to expect, and he was ready for it, and he was there for her when it came, ready with the tissues.

VIRGO *(23 August–22 September)*

15

Out of character. An act of desperation.

Once every four weeks, Felix sat in the local magistrates' court, tracking the progress of any Social Services client through the criminal justice system, and once in a while contributing to the proceedings if someone on his caseload came before the bench. The days could be long and tedious. With all the remands, bail applications, stand-downs, delays, adjournments and a whole bunch of other tricks designed to stave off the day of judgement, it was rare that a case ever resulted in a decision and rarer still for a matter to be considered finalized or in any way 'closed'. At first Felix had enjoyed listening to the bantering that went on between the lawyers and the clerks, but after so many years of the same jargon, the same arguments and identical replies, he now thought of his monthly day of court duty as something of a chore.

Neville had become so impatient he had flatly refused to do his stint and had removed his name from the rota. The magistrates, he said, were Freemasons on a power trip or nosy Women's Institute types with nothing better to do. The lawyers were dunderheads and losers, criminal work being to the legal profession what road sweeping is to landscape gardening. The clerks were failed lawyers who secretly thought of themselves as judges, and the criminals were not just small-time thieves and petty crooks but hopeless amateurs as well, as evidenced by the very fact they had been caught. He said he found it beyond his dignity to spend time in such pathetic and miserable company. Bernard, in a rather embarrassing attempt to exert his authority, had called Neville into his office and explained that in his opinion the magistracy of the local court was among the most informed he had ever come into contact with and he had no reason to suppose that the clerks and solicitors were of anything other than the highest calibre.

'So why are they working in *this* town?' Neville wanted to know.

It was the end of the argument and Neville hadn't been seen in court again, except for that time when a man was half eaten by two 'healers' attempting to purify him of his sins, and on that occasion everyone in the department had turned up for a look at the alleged cannibals, including two temps from the typing pool and the office cleaner.

Bernard wasn't on the court-duty rota because he was the boss. And Thelma was excused on account of a previous whiplash injury to her neck, a condition aggravated by the constant nodding and bowing to the magistrates each time they entered or exited the courtroom.

Roy was very often denied access. It had taken a lot of hard work for him to convince the ushers, who 'knew him of old', that he was now a fully qualified social worker, and on one occasion when he had actually made it into the courtroom he had been turned away by the clerk on the grounds that jeans and a denim jacket were not a sufficiently respectful form of attire. The quick addition of a pink nylon tie, bought from the charity shop round the corner and worn loosely beneath the frayed collar of his green polo shirt, had almost earned him a conviction for contempt.

This left Mo, Marjorie and Felix to man the barricades, or 'staff' the barricades, as Mo had once corrected him, and Felix being Felix, the gaps in the schedule had become his responsibility. Sitting at the back, he would spend the first hour of every morning reading through the numerous court reports supplied by either his agency or the probation service, reports which were full of stock phrases used to explain or excuse the behaviour of individuals. Phrases such as 'out of character' and 'an act of desperation'. 'Looking at Mr Bloggs's record, it can be said that the attack on the garage that night and the injuries he caused to the woman in the kiosk were very much *out of character*.' 'In interview, Mr Bloggs presents as a thoughtful and unassuming man, a husband and a father with a family to support, and in that light, his obtaining money by deception over the past two years can only be seen as *an act of desperation.*' 'Mr Bloggs tells me that the gun was fired in the heat of the moment. The incident itself was *an act of desperation* and *very much out of character.*' It wasn't Felix's job to doubt the phrases – the cynicism could be left to the likes of Neville, or the magistrates, who presumably scoffed at the reports over their tea and biscuits in the retiring room before returning their decision. But people doing things that were out of character, or doing things as an act of desperation, or even doing them in the heat of the moment – these were concepts that Felix struggled hard to come to terms with. They were far-fetched.

Until, that is, the sunlit Tuesday morning, not long after nine fifteen, when he knocked at the house of Jed, his closest friend and next-door neighbour. That was the instant. That was the precise point the normally level-headed, calm and collected Felix did something which was well and truly out of character, and quite possibly beyond the character of anyone he had ever known, alive or dead. Jed was still in his pyjamas and midway through an enormous yawn as he pulled open the door.

'Thought you were the paper boy,' he managed to say, when his mouth had fallen back into position.

Felix rocked from one foot to another, and let out a long stream of breath, like a weightlifter about to attempt some huge feat of strength. 'I need your help, Jed.'

'What's up? Won't the car start? I think the jump leads are still in your garage – is that what you're after?'

'Jump leads? Er . . . kind of.'

'Jesus, man, you're sweatin' like a racehorse. What's up?'

'Can I come in?'

Felix sat on one of the high stools at the breakfast bar and drank a glass of cold apple juice from the fridge while Jed went upstairs to get dressed. When he came back down he put his hand on Felix's shoulder and said, 'You and Abbie had a domestic?'

'No. But if I don't sort this mess out we'll have the biggest domestic of all time, and I don't know if we'll ever get over it.'

'Aw, come on, man. Look at me an' my Max. We have the mother of all slanging matches but it's always OK again in the morning. Nothing seems as bad in the cold light of day.'

Felix gestured towards the window and the clear blue sky filling it, making the point that it *was* morning, that here they were in the cold light of day and there was still a problem. The sweat had begun to collect on his forehead again. Jed tore off a sheet of kitchen roll and passed it to him. 'So . . . have you been . . . playing around?'

Felix didn't even bother to answer. Instead, he reached into his pocket and produced a small plastic bottle with a yellow screw top, which he placed on the Formica surface. 'Do you know what that is?'

Jed lifted the empty bottle to the light. 'Air?'

'The bottle. Do you know what it's for?'

'Tell me.'

'Sperm.'

'Right.'

'My sperm.'

'Right.'

'My sperm, to take to the hospital this morning, to be specially prepared for this afternoon.'

'Right. So what happens this afternoon?'

'IUI.'

'Good. What's that?'

'Intra-uterine insemination. Seven hundred and fifty quid a shot. They inject the sperm into Abbie, and fingers crossed she gets pregnant.'

'Right. So . . . what's the problem?'

Felix helped himself to another glass of juice and another sheet of kitchen roll. It was almost half past nine now. There wasn't time for all this conversation, all this chat.

'I can't get it up,' he said. He was facing the window so he didn't have to look at Jed when he said it.

There was a quiet, understanding pause before Jed said, 'Right,' again, but this time with a gentler voice, without any hint of comedy.

'You see, Jed, it's kind of now or never. We can't afford another go after this, and Abbie says she can't stand any more disappointment, on top of the stuff about her mum and everything. So this is the big one. We're banking on it. And it must be the pressure or something, because I just can't . . .'

'OK, OK, wait there. Don't go away.'

Jed opened the internal door to the garage and was gone for three or four minutes. When he came back he was carrying a large plastic bag in his hand, which he dropped on to the breakfast bar. 'There you go.'

'What?' said Felix, prying into the bag.

'Bash mags. Some of the lads at work . . . Anyway, what the fuck. There's all sorts in there, Swedish mainly. You can chuck 'em once you've finished, just don't let on to Max, all right? She'll brain me.'

Felix pulled out one of the magazines. A naked woman looked at him from between her legs. He slid it back into the bag. 'Jed, this isn't really . . .'

'Go on. Take 'em. That's what they're for. And here, don't forget your bottle.'

Felix left Jed's house and walked across the driveway to his own home. Now would have been the time to stop what he was doing, to pull back from the edge, but he didn't. Desperation. The heat of the moment. Only the moment had lasted a good twenty minutes now and was still simmering. He sat in the living room for a while, then crossed back to Jed's house and knocked at the door, by which time his actions were becoming not only out of character but altogether alien – one of those out-of-body experiences people talk about. He could see his arm rising towards the glass panel, he could hear the rapping of his knuckles against the pane, but his true self was elsewhere, watching from a distance, horrified and appalled.

'Did the trick, did they?' said Jed, grinning.

Felix pushed past him and dropped the bag of magazines in the corner by the bin. He produced the empty plastic pot again and put it down on the worktop. He tapped on the lid.

'Jed, listen. I need you to help. Do you know what I'm saying? I'm asking for your help. As a friend. Do you see what I'm saying?'

Jed obviously didn't understand, because he scrunched his face into a strange, quizzical expression and rubbed at the stubble under his chin. Then a darker, more serious look came over him. He stood up straight, six feet and four inches tall, and peered down towards where Felix was hunched over the table. 'Don't tell me . . .'

Felix looked up at him, waiting for the penny to drop.

'You mean you want me to . . .'

Felix nodded, encouragingly.

'You want me to . . . toss you off?'

'NO! NO!'

'Well, thank fuck for that. I know we're mates but . . . Christ Almighty.'

'Jed . . .'

'I know. Stupid. I mean, if you can't get a bone on looking at those porno mags, you're not going to want me to . . .'

'Will you just listen?'

'What about a film? Come and have a flick through the satellite channels, there's that Dutch station . . .'

'I want you to do it.'

Felix picked up the transparent plastic pot and took a couple of steps towards where Jed was standing. He felt his arm rising again and his hand opening. Now the container was there, between his thumb and finger, right in front of his face. All that Jed needed to do was to reach out and take it.

'It's not *how*. It's *who*. I can't do it. I want you to do it.'

It was as if the container was red-hot or radioactive. Ever so slightly, Jed backed away and took his hands out of his pockets and curled his fingers around the metal towel rail behind him. Then he forced himself to smile and said, 'You're kidding, right?'

Felix shook his head. He wasn't kidding. It was nine forty-one on a weekday morning. He was standing in another man's house, holding a plastic container in his hand designed for the collection of semen. He was pouring with sweat, holding the container under the other man's nose. Did this look like a joke? Would he be doing this if he was kidding, if he wasn't absolutely 100 per cent serious?

They sat on the front step. Jed had made a pot of tea and was smoking a cigarette. He hadn't spoken for a while. It was now ten to ten. He let the smoke stay in his lungs, then blew it out of his nose. He went back into the house, and Felix heard the sound of him peeing in the downstairs loo and the toilet flushing. Then he came out again, sat down and picked up his cigarette, which he'd balanced on the rim of a garden tub. A garden gnome looked at them from the window of his windmill. If the wind blew, the sails went round and it played a tune, but today there was no wind and the windmill was stationary and silent.

'Supposing . . .' said Jed. He took another drag on the cigarette, then dimped it in the dry soil among the dead geranium leaves. 'Supposing I did. Just supposing, mind.'

'Go on.'

'What if it works?'

'I don't know. We could move house.'

'And what if . . .'

He didn't finish the sentence. What was the point? There were too many 'what ifs' to choose from. They'd be here all day. Instead he said, 'Felix, let's stop pussyfooting around. You want me to wank in that pot, then you're gonna take it up the 'ossie and they're gonna squirt it into your wife, and if she gets pregnant you're gonna pretend it's yours, and we'll all live happily ever after? Is that it?'

Felix nodded his head. 'I know it's mad. But if I don't come up with the goods I think this could be the end of the line. She's obsessed. Nothing else matters.'

'But have you thought it through?'

'Course I haven't thought it through. Half an hour ago I was sat on the edge of the bed with my trousers round my ankles, and now I'm here asking you to do this. It's crazy, of course it is. But I'll tell you this: I know Abbie, and I know what's going on in her head. She wants a kid. That's what her life is all about now. Having a child. There's nothing else. And if it doesn't come from me it will come from somewhere else. So it might as well be you. It's terrible, I know. Terrible on her, on you, on Maxine . . .'

Jed stepped inside the house again and didn't come back. Felix went to look for him. He was standing by the oven, staring at the floor. Felix sat down at the table. It was exactly ten o'clock. Jed's watch gave a little electronic beep. He held out his open palm. 'Give us that pot, then.'

The sticky label had started to peel, a reaction to the heat and sweat generated by the trembling hands of a very frightened man.

'Are you sure?'

'Am I fuck. So pass it here before I change mi mind.'

Felix dropped it into Jed's big red hand.

'Never breathe a word,' he said. It wasn't exactly a threat, but it was more than the extraction of a promise.

Felix nodded his head.

'Or it's two marriages down the toilet. Not just yours.'

'Thanks,' said Felix feebly, almost tearfully. 'You're a friend.'

'I'm a mentalist that needs his head seeing to,' he said, and slapped Felix hard on the shoulder. He walked out of the kitchen and went up the stairs. It was five past ten, there was still time. Just. Felix stood motionless in the kitchen, trying not to think about anything. If an image or idea came into his mind he blocked it, visualized an empty road, a windscreen, white lines and streetlights flying past, the pedal full to the floor, the needles on the dials way over into the red.

'Felix. Felix,' he heard Jed shouting from somewhere above him.

'What?' he called back from the foot of the stairs.

'Throw us one of those magazines up, will you? Might as well have a quick squint while I'm at it.'

It was almost a fortnight till they saw each other again. Felix was busy at work. Jed was busy at work. They were busy at home too.

Jed was boarding out the attic for a playroom for the twins. Felix was devising a new filing system for all the receipts, guarantees, policies and other important documents that were presently stuffed in a shoebox in the spare bedroom. As he sorted the paperwork into separate piles and wrote out neat headings on sheets of coloured card, he could hear the thump of a hammer somewhere above him, the sound of nails being driven through panels of chipboard into the beams and joists. Occasionally he heard a power tool, the screaming of a drill as it bored through timber and into the block-work or stone behind, or the drone of an electric sander, or the deep, unfamiliar rumble of some altogether more complicated piece of equipment performing a more esoteric task. Then just when Felix was wondering if he should phone and make contact, Jed left a message on the answering machine at work saying he'd be 'testing a new batch' next Friday morning and why didn't he join him. 'You can phone in sick, can't you? For once.'

Felix had driven past the gates of Kingfisher Fireworks many times on his way to the golf club but had never actually been inside. He entered the drive and followed the signs in the shape of a bird with the word 'Visitors' written across its breast and its beak pointing towards a Portakabin on a mound of cinders. The door was locked. Felix sat on the metal step and looked out across the site, which appeared more like an army barracks or military hospital than a factory. The sheds, of which there were thirty or forty, were made from dark-green corrugated iron, semicircular in shape like Nissen huts, with as much space between them as was geometrically possible, the principle being that if one shed blew it wouldn't take the whole factory with it. Three larger constructions to the right were rectangular, with a row of windows along the side protected by bars and mesh. Each building had a sign attached to the door. Although Felix couldn't read the words from where he was sitting, it was clear the red and white lettering was a warning against some pretty serious type of danger. Jed had told him that the buildings were made from metal to cut down the risk of fire, which meant that each hut was like a kiln in summer, with the sun beating down on the curved roof. In winter they were cold and a lot of the employees wore thermal underwear, gloves and even balaclavas.

Looking to his left, Felix could see two small patches of charred earth. He'd read in the paper about one disaster when lightning had struck Kingfisher Fireworks during a storm. And Jed often talked about a legendary incident from a few years back when a man and a woman had lost their lives. A stock of gunpowder had exploded, and although it had never been proved, it was rumoured that the couple were misbehaving during their lunch hour. A flash of static electricity had been generated as the man removed his nylon underpants, causing a spark that blew them both to kingdom come. Felix started to imagine cameos of sexual activity going on inside each of the little green sheds. Perhaps those red and white signs on every door were a set of rules prohibiting heavy petting and postcoital cigarettes as well as a warning about the dangers of underwear made from anything less than 100 per cent cotton.

A small man with a shaved head walked from one hut to another with a tray in his arms, then closed the door behind him. Followed by another man pushing a handcart, then a woman with a long pole in her hands. Everyone wore the same regulation brown overalls. The area was zigzagged with paths, some of them tarmacked or paved with flagstones, others being muddy short cuts across areas of grass. For a further ten minutes or so Felix watched the workers coming and going. At half past ten there was a long, high-pitched blast from a hooter somewhere behind the Portakabin, and instantly every door on the site opened and out of every green shed came two or three workers, some of them unbuttoning their work clothes, some carrying newspapers under their arms, all walking in the direction of a bigger, stone-built building on its own with steam rising from an aluminium chimney stack and a row of wheelie bins parked along the side. Some of the younger men were running to be first through the door. As it opened, Felix could see a counter at the far end with an enormous tea urn next to a trolley full of cups and saucers. Two women stood behind it in blue pinnies and white cotton hats. Turning back towards the stream of workers,

Felix caught sight of Jed making his way up the central path towards him, head and shoulders taller than most of the people at his side. A young woman stopped him and put a notepad in his hand. There was a brief conversation before Jed took a pen from his top pocket, signed the docket and handed it back. He was stopped three or four more times before he reached the steps where Felix was sitting.

'All right?'

'All right.'

He unlocked the Portakabin and they went inside. He had a couple of phone calls to make and a fax to send. Then he opened a wooden shutter in the wall and took a key from a hook, and Felix followed him to a parking area at the rear, where they jumped into a battered old Transit van with the Kingfisher logo on the side and set off.

No weapon had been discharged at the town firing range for several years now and most people knew that the bangs and thumps coming from the edge of the moor every second Friday did not originate from side arms or shotguns but from the trying and testing of Kingfisher Fireworks' latest products. The reverberation of air-bomb repeaters between the walls of the valley and the occasional twist of grey smoke hanging in the afternoon sky reminded people down in the streets and houses that the town's fourth-biggest employer was still in business. It was a tradition and, in an age of economic uncertainty, a comfort. But what they couldn't have known was the way in which the tests were conducted. Whenever Jed had talked about his Friday afternoons 'in the field', Felix had pictured a series of controlled explosions. At the very least he had envisaged electronically detonated pyrotechnics and the close monitoring of their behaviour from a safe distance. In reality, the research and development arm of Kingfisher Fireworks consisted of Jed and a dwarf called Keith, and its equipment extended no further than a van full of gunpowder, several assorted wellington boots and a box of matches.

For two hours, Felix sat on top of a wooden dugout covered with turf and watched as Jed and Keith loosed off a hundred or so explosions. In what looked to be more of a routine than a system, Jed would select a firework from the back of the van and throw it down over a wicker barricade to Keith. Then Keith would amble to a launch site about fifty yards away and either attach the firework to a plinth on the ground or mount it on an upright metal frame. When Jed gave the signal by raising his arm in the air, Keith bent over the touchpaper and, if he was lucky, ignited it with the first strike of a match. Sometimes it would take two or three strikes, and one in every ten fireworks refused to light at all. Keith would confirm this failure with a downturned thumb, at which point Jed would make a little note in his pocketbook, then go back to the van and select the next squib. Some of the fireworks were little more than common bangers or bog-standard Roman candles. Very often Keith took no more than a couple of steps backwards and Jed hardly bothered to look. But then came the big ones, the display models, more like weapons of mass destruction than anything designed for the purpose of entertainment. Keith tottered out to the launch pad with them, stumbling under the load, and had to go down on one knee to lay his payload on the ground. On these occasions the match would be struck with more purpose and held out with a stiff, fully extended arm. As the touchpaper started to fizz, he'd scuttle backwards, then turn and leg it towards some sort of trench or foxhole in the ground, completing his retreat with a well-practised commando roll. Then he'd peep from behind the mound of earth, using the flat of his hand as a visor. Invariably, there would be several detonations, each one sending up a cluster of smaller fireworks, which exploded in turn, and although it was hard to detect the colour or even the shape of the flaming gun- powder against the brightness of the sky, there was something about the timing of each explosion – as a sequence – that implied success.

One of the bigger fireworks, which looked to Felix like a real heavy-duty piece of kit, smouldered on the ground for a while and let out a couple of dull thuds, but nothing appropriate to its size. In fact if size was anything to go by, a sustained barrage of anti-aircraft fire would have issued from the thick black cylinders pointing into the heavens. From his trench, Keith gave the thumbs-down to Jed. Then a series of more convoluted hand signals was exchanged, resulting in Keith pulling a pair of goggles over his face, approaching on all fours and, with the aid of a long-handled spade, flipping the rocket launcher on to its front. Jed vaulted over the barricade and jogged to the launch site. They kicked and prodded with their feet and pointed with their fingers. Jed made a few notes as Keith dragged the piece to one side. Then Jed went back to the van, but this time produced a flask of coffee and a paper bag, and held them in the air for Felix to see. There was an Eccles cake each and a vanilla slice to share, though by the time Jed had torn it in two, squeezing the custard out on each side and covering his hands in icing sugar, there wasn't much worth having. They'd climbed up the metal ladders on the side of the van and were sitting on a narrow wooden platform that formed part of the roof rack. Their feet hung down over the open back door. Jed drank half a cup of coffee from the lid of the Thermos and handed it across for Felix to finish. It was sweet and syrupy. As they sat there, Keith raked all the duds into a large black pile to one side of the launch pad, then set about shovelling them into a wheelbarrow with the long-handled spade. The spade was at least a foot taller than he was.

'Why don't you get him a shorter one?' Felix asked, after a while.

'He likes the big one. Stops him getting too close.'

'He doesn't say much, does he?'

'Not since he got that rocket in the mouth.'

'Really?'

'Yep.'

'When did that happen?'

'1985.'

Felix helped himself to another cup of coffee and Jed set about licking the icing sugar from between his fingers and out from behind his wedding ring.

'Did he sue?'

'How d'you mean?'

'Did he sue his employers? An industrial injury like that, he could get millions.'

'Oh, he doesn't work here,' said Jed. 'He just does it for fun.'

Keith had finished loading the wheelbarrow with the spent casings and other bits and pieces, including the big rocket contraption that had gone off at half-cock, and was wheeling it across the moor along a length of chestnut paling laid flat to act as a path. The two metal rests at the back of the barrow kept catching on the wooden struts. To lift it higher, he hoisted the handles on to his shoulders. Then he walked back to the launch site for the spade.

'Not very scientific, is it?' said Felix.

Jed shrugged his shoulders. 'Sometimes they work, sometimes they don't. What more do you want?'

'Well, don't you make note of what they look like? Don't you take pictures or anything?'

'Can't see anything during the day and we're not allowed to test at night. Anyway, that's not my department. They sort all that out on computers. As far as I'm concerned, it's either a tick or a cross. Did it get off the ground? Yes. Did it make a big fucking bang? Yes. Job done.'

Keith was now digging a hole in the moor and piling the peaty earth to one side. He stood on the metal edges of the spade to chop a large piece of turf.

'Are we still talking about fireworks?' asked Felix.

'Probably not,' said Jed. Then after a pause added, 'So is she or isn't she?'

'She's doing a test tonight.'

'Right.'

'But she's a day late.'

Jed shook his head and looked up towards the long, dark quarry about a mile or so beyond the back of the firing range, and Felix followed his stare. The stone face must have been sand yellow at one time, when the quarry was in use, but there hadn't been a grain of rock taken from that hill in a couple of hundred years. Two centuries of smog and bad weather had stained it black. Sometimes from the town you might look up and see the last of the sun catching the giant slabs, and almost anything will shine in direct sunlight. But mostly it was a gloomy, brooding mass on the skyline, the geological equivalent of the Lakeland Estate on the opposite hill. A rock and a hard place, with the town in between. Down below, the Horseshoe roundabout appeared busy with cars, people knocking off early for the weekend. Then Felix looked at Prospect House, and counted the floors and the windows until he was looking at his office, and wondered if Neville was there at the end of his telescope, looking back.

'Do you want me to call you tonight, to tell you what's happened?'

'Apparently you're coming round to ours. Max is cooking.'

'Isn't it our turn?'

'Yeah, but we can't get a sitter. Listen, whatever happens, try and put it off till later, all right? I can just see it, Abbie going upstairs to the loo with her handbag, then coming back down all smiley and full of it, making the big announcement, and Max opening a bottle of champagne, and me and you sat there like a right pair of . . .' He slithered down from the van roof. 'Wankers, I was gonna say.'

He rummaged in the glove compartment for something, which turned out to be a packet of cigarettes. Felix looked down through his legs and saw that one side of the van was still piled high with fireworks, some packed neatly in boxes, others loose, rolling around on the floor.

'Don't worry,' said Jed. 'I'm not that stupid.'

Felix watched him as he jumped the barricade and strolled over to where Keith had finished digging the pit. He was leaning on the spade, having a breather. As Jed approached, Keith reached into his inside pocket and handed over the box of matches. Jed turned out of the wind and lit a cigarette, facing the quarry. Smoke streamed away from him, over the moor. With Keith at his side, holding the long spade like a primitive flag, they could have been Don Quixote and Sancho Panza staring out over the plain, contemplating their next adventure or their latest farce. Keith lifted the wheelbarrow by its handles and with some effort managed to tip the contents into the pit. Then, with the spade, he began digging at the pile of loose earth and heaping it over the cache of tested fireworks. Before the hole was completely covered over, Jed stooped over the mound and planted what looked like a black metal tube in the middle. Keith raked the soil more carefully around the tube until it stood on its own, wedged in the ground like a tiny chimney.

'Felix, watch this,' Jed shouted towards the van.

Keith was already hurrying away, dragging the spade behind him. Jed took a long drag on the cigarette and seemed to examine the burning tip before dropping it into the top of the tube.

Keith had made it to his bunker before the blast occurred, but Jed was only about halfway back to the barricade. The noise was low and heavy, as if from several miles away, and the eruption that followed must have been spectacular, although Felix saw little of it. The expression on Jed's face as he studied the glowing cigarette had told him what was coming and in one seamless move he had swung down from the roof of the van and yanked the door closed behind him. As he cowered by the wheel arch and removed his hands from his ears, cinders and dirt began raining from the air. It was like being in the caravan when he was small, the night of the hailstorm. Then two bigger clumps of soil thumped down and a pebble ricocheted off the bonnet.

When the fall-out had stopped, Felix looked up and saw Jed girning through the back window. 'BOOM!' he said, and pressed his face against the sooty blotches on the glass. 'Now that's what I call a firework.'

The twins were in bed. Maxine hadn't cooked but they'd phoned for a pizza. Abbie and Felix were on the sofa. Jed was in the comfy chair with a large mug of tea resting at a dangerous angle on the arm. Maxine sat on the rug in front of the fire. 'Only me drinking?' she said, reaching out for the bottle of red on the coffee table. Abbie wanted a glass of water, please. They talked about work. Maxine said she once worked in a hotel in London, as a chambermaid to begin with, then in the restaurant and behind the bar. Just for a while, until she knew what she wanted to do. With her life. It was a big hotel used more by businessmen than tourists. One evening she was chatting with a friend of hers in the kitchen, when the chef told her to make herself useful. He put a tray in her hand and said to take it to a room on the top floor. She went up in the lift and walked along the corridor. The door was ajar, so she knocked and she heard a man's voice telling her to come in. She went in. At the far end, in front of an enormous pile of books, was a tiny little man in his underpants. He didn't turn round. He just sat there in his underpants. Red ones. He was taking books from a great big pile on one side, signing them and putting them on a great big pile on the other side. There must have been a thousand books in the room. He was skinny as well, she could see his ribs. He just said, 'Leave it on the bed.'

'Who was it?' said Abbie.

'That jockey. The one who writes thrillers.'

'Never.'

'Just sat there in his knickers, signing books.'

Abbie described a job interview she'd been for once in an umbrella factory. The man doing the interview had asked her what her favourite kind of weather was, and she'd said clear winter skies, and she didn't get the job. Maxine said that she'd once been for an interview in a bank and the manager had no arms. The sleeves of his suit were folded over in front of him and stitched together to make it look as if he had his arms crossed. She realized she couldn't shake hands with him so she kissed him on the cheek. Just like that. He'd been in an accident on a farm. She got the job but didn't accept it because she'd been offered something better on the perfume counter in Boots. A couple of month later she'd seen him driving a car.

'How can you drive a car with no arms, Jed?'

'Huh?'

'Haven't you been listening to me?'

'Yeah.'

'I said how can you drive a car if you've got no arms?'

'Dunno. With your knees?'

Abbie asked Felix if he would slide the stool under her feet, then she sat holding a cushion to her stomach. Could she have another glass of water? Jed went for a smoke at the back door, then came back. Maxine drank more wine. They talked about perfume, about sunglasses, about wedding photographs, about a stag night that Jed had been invited to at the weekend. There was a spare place on the coach if Felix wanted to go. Felix said he wouldn't know anyone. Abbie said go on, he should do, it was OK with her if he wanted to, so long as she got the full story when he came home. They talked about Jed's stag party at Doncaster races, and a game that Jed and Maxine played sometimes called St Leger. According to Jed, the races were one of the few places in the world where toffs and scruffs mingled together. To play St Leger you had to think of things the upper classes and the working classes had in common, something the middle classes didn't do. Like swearing. Like debt.

'Give us an example,' said Abbie.

'Flat caps,' said Maxine. 'The blokes in the taproom wear them and so do the horsy people.'

'I thought they wore red underpants,' said Jed. It was one of the few things he said all night.

'I get it,' said Abbie.

'Go on, then, your turn.'

'BMWs.'

'Do you think?'

'Yes. Posh people have them and so do drug dealers. And gypsies. Felix worked with some gypsies in those caravans parked behind the railway station and he told me they all had BMWs. Didn't they, Felix?'

'Huh?'

'What's the matter with you two tonight? You're like Gloomy and Doomy. I'm telling Maxine about how those gypsies all had BMWs.'

'Travellers, you mean.'

'Whatever.'

'I think one of them did. It wasn't new.'

'All right, it's your turn now, Felix,' said Maxine, pouring herself what was left of the wine.

'My turn for what?'

The pizza arrived. Three pizzas in fact, and bread. Not all of it was eaten. At about half past nine Abbie stood up and said she needed to go next door for something. Felix asked if she wanted him to come with her. Abbie said no but brushed his hand as she went past him. Maxine was a little bit drunk and was feeding long, rubbery strands of cheese to Smutty. Jed told Felix about the stag do, how it was a guy at work who was getting married to a woman from Thailand. He was welcome to come and the bus was picking them all up outside the Man with No Name at ten o'clock.

'That's a late start,' said Felix.

'Ten in the morning.'

The phone rang and Maxine answered it.

'It's Abbie, she wants you to go home,' she said to Felix.

Felix got up to go. He could feel his heart bumping inside his chest and didn't say goodbye in case his voice started to shake. As he passed Jed, he looked quickly into his face, but Jed was leaning forward in his chair, his head down, stroking the dog.

There was a light on upstairs, on the landing. As he turned the corner at the top of the banister, Abbie was standing in the bathroom door. In her hand was what appeared at first to be a white tooth-brush. She was staring at it, peering into the little window. Felix waited in front of her until she looked up from behind her fringe.

It was an hour later when he came back downstairs, closing the bedroom door quietly behind him and padding softly into the kitchen. He boiled the kettle and poured the water, then watched as the tea bag became fuzzy and blurred inside the teapot, emitting its inky brown dye. He went to the back door and looked through the glass panel. With his right hand he flicked the switch that lit up the carriage lamp on the outside wall. It glowed with energy. It illuminated the yard and the driveway next door. It was a signal. It was the signal that told Jed that Abbie was not pregnant. It was prearranged. Felix took a sip of tea, then pulled down a bottle of whisky from the cupboard above the microwave. He took a few slugs from the neck and rested his head on the table. He might easily have fallen asleep, but after a few minutes he heard music coming through the wall. From next door. Not loud music, but music all the same on an otherwise quiet night, and also the sound of singing.

The Stag Night

*They are apparitions. The first half a dozen of them seem to evolve out of
the morning mist, noticeable only by the light of their cigarettes, the sound
of their coughing and the occasional bout of laughter. Then a small
hatchback arrives, driven by a girlfriend or wife, and another five are
delivered, four of them clambering out of the front passenger door and one
emerging from the boot. Three more come in a taxi. Others have walked.
Soon there are twenty, then thirty of them, coughing and smoking and
laughing and waiting outside the Man with No Name. It is five to ten on
Saturday morning. The dress code is smart-casual. No jeans or trainers
but no suits or jackets. They could be on their way to a court hearing,
lager louts charged with a breach of the peace, or a firm of football
hooligans pleading not guilty to a more serious public order offence such
as criminal damage or affray.*

*Just after ten, a light comes on in the frosted glass panel above the big,
scuff-marked door and the noise from inside is that of a bolt sliding out of
its keep, then the rattling of a chain, then the turning of a key and the
snapping of a lock. A small cheer goes up as the thirty men push into the
pub and the last of them closes the door behind him. The curtains are
drawn. Inside it is murky apart from the fairy lights around the optics
and the glow of the beer pumps along the bar and the triangle of rich,
yellow light that angles down on to the green baize of the pool table. The
stink of smoke still hasn't cleared from the night before. The landlord, in
football shirt, shorts and slippers, leans behind a table to plug in the
jukebox and the cigarette dispenser. When he switches on the slot machine
it jolts into life, fluttering its lights and spinning its reels and piping out
'Yankee Doodle Dandy' at twice the normal speed. Back behind the bar
he points the remote at a large TV bolted to the wall and scrolls through*

the programmes until he finds a man in a brown trilby talking about
horses and money.

The first round comes to forty-eight pounds and ninety-three pence,
fifty for cash, and is paid for by the groom, Stevo, who already has a
condom stapled to the back of his shirt. The second round comes to the
same price and is paid for by the best man, Bez, who is running a
sweepstake on the first person to vomit. A lean, well-scrubbed man in
silver glasses and a yellow Pringle jumper, known as Virgil, is favourite,
followed by a man known as Sickbreath, who is diabetic. No one has a
proper name. There is Muppetman, Caddy, Robbo, Rollo, Tupps, Bloodbath, Jenks, Jackpot, Big Ted, Little Ted, China, Rabbit, Sox . . . and so
on. They sit in a circle, apart from a dwarf, standing on tiptoe playing
the fruit machine. His name is Keith. At half past ten a tray of warm pork
pies arrives from the kitchen and is left on the bar, along with a large pan
of mushy peas, a dish of jellied mint sauce and a bottle of Lea and Perrins.
They have all had three pints, apart from the groom, Stevo, who has also
consumed a double vodka, although he is not aware of the fact, vodka
being pretty much undetectable in taste and smell when mixed with a pint
of Mansfield Smoothflow bitter. At eleven o'clock a horn sounds outside,
the signal to sup up and leave. The coach is parked on the road with its
engine running, and as the last man leaves the pub he hears the door close
behind him and the sliding of bolts and the rattling of chains.

First stop is a karting circuit on an industrial estate on the edge of
town. There is no bar and, as the large sign in reception points out, any
person believed to be under the influence of alcohol will be asked to leave
the premises without the return of his deposit. Nevertheless the occasional
hip flask is passed among the thirty men milling about in the pit lane in
the brightening sun, although the whiff of brandy or whisky is masked by
the stench of petrol fumes and burning rubber. In leather jackets and crash
helmets, the men race eight laps of the circuit, five karts at a time, until
a member of staff leans over the tyre wall and waves a chequered flag.
Some karts are obviously quicker than others, and the groom, Stevo, sulks,
sitting alone and reading the paper after being allocated a vehicle with a
dodgy exhaust and finishing last in his heat. One race has only four
drivers because Keith cannot reach the pedals. Virgil is rammed in the

back by Little Ted and retires, hobbling to the grandstand like someone suffering from the after-effects of a lumbar puncture. China and Muppet-man lock wheels on the first corner and slide off into a bale of hay. Bez is taking bets on the result. Sickbreath has brought his own driving gloves and, despite being identified as a rank outsider, finishes with the fastest time and claims pole position for the final. When the black and white flag is flourished for the last time, he crosses the line with a leatherette fist above a raised arm, and licks the froth from his face as the rest of the men stand around the base of the podium, showering him with Pomagne.

The coach makes two unscheduled stops, one at the Wren's Nest for more beer and one at the Whacky Warehouse, just off the motorway slip road, where parents protect their children in their arms until the last of the stag party has quit the toilets and vacated the premises. Stevo and Bez, though, are unable to resist the brightly coloured climbing apparatus and are chased from the play room by the duty manager after belly-splashing into the ball pool from the top of the rope ladder.

At Megakill, bespattered boiler suits are handed out by the man behind the counter, who then gives a practical but perfunctory demonstration of the automatic paint-gun, illustrating his talk with anecdotes of skull fractures and burst eyeballs before handing out the weapons. One team will shoot red pellets, the other team blue. Even before battle has commenced, Big Ted has accidentally triggered a pellet of blood-coloured paint against the ceiling panel of the reception hut, and Tupps has blasted Muppetman in the thigh at point-blank range, causing an indigo stain that spreads from his hip to his knee. Outside on the bulldozed landscape of hillocks and dunes, the men run and jump and roll, firing their weapons as often as possible, until excitement and adrenalin give way to tiredness and cruelty, making for a more strategic and tactically fought battle. Jackpot sits in a treehouse picking off anyone who emerges into the open ground in front of the hawthorn bushes or makes a run for it along the sniper's alley between the wicker fence and the pond. Although the wooden slats of his tree-top den are splattered with blue paint, he is uncoloured by war. When Little Ted tries to climb the ladder beneath him, he simply points his gun through the trap door and fires a shot which in real life would have entered Little Ted's skull at the crown of his head and exited *through his scrotum. For the blue team, Stevo and Bez have fortified their position at the top end of the battlefield with a row of oil drums and two sheets of plastic. Their resistance lasts a good twenty minutes until China, Bloodbath and Caddy perform a well-thought-out pincer movement and overrun the groom and his best man. Dispossessed of his weapon, Stevo is frogmarched to enemy headquarters and tied to a chair with a length of dirty rope. He sulks, and when he is finally unbound, Bez has to step in to dissuade his brother-in-arms from engaging in actual hand-to-hand combat. Elsewhere, as retaliation for the capture of their leader, four men from the red army have ambushed Keith, the dwarf, blindfolded him with a sock and positioned him against the outer wall of the reception hut. He is informed of his guilt. One of the soldiers asks Keith for any final request, but there is no reply. The firing squad lift their weapons to eye level, take aim and the execution is complete. Keith falls to the ground. Then, in a scene of almost filmic intensity, one of the soldiers strides towards the body, reloads and, from a distance of no more than six inches, discharges a single shot against the head of the man on the floor. 'To make sure.' Even through his safety helmet the blow must be painful. His body flinches in the dirt.*

When all ammo is finally spent, a truce is declared. Both sets of infantry meet in no man's land, shake hands and amble back towards the shower block, some making accusations of foul play, some revelling in their best kills or showing off their wounds, and others keeping quiet about actual contusions to their flesh and bruises to their pride. No one will admit to targeting Virgil in the groin, but he follows the other combatants away from the theatre of war like the victim of some ritual and frantic dismemberment, so profuse is the redness. Showered and dressed, they are all heroes and friends. The bus is waiting with its engine running and there is just enough time for a pint or three in the Cobbler's Arms before kick-off.

Third Division football is made for stag parties. Of course, to the 2,000 or so die-hard fans, many of them serial masochists with season tickets, the result is important. And to the hopelessly insane band of travelling supporters huddled together in an open terrace designed for maximum exposure to verbal abuse, violent incursion and wind chill, the possibility of an away win is the only hope in an otherwise empty and Godless universe. But the future of Third Division football rests not with the loyal fan of questionable sanity. It rests with the drunken tourists for whom there is no tomorrow. It lies not with the dwindling bunch of disciples whose disposable incomes extend no further than one replica shirt per season and a meat pie at half-time, but with groups of young, inebriated men on pre-nuptial spending sprees. It depends not on football at all, but on weddings, on the likes of Stevo et al., who have forked out seventy-five pounds each for an afternoon which has little to do with sport and everything to do with alcohol and companionship. At least five of the party have never been to a football match in their life, and Sickbreath has to be told which colour his local team will appear in. The party are warmly received in the staff car park and escorted through the offices under the grandstand. They make a quick tour of the trophy room, which contains an astonishing array of cups and medals for a team whose one claim to fame is its complete lack of success. The pennants and flags of visiting teams make up the bulk of the decorations. It could be the committee room of some now defunct trade union, hung with the banners of its many guilds and branches, proud of its affiliations with comrades in the struggle. A flight of temporary iron stairs finally brings them to their accommodation for the afternoon, a 'box', which is little more than its name suggests, even though it is referred to in the sales brochure as an executive suite. The floor is laid with beige lino and dotted with flattened grey blobs of chewing gum. Three of the walls are panelled out in wood-effect hardboard, and the ceiling is fitted with two electric heaters and three fluorescent striplights, one of which flickers on and off. The front wall is made of toughened glass, and it is from behind this window, shielded from the weather and inoculated against the moans and groans of the crowd, that the game can be viewed. Bez has opened a sweepstake on the first person to score and has extracted a fiver from each member of the party, even from Virgil, who has drawn the substitute goalkeeper of the visiting team. Down on the pitch, a mascot in the shape of a ten-foot badger galumphs along the touchline, and a boy with leukaemia gets to take a penalty into an open goal. The supporter of the month, a woman in lumber jacket and snow-washed jeans, collects her award in the centre

*circle and has her photograph taken with the manager. Then the teams
are announced over the PA system, the away side to some half-hearted
booing, the home team to some lacklustre cheering, except for the blond,
frizzy-haired centre forward with the headband, whose name is greeted
with laughter. The match gets under way almost unnoticed. The stag
party are served with a selection of sandwiches and crinkle-cut chips and
have access to a free bar, the only limit to their drinking being the speed
at which Reg, their allocated waiter for the afternoon, can make his way
up and down the metal stairway with their order and the amount of beer
he manages to spill on each journey. At half-time, an official from the club
comes into the box and makes a brief speech about their valued custom.
In his grey suit and pink tie, he also says a little something about the long
and proud history of the club, and, as he leaves, very much hopes they are
enjoying the football. This comment is made with something of an ironic
smile, since the score is nil–nil, just as it is at the end of the match, by
which time half of the stag party are involved in a game of cards and
three others have gone outside to admire the mid-range Mercs and Beamers
in the players' car park. By four thirty, most of the men are happily drunk.
Sickbreath denies the allegation of vomiting put to him by Bez, pointing
out that his most recent and prolonged visit to the toilets was necessitated
by his desire for privacy during the intravenous administering of insulin.
Bez counters this alibi with the statement, 'That's bollox 'cos Jackpot
heard yer ralphin' and anyways yer've getten puke down yer bib, yer
fuckin' lightweight.' An argument is avoided when the door opens and
the club official in the pink tie thanks them again for their patronage and
reminds Stevo that it is his privilege, as groom, to nominate the man of the
match. Putting down his hand of cards, Stevo nominates the blond-haired
striker with the headband, and is adamant about his choice, even when
it is pointed out to him that the same player had missed a penalty and
been booked for throwing the ball at the linesman. It is now almost five
o'clock, and the stag party decline the guided tour of the dressing-room
area and the pitch in favour of a burger on the way back to town, before
the real drinking begins. The bus is waiting for them. A coach carrying
the entire contingent of away support pulls up alongside them at the traffic
lights and a dialogue of body language takes place, beginning with fingers*

and concluding with several bare arses squashed against glass on both sides of the divide.

After this, things become hazy. Three of the party get chatting to a couple of girls in the drive-through McDonald's and do not get back on the bus. Five more are refused entrance to a pub because they are too drunk or not wearing the right clothes, but two of them manage to climb in through the toilet window. The three who missed the bus turn up again in the queue for the nightclub. The party fragments, then recombines. Splinter groups go in search of cashpoints and are lost, then are found again and brought back into the fold. Virgil hangs off the back of the pack, then sidesteps into an arcade and runs away in search of a taxi home. Sickbreath, insensate with drink, confesses to chundering in the toilets of the football stadium, at which point Bez pays the winner of the first-to-puke sweepstake with his profit from his first-to-score sweepstake and orders another round of drinks. Most of the men are now drinking alcopops or shorts, apart from Bez, who seems inhumanly unaffected by the strength, gassiness or volume of premium continental lager, and continues to down pints of it. Little Ted has picked up a bloody nose somewhere along the route, caused by a handbag. Stevo is overheard talking to his bride-to-be on his mobile phone, telling her he is sober, telling her he loves her and won't do anything stupid, telling her they are going to a club but only for a nightcap, only because it's expected of him, and no, it won't be Cinderella's, and even if it is, there won't be any strippers, and even if there are, he won't watch. And he loves her. On the way to Cinderella's they stop for a kebab and a roll call. They are twenty by now, the hard core. Others have faded, fallen asleep in the corner, sneaked off home, or have been left in the gutter. But the hard core remain.

'My true mates,' sobs Stevo.

Bez tells Stevo to stop making the corny speeches and get his arse in gear or they'll be late.

'Late for what?'

'You'll see.'

In a private room at the back of the club, a spotlight illuminates a large circle of glitter curtain, like the shimmering moon, through which strides Cat Woman, their feline entertainment for the evening. Stevo gawps as *she peels off the layers – her satin cape; her elbow-length gloves with long, sharp claws; her boots with the pointy toes and stiletto heels; her fishnet tights; her leopard-skin bra; her leopard-skin pants; until she stands above them in nothing but a cat mask, a pair of small, velvety ears and a furry tail. Suddenly the music stops. 'So does anybody here like pussy?'*

From the cheer that goes up, it appears that everyone does.

'Well, let's see how much,' she purrs, handing a metal tray down to the crowd of whooping and whistling men before slinking off into the wings.

'Get yer hands in yer pockets, lads. Silver tray,' yells Bez.

Upon hearing the magic words, the men delve deep into their pockets, pulling out all the loose change they can find and tossing it on to the tray as it passes in front of them. Upon hearing the magic words, men from other rooms in the club stream in through several doors, heaping their coins on to the growing pile, until the tray is spilling over with money and buckling under the weight. A man on the stage in a dinner jacket receives the offering and pours the money into a cloth bag. From the wings, he produces a theatrical set of weighing scales and hangs the cloth bag by its straps on the hook. The needle on the scales swings sharply to the right, stopping just short of the red area on the dial. There is a loud, comic groan from the men in the room and more coins are showered on to the stage. The man in the dinner jacket sweeps the coins into a dustpan and tips them into the bag, and this time the needle passes the critical mark. A huge roar goes up, including barking noises and, from a man stood on a table, the braying of a donkey. The music starts again, the lights go down and Cat Woman re-enters through the glitter curtain, her tail swinging and her cape swishing from side to side, giving flashes of her bare body. Stevo is pushed forward but resists, clinging to a table. Two or three men grab him, pull him loose and again force him in the direction of the stage, but he wrestles free and barges his way past the crowd, the fear in his face only subsiding when he reaches the back of the room and clamps hold of the radiator. Names are called out. Scuffles take place as men are hauled forward, bundled towards the light, but break loose and scuttle back into the darkness. Just as Cat Woman is losing her patience and seems ready to bring the show to an end, a volunteer is produced. He is carried by his arms and legs, then rolled across the heads and shoulders

*of the men at the front of the crowd and dumped on the stage. It is Keith.
Keith the dwarf. Keith who is literally mouse-like in front of the high-heeled,
long-tailed Cat Woman. The laughter in the room is riotous. It is overtaken
by shouts of, 'Go on,' and finally by a chant of 'Keith, Keith, Keith'. Cat
Woman's mask still wears its cunning smile, although her tail has stopped
swinging now and her cape hangs lifelessly in front of her. But the money
has been weighed, the target met and the man in the dinner jacket looks
on from the wings with a face like a hammer. Stevo is at the back of the
room, on tiptoes. Somewhere in the middle of the crowd are Big Ted and
Little Ted, Jackpot, Muppetman, Caddy, Robbo, Rollo, Tupps, Bloodbath,
Jenks, China, Rabbit, Sox, even Sickbreath. The hard core. And at the
front is Bez, close enough to lean forward and yank Keith's trousers to the
floor, then his underpants, bringing Keith to his knees and the crowd to
their feet. Taking three strides forward in her pointy boots, Cat Woman
envelops Keith in her cape, rocks him on to his back and, with her hands
inside her cloak, lowers herself on to him. From behind her cat smile, she
turns to the audience and lets out a long, howling, 'Meow.' The man in
the wings yawns and glances at his watch. Keith turns away, facing the
back of the stage, and the redness around his ears and behind his neck is
the burst of red paint from earlier in the day, when he was shot dead.*

SAGITTARIUS *(22 November–21 December)*

16

The decision to remove Ruby Moffat from the family home and place her in the care of the local authority was taken at a case conference. The vote was not unanimous, but was carried by a majority verdict, and from where Felix was sitting it seemed that those people whose opinion really mattered were all of the same mind. A crisis point had been reached during the past couple of days. After a month or so of relatively calm behaviour, there had been problems at home and three or four altercations at school, including a very ugly scene in which Captain Roderick had tried to remove Ruby from one of the cubicles in the girls' lavatory. She had locked herself in not long after assembly and was still there at the end of the lunch period. When the head teacher peered in over the top of the door Ruby had jabbed at him with a twelve-inch ruler, causing a cut to his chin and a thick lip. For a high-ranking military man with a tactical mind, the Captain's response had been surprisingly crude, his immediate reaction being to remove the door with a crowbar borrowed from the metalwork department, then attempt to prise Ruby's arms apart with his bare hands as she clung to the base of the toilet. When Ruby lashed out with her feet he sustained further bruises to his chest and shoulders, but, according to one of the dinner ladies interviewed by PC Lily, the Captain 'really went apeshit' when one of Ruby's kicks caused blood to spill from his nose, blood which stained not only his shirt but his regimental tie. Captain Roderick was eventually restrained by two male teachers. After a long, quiet chat with Mrs Dobson from RE, Ruby was finally persuaded to let go. She was taken to the matron's room, wrapped in a blanket and given a mug of warm orange juice. Eventually she had fallen asleep.

Captain Roderick's action would have been more than enough to warrant disciplinary proceedings or even a sacking under normal circumstances, but when Ruby's parents were visited by a member of the education department, Mrs Moffat admitted that similar incidents had taken place at home over the previous week. Only last Sunday Ruby had barricaded herself in her bedroom for several hours; when one of the boys broke in through the bedroom window he received a broken tooth for his trouble as Ruby greeted his arrival with a wooden tennis racquet. Mrs Moffat said they couldn't expect Captain Roderick to be punished for something they had done themselves. Mr Moffat had remained silent during the inter-view, which rightly or wrongly had raised PC Lily's suspicions. Two days later, Ruby had gone missing from her bedroom during the night, via the ladder that had been left there by her brother. She was not found until six o'clock the following evening, hiding in a skip on the far side of the estate with a large sheet of polythene pulled over her to keep the spiders away. Her thing about spiders had now developed into full-blown arachnophobia, and not only that, she didn't want to go home. The case conference was called the very next afternoon, and although Felix had some doubts about placing her in an alien environment full of strangers with problems of their own, he agreed that for now she would be better off in more neutral surroundings. So when it came to the vote, he raised his hand. The interests of the child always came first, and until somebody figured out what the danger was, exactly, and where it was coming from, she was best on her own, away from everyone.

Mrs Moffat came with them in the car as Felix drove Ruby to the children's home. Carlos was on duty and came outside to meet them, opening the car door for Ruby and introducing himself. Ruby was carrying a black holdall over her shoulder and a smaller, tartan-coloured case. Mrs Moffat carried another two plastic shop-ping bags full of shoes and cassette tapes. Inside the home, Carlos showed them to the room, and Ruby waited outside until Felix and

Mrs Moffat had checked that the wardrobe and the set of drawers were free of spiders. Then Ruby entered, crossed to the far side of the room to check the lock on the window and sat down on the bed. Mrs Moffat unpacked the bag, loading the shoes into a hollow section in the base of the wardrobe, folding the sweatshirts and trousers into one drawer and the underwear into another, then hanging the skirt, blouse and jacket of Ruby's school uniform on the rail. The collection of a dozen or so Beanie Babies was lined up on the bookshelf. She stacked the cassettes along the window-sill, found a place above the vanity unit for the tape recorder and trailed the flex to a socket a couple of inches above the skirting board.

'Want to listen to some music, Rubes?'

Ruby shook her head.

'If you'd only tell us what the matter was we wouldn't be here. Why don't you tell Mr Felix what it's all about, eh?'

Ruby rolled backwards on to the bed and pulled the pillow up over her ears.

Felix said, 'Why don't you have some time together? I'll be in the office.'

Felix handed Carlos copies of various documents and important papers. He'd been through the details of the case with him on the phone and went over the main points again as they waited for Mrs Moffat to return. After about ten minutes she came along the corridor from Ruby's room. Her eyes were red and she was holding a paper tissue to her face.

'Don't worry, Mrs Moffat, we'll take good care of her, and I'm sure she'll be home soon,' Carlos told her.

Mrs Moffat nodded through her tears.

'Shall I show you around the kitchens and the laundry? We've got a games room where we organize a lot of activities.'

'I'm sure it's all very nice,' she said flatly.

Outside, Mrs Moffat walked across the row of paving slabs that ran alongside the building and peered into each window until she found Ruby's room. She tapped on the glass, then rapped a little harder with her knuckle. Then she walked back towards Felix, shaking her head and reaching into her coat pocket for another tissue. In the car, she sat upright and formally in the seat, with her hands on her lap, and looked straight ahead. After a few minutes she reached down for her handbag, took out a compact and inspected her face in the mirror. With her fingertips she pushed her hair out of her face and hooked the longer, wispier locks back behind her ear. Then, snapping the mirror closed, she said, 'That's no place for my wee girl.'

Felix nodded. 'It's only till we find out what's going on.'

'It's not what, it's who,' she said, still looking straight out in front through the windscreen.

'What makes you say that?'

'I'm her mother, aren't I?'

'You would say if you knew anything, wouldn't you? You would tell me?'

Felix felt her stare.

'Do you honestly think I'd let my wee girl stay in a place like that for one minute, even for one second, if . . . Do you?'

'No. Of course you wouldn't.'

When they pulled up outside the house on Coleridge Avenue, half a dozen of the Moffat lads were hanging around by the door, including Teddy, the eldest. Mr Moffat was standing in the living room, looking out of the window. Mrs Moffat checked her face in the mirror again and asked Felix how she looked.

'You look fine,' he told her.

'Won't be having this lot thinking I can't deal with it.'

Then she walked up the path, picking up a soggy egg box on the way and dropping it into the wheelie bin before going inside. The boys never moved. Just stood there in their shabby donkey jackets and filthy overalls, each with a cigarette in his mouth or hand. As Felix nodded his acquaintance in their general direction, Teddy fixed him with a hard, open-eyed stare that lasted for several long seconds. And then he winked.

*

Felix had three more visits to make, the final one being at the Sunnyview Nursing Home in the town's only leafy suburb, though nearly all of the leaves were on the ground by now, raked into piles at the bottom of some of the better-kept gardens, dappling the lawns of others and lining the gutter on both sides of the road. It was at least three months since his last visit, not good enough, but he had been busy. He carried his briefcase with him to the door. Through the glass the receptionist recognized him and buzzed to let him in. In the hallway, a woman on a metallic blue Zimmer with her stockings rolled down to her ankles stood motionless and bewildered. In the dining room, a handful of residents were either asleep behind the remains of their meals or slowly spooning what looked like chocolate custard towards their mouths.

'She's down here,' said one of the nurses, showing him along a carpeted corridor and through an open door at the far end. In one corner, a large television shone brightly, lighting up what was an otherwise dark and rather gloomy room. About twenty residents were seated around the outside, most of them women. From previous experience, Felix had taught himself not to look, but the sounds alone reminded him of what he didn't want to see, and he couldn't shut out the sounds. The mumbling and the chunnering. The sighs. The panicky struggle for breath and the mechanized hiss of an oxygen bottle. The sobbing. The woman saying her prayers. The woman shouting, 'Bill, Bill, stay at home with me. Don't be going with her. What's she got that I haven't, Bill? Bill?' The man still fighting the Second World War in his dreams. The moans. And the noises of boredom and uselessness and fear. Felix kept his eyes to the floor, but in his mind's eye he could see. The hunched spines. The knotted fingers. The inflated ankles and bandaged legs. The faces. The eyes, weepy and afraid, or closed against the pressure of light, or magnified by thick glasses, or bloodshot, or marbled, or glazed. And the eyes of the man in the corner chair by the window, wide open and blind.

'Elsie, you've got a visitor. Come on, love, wake up.'

The old lady roused and looked towards the nurse.

'Someone to see you. Come on, love, wakey-wakey.'

Putting her hand under Elsie's chin, the nurse gently turned her face through ninety degrees until she was looking at Felix. Felix bent down towards her.

'It's Felix,' he said.

The old woman smiled vaguely, then looked back at the nurse and shook her head. She was drooling slightly. The nurse pulled out Elsie's handkerchief from the sleeve of her cardigan and wiped her mouth.

'It's Felix,' said Felix again. 'I've come to see you.'

This time the old woman seemed to understand. She looked again for his face, then reached out towards him with her hand, which had curled and shrunk into a tight, crooked fist, almost a claw. Felix pushed his index finger into the hole between her palm and her thumb and sat down beside her.

'How are you?'

'Is it Felix?' she said. Her voice was dry, coarse-sounding but strong all the same, and her words were clear.

'Yes. Do you want a glass of water?'

She shook her head.

'Billy, don't be going with her. You married me, Billy,' shouted the woman across the other side of the room.

'Is it Felix?'

'Yes.'

He felt her hand tighten ever so slightly around his finger.

'Are they looking after you, then?' he asked cheerily.

There was a pause. 'I don't eat rabbit, do I?'

'No. You don't.' Then, adding some laughter into his voice, he said, 'Have they been feeding you rabbit?'

With her other hand she lifted the handkerchief towards her face and dabbed at the corner of her mouth. Her cane walking stick with the horn handle was resting against the arm of the chair, the one that had belonged to her father. He was a gentleman, who wore a tie on Sundays and never went out without a hat. He was a stickler for timekeeping and cleanliness. He kept a fob watch in his breast pocket. He was proud, because when you were poor you had nothing but your pride and a few possessions to last a lifetime. Like a tie and a hat, and a stick, and a fob watch if you were lucky. Elsie had told all this to Felix over the years, but she was quiet now and, whatever thoughts she had, few of them came out as words.

'Is it Felix?'

'Yes.'

'I don't eat rabbit, do I?'

'No, you don't eat rabbit.'

Then from behind, 'Oh, Billy. Shame on you. You married me, not her. Shame on you, Billy.'

Between the muttering and the breathing, the silences were heavy and slow, as if quietness were congealing in the air or gathering in the dark corners of the room. As if the spores of time were hanging in the atmosphere, feeding on silence. Someone would cough or shout, or the woman by the door would whisper her prayers, and for a moment time would disperse. Then the silence would creep back, filling the gaps, multiplying until its presence could be touched or smelt. It wasn't clear to Felix which was worse, the noiselessness or the noise. Two nurses came in and wheeled out the man from the war without waking him up. The television was still on but the sound was inaudible and no one was watching. With his finger still tight in her hand, Felix imagined she had nodded off or was lost in some daydream. Then her head rotated towards his wrist. Suddenly she slid her free arm across her body towards him and with her thumbnail tapped on the face of his watch.

'Still shiny and clean,' she said.

He was astonished she had remembered, and lifted the watch up so she could see it more clearly. 'Sapphire glass. It won't ever scratch,' he said.

She shook her head. Either she was marvelling at the glass face and the science that kept it so polished and clear, or she had already forgotten why she was examining this expensive timepiece with its golden hands and brilliant white dial.

'It's Felix, isn't it?' she said.

'Yes, it is.'

She looked away from him, towards the picture of the buttercup meadow on the far wall, and shook her head again.

Outside in the car, he unfastened the clasp of the watch and hung it over the outstretched fingers of his right hand, the way a jeweller might present such a watch to a customer. Bringing the face close to his eye and angling it towards the light, he could see the sheen of the glass. There wasn't a mark on it. He flipped it over and traced the message engraved in neat, curvy writing on the back of the case. 'To Felix on his eighteenth. All my love. Mum.' Then he drove home.

Men may be forgetful and sloppy and not as tidy as they should, but they have a knack of hanging on to things and holding them safe. That's not so difficult with something like a watch, which is basically a handcuff that tells the time. But even with small, apparently insignificant objects, men have a way of keeping them in their life for years, against all the odds. One night in the park with Jed and Smutty, after an argument with Maxine, Jed asked Felix which of his possessions he valued the most. Under normal circumstances, Jed wouldn't go anywhere near this kind of conversation, but sat on top of a slide in the early hours of the morning after a gallon of beer, his mind turned to matters of a philosophical nature. Felix talked about his wedding ring, and about his watch, which was all the more special since his mother had gone into the nursing home, and how the writing on the back was important because it said something his mother was no longer capable of speaking.

'But you wear the ring and the watch all the time. What if the house was on fire? What would you go in and get?'

'I don't know. Photographs?'

'Yeah, that's a good answer. That's a woman's answer.'

'What do you mean?'

'That's the kind of thing you'd say if Abbie asked you. But she's not here, so what would you really get?'

'My wallet,' he answered.

'Exactly. Your wallet. The floppy disks. The train set in the attic. That's what you'd go for.'

'And what about you? Would you get the twins or would that be too girly?'

Jed scratched his chin for a moment. 'Fair enough. Checkmate.'

Smutty was pawing at a mole hill over by the privet hedge. It was a cloudless night and Jed was staring into the sky in the direction of the Plough. After a while there was something he wanted to say. 'You got that watch for your eighteenth, right?'

'Yes.'

'When I was eighteen, mi mum and dad gave me this electric shaver. I only had a bum-fluff moustache but it was a good pressie 'cos it was all about becoming a man. Must have cost 'em a fair whack. Came in a case with a mirror on the inside and space for the flex. Dead neat. Still using it. And it had this little brush with it, right, just a tiny black brush for dusting the bristles off the foil and cleaning the gunk out of the head. There was a little slot in the case for this brush. I had it eleven years and never lost it. Always put it back in the slot. All those mornings when I was late for work, or still pissed from the night before, or hungover, or on holiday with mi mates, and it was still there. Then two days after we got married, I looks in the case and it was gone. And I says to Max, "Hey, have you seen a little black brush anywhere?" And she says, "If it was that manky little thing I found on the side of the sink, I've thrown it out. I thought it was rubbish." And I told her what it was, and she said, "They're twenty-five pence in Boots, go and get another."' He stopped to light a cigarette. Then he said, 'Do you see what I mean?'

'Was it a Braun?' asked Felix.

'Yep.'

'With the green felt on the inside of the case?'

'That's the bunny. Don't tell me you've got one too?'

Felix nodded.

'But have you got the little brush? You haven't, have you? Have you?'

Another thing that Felix had kept safe and sound for many years was the miniature treasure chest Abbie had given him not long after they had started going out. She called it a 'love gift' – he can still remember her saying the words – and it was no bigger than a matchbox with a press-stud clasp on the front in the shape of a padlock. When he opened it with his thumb, he found seven or eight of her hairs, twisted together to make one length of braid, tied in a ball. Where the hairs were tightly bound their blackness seemed stronger, more intense, as if pulling them into a knot had wrung a deeper, darker shade from the strands. They were sitting in the snug room of the pub, in one of the booths. He'd kissed her, then she'd whispered in his ear that in Italy lovers give each other gifts of their hair, but not the hairs from their head. He could feel the redness in her cheek, next to his. She said, 'I was too embarrassed, though. I didn't know what you'd think.' He can't remember what his answer was, but a few days later there was another little treasure chest waiting for him. With more hairs in it. Hairs not from her head. He had kept both boxes, along with all the letters she sent him and other mementoes of their first few years together.

Abbie hadn't changed much to look at. Not in Felix's eyes. But as they sat in the waiting area of the clinic, she let a thick shank of her hair fall in front of her eyes and, by sifting it through her hands, teased out several long, grey strands. With her fingers she followed each one back to its root somewhere in the top of her scalp, then tugged it out and presented it to Felix. Each hair was at least eight inches long, black at the tip but undeniably grey at the other end, even white or silver. They were presented to Felix one at a time. He duly examined them and nodded.

'I'm not the only one,' she said, touching several places on his head just above his ears. He nodded again.

Their appointment had been for twenty past three but it was half past four by the time they were asked to go in. Dr Tremlett, the consultant, was not in his office, and they waited another ten minutes before he swept through the door, snapping off a pair of transparent latex gloves and tossing them into the bin under the sink.

'Sorry about that. Minor crisis. Tremlett called in to save the day, as per.'

In combination with the sunshine from the window, his blond hair, gold-rimmed glasses, ginger eyebrows and tanned face created a peculiar effect, as if his head were emitting an aura of yellow light. He flipped open the case file on his desk and read quickly through the notes, nodding in agreement or frowning in sympathy.

'So it's Felix and Abbie, yes? And you were referred to me in April.'

'March,' said Abbie.

He looked back at the file. 'March it was. Apologies. And you've been waiting for the results of the biopsy following a D&C following a . . . Was that your first miscarriage?'

'Third,' said Abbie.

He looked at the notes again, turning back a couple of pages. 'Your third. That's correct. Hence your concerns and your request for the biopsy. And a chromosome test as well.'

'Yes.'

He scanned the last two pages of the notes, nodding and frowning again, and at one point pulling his face as if in pain. Then he closed the file and took off his glasses.

'Afraid to say there's been a bit of a cock-up.'

'In what way?' asked Felix.

'Seems like the foetal matter taken away for analysis became contaminated. Broken seal most likely, so the lab weren't able to carry out the tests. Seems you've had a bit of a wasted journey.'

Felix turned to look at Abbie. There was a terrible sense of resignation in her face. She was appalled, yes, and disgusted, sure, but more than that she was exhausted and defeated and without hope. She was blank and pale. She had lost.

'So we'll never know what caused it?' said Felix. He was trying to talk for Abbie. He wanted to prove to her that he was on her side, that he wouldn't let her down.

'You know, we could have run a thousand tests and not come up with any answers. Chances are, it was just one of those things,' asserted the doctor.

'I see,' said Felix. He had meant it to sound challenging. Sarcastic, even. As if he didn't accept what he had been told and would be taking the matter further. But it sounded lame, as if he'd said, 'I understand,' or, 'Oh well, not to worry.'

'While you're here, I should mention this other thing. Have you read about it in the paper?'

'What's that?'

'Had some trouble with the locals. Didn't want any bio-matter incinerated. Said they were breathing in the smoke. Moral and religious grounds, that sort of thing. Possible lawsuit, but it's all blown over now. To coin a phrase. Been settled, I should say. So, question is, what do you want doing with the remains?'

'Pardon me?'

'We can get rid of them now, or if you'd rather have them back for a burial . . . Totally up to you. I'll just pop out while you talk it through. Back in a mo.'

He jumped up from the desk and went out of a side door, through which he could be heard chatting with two of the nurses.

Abbie still wore the same expression.

'So it . . . the baby . . . has been lying around in a lab for eight months. Is that what he means?'

'Yes,' she whispered. A semicircle of clear liquid began to form in the bottom half of each eye.

'Did you know?'

She shook her head.

'What shall we do?'

Unexpectedly, Abbie stood up and folded her coat over her arm.

'You decide,' she said, and went out into the waiting area, closing the door behind her.

After three or four minutes Dr Tremlett came back and took his place behind his desk.

'Has she . . .' he inquired, gesturing towards the seat where Abbie had been sitting.

'She's very upset,' said Felix.

'Understandable. Understandable. So what's it to be, then?' He drew a silver fountain pen out of his top pocket, unscrewed the lid and held it above an empty box on one of the forms in front of him, waiting for Felix's answer.

They hadn't asked permission, just in case they were refused, and Abbie didn't want a vicar involved. It was too complicated to explain. Although the vase had fallen over, the bunch of lilies they had left on their last visit were still on the grave, the heads brown and perished and the stalks wizened and hard. There was also a single red rose thrown on to the green stone chippings, with a card attached. It read, 'From B.'

'Just like last time,' said Felix.

'What is?'

'A gift tag with this message on.'

'Maybe it's the same one.'

'But this is tied to a flower.'

Abbie shrugged. With the trowel he had brought, Felix scraped away some of the loose stones, then dug into the earth in the middle of the grave. He had always assumed that graves were solid and covered over with a stone slab. Maybe the better ones were. But the grave of Maria Rosales was just a headstone, bordered by three sides of stone edging. When the hole was deep enough, Abbie took the small pine box from under her coat. Kneeling in the dirt, she placed it in the centre of the hole, then took off her gloves to scrape a few handfuls of soil over the lid. She stood up and Felix levelled the grave with the trowel and scattered the green chippings back on top. The grave looked disturbed but not desecrated or spoiled. A few days of weather would heal the wound. There was a chill in the air and for the first time that year Felix noticed his breath steaming in front of his face. It was also the first time he had done any physical exercise in a long while. Abbie dusted the dirt from her knees.

'They won't be on their own now. They'll be company for each other.'

Felix nodded in agreement. He tapped the trowel gently against the headstone to clean it.

Abbie said, 'My mother and my child, and I didn't know either of them.'

The Godfather

Children who are baptized are brought up in the Christian faith. Jesus tells us that unless a person has been born again, he or she cannot see the Kingdom of God, and baptism is the sign and seal of this new birth. Furthermore, under section seven of its rules and regulations, it is clearly stated that only those children who are baptized will be offered a place at Mount Rose Church of England Junior School, with its impressive Ofsted report, consistently high examination results and distinctive green and mauve uniform. Pupils educated outside the Church of England will take their chances in the failing junior school on the other side of town, with its reputation for truancy, bullying and even drugs.

The priest will ask if the parents and godparents are willing to give the children the help and encouragement they need through prayers, through example and through teaching. They will mumble that they are willing.

'Alice and Molly, when you are baptized, you become members of a new family. God takes you for his own children, and all Christian people will be your brothers and sisters.'

Priest: The Lord is loving to everyone.

All: And his mercy is over all his works.

The parents stand. Maxine appears more tiny than usual alongside her very tall husband, who has raised himself to his full height in the presence of God. The godparents also stand. Two couples. To the left of the font, Auntie Lynn and Uncle Graham from Colchester. To the right, Felix and Abbie. Felix in a collar and tie. Abbie in tears. The twins rustle and shine in their homemade satin dresses. Sunlight enters the nave through a spectrum of stained glass, making the jewels of their plastic tiaras sparkle and glow.

'It is your duty to bring up these children to fight against evil and to

follow Christ. Therefore I ask these questions which you must answer for yourself and for these children. Do you turn to Christ?'

Maxine and Jed turn to Christ, holding hands as they do so. The Colchester branch of the family affirm in unison, though due to an unfortunate speech impediment it is Chwist that Uncle Graham turns to, and in an Essex accent. Abbie, swallowing back her tears, is unable to speak, but Felix turns to Christ on behalf of himself and his wife.

'Do you repent of your sins?'

They repent.

'Do you renounce evil?'

They renounce.

Having wepented and wenounced, Uncle Graham extrudes an apparently endless handkerchief from his breast pocket and blows his nose, the comedy-style trumpeting of his nasal passages echoing through the church. Felix makes a quick dash to the tripod positioned several feet away and checks the auto-focus on the camcorder and replaces the battery. Auntie Lynn steps forward with an offering of oil. The priest unscrews the small green and black jar, labelled Body Shop, and dips his index finger into the liquefied extract of coconut and aloe vera, specially blessed for the occasion. Turning to the twins, he smears the sign of the cross on the forehead of the smiling Molly, recharges his finger in the pot, then smears the same shape on the forehead of the giggling Alice. A bead of oil runs between her eyebrows, which she follows with her inturned eyes until it comes to rest at the end of her nose. Maxine offers a tissue, but Alice pushes it away, waiting for the moment when the trembling drop of oil has enough critical mass to detach itself and fall. The priest implores everyone not to be ashamed to confess the faith of Christ crucified, and a long response about fighting valiantly under the banner of Christ peters out before the last bit about soldiers and servants. A hymn is sung. Then the lid of the enormous font is raised by means of a hand-crank attached to a series of pulleys and ropes suspended from the ceiling. The priest demands to know if the parents and godparents believe in God the Father, who made the world, and Jesus Christ, who redeemed mankind, and the Holy Spirit, who gives life to the people of God.

They do.

The priest reaches backwards into the font and scoops out a handful of dripping water.

'Alice, I baptize you in the name of the Father, and of the Son, and of the Holy Spirit.'

'I'm Molly.'

'I beg your pardon. Molly, I baptize you in the name of the Father, and of the Son, and of the Holy Spirit.' *He lets the water dribble from his fingers on to her head.*

Molly closes her eyes as it runs down her cheeks and on to her chin. 'Amen?' *she asks.*

The priest fishes behind him in the font again and scoops water on to Alice.

It runs behind her ears and she shrieks as the icy liquid trickles down her neck and between her shoulders.

'Shhh,' *says Jed.*

'But it's freezing.'

Candles are handed out to parents and godparents. One per hand. Twelve in all. Jed tucks one of his candles behind his ear as he passes among the small circle of adults with his fag lighter. The buds of flame are barely visible in the strong sunlight projected through the coloured glass above them. The priest welcomes the twins into God's Church. The enthusiasm of the congregation is flagging, until the commencement of the Lord's Prayer. The priest says it his way. The new way. The six adults who never go to church say it their way. The right way. Then the baptism comes to an end.

'The grace of our Lord Jesus Christ, and the love of God, and the fellowship of the Holy Spirit be with us evermore. Amen.'

'Amen.'

At the door, in the large wooden porch, each member of the gathering files past the priest. The twins have run ahead to look for ghosts in the graveyard. Maxine and Jed are grateful that the service could be fitted in at such short notice and the priest hopes to see them again in the future. Lynn and Graham are wished a safe drive back to Colchester. It was a lovely service, says Lynn. Weally special, Graham agrees. Felix is next.

'There, that wasn't so bad,' *says the priest.*

'It was very nice,' says Felix.

'Great thing about being a godparent – at least you can give them back at the end of the day!' says the priest.

'Exactly,' agrees Felix.

'Love 'em to bits but wouldn't want one in the house!'

'Quite.'

The priest laughs. Felix laughs too.

Behind him Abbie does not laugh. When the priest offers to shake her by the hand, she holds out the two burning candles, one in each glove, then circles past him and leaves. Later, when they climb into the car, after the smiling and the thanks and the goodbyes have ended, she will despair of her husband. 'Is it any wonder I can't get pregnant, if that's how you feel.'

17

It was to be a week of surprises and shocks both at home and at work. Maybe the stars and planets were lined up in a particular direction, bringing about a new phase. Maybe it was a turn in the weather, a coolness entering the lungs and the blood, a chill in the marrow of the bones causing a change in mood. Maybe it was a biorhythmical blip, or the psycho-physical effects of the central heating, or a consequence of the dark nights drawing in. Felix didn't think it was any of those things, but in the absence of a logical explanation, he allowed himself to speculate and to fantasize.

On Monday Marjorie was missing from the team meeting. Bernard glossed over her absence by agreeing that she wasn't present but offering no explanation or apology. He had recently switched to a type of cherry-flavoured tobacco; even though he only smoked in his own office, the smell had already impregnated his clothing and radiated outwards as he sat at the head of the table, announcing the agenda.

'Agendum,' said Neville.

'I beg your pardon, Neville.'

'How many items will we be discussing?'

'Just one, the allocation of cases.'

'So it's singular. Agendum.'

Mo snorted.

'Is that animal noise something you'd like putting in the minutes, Mo? If so, I wonder if you could help me with the spelling,' sneered Neville.

'No. I just thought this was a team meeting. Not *Call My Bluff.*'

'Well, if I'm writing this down I might as well use the English language as it was intended to be used. That is the *criterion* we should be working to, wouldn't you say?'

Mo shook her head and mouthed a word in his direction. Neville tutted theatrically and wrote it down. Roy came in late, reeking of a less perfumed brand of tobacco. 'Where's Marjorie?' he asked, glad that someone else hadn't made it on time.

'She's not here,' replied Bernard. 'I think we should press ahead.'

Sandwiched between Old Holborn and Maraschino ready-rubbed, Thelma shrank in her chair until she was barely visible inside her thick winter coat. At one point she raised her mouth above the top button and croaked, 'Is it pears?'

'Is what pears?'

'That smell.'

'Cherries. My sister brought me two dozen packets back from New Orleans. It's rather pleasant, don't you think?'

He unzipped a small leather pouch and with his hand wafted the scent in Thelma's direction. Like a rabbit that had seen a fox, she disappeared inside the burrow of her coat and wasn't seen again until the end of the meeting. Afterwards, Felix went along to Marjorie's office to deliver a memo, but her door was locked. Checking the rota, he saw that she hadn't booked any leave, and Cathy on reception told him that she hadn't phoned in sick or left any message regarding her whereabouts. There was still no word from her on Tuesday, and on Wednesday even Neville was worried enough to voice his concerns. 'She might be lying at home with her throat cut and that spaniel of hers sniffing round the rotting corpse, thinking about its next meal.'

They were all in the staffroom at lunchtime and Thelma was just lifting a spoonful of tomato soup to her lips when the smell of ripe cherries entered the atmosphere, followed by Bernard carrying an orange Tupperware box.

'Any news on Marjorie, boss?' asked Roy.

'Marjorie's not here,' he said, and turned away from them to unpack his lunch.

194

'Will she be here on Friday, because she's doing court duty?' Felix wanted to know.

Sensing that Bernard knew more than he was saying, Neville went over to the door, removed the wooden chock that held it open and let it swing closed. Ambushed, Bernard busied himself with his meal, going through the elaborate process of removing the top slice of bread from each triangular sandwich and smearing the ham inside with a thin layer of English mustard. There were eight sandwiches in total, a fact made clear by the way he counted them on to a plate, arranging them in a pyramid formation with a hard-boiled egg placed ornamentally on top. This diversion bought him at least five minutes, at the end of which he produced a teapot from under the sink and asked if anyone wanted a cuppa. There were no takers. Having exhausted all options, and noticing that Neville was actually barring the door with his arms folded across his chest, he took a deep breath and turned around.

'Er, bit awkward this. My line manager asked me to keep it quiet but, since you're ... er ... concerned. About a colleague.' He swallowed and pushed the plate of sandwiches to one side. 'Mind if I smoke?'

Through clouds of fruit-scented fumes and between vigorous puffs on his pipe, Bernard explained that as of last Friday Marjorie was no longer a Social Services employee and would not be returning to her post. In preparation for her retirement, pensions section had been going back through her file and had noticed a few 'irregularities, relating to qualifications, references, that sort of thing'.

'Like she didn't have any?' prompted Neville.

'Er, in a word, no.'

'And how long had she been working here?' asked Mo.

'Thirty-two years.'

'Bloody hell.'

'Precisely.'

He shifted nervously from one foot to the next, cleared his throat, then gave a little speech of such confidence and clarity that not only did it surprise everyone in the room but it must have come as something of a shock to Bernard himself. 'Now, I'm a quiet sort of person. I don't ask much from my staff, and my staff don't ask much from me either. For which I'm grateful. But if it comes to the attention of the court or the press that hundreds of adoption orders have been signed illegally through this office, or that hundreds of adoptive parents are not the true, legal guardians of their sons and daughters, then Marjorie Stanmore is not the only person who will fail to qualify for a superannuated, index-linked pension. I have six months to go and a sizeable deposit on a small property overlooking the sea above Colwyn Bay. And I can promise with absolute certainty that if my retirement plan gets flushed away between now and next May, then some, if not all, of you will be coming down the toilet with me. Therefore, I'll do you the favour of staying in my office, topping up the coffee fund out of my own pocket, signing your preposterous expenses claims and turning a blind eye to everything else that goes on in this building, and in return you'll do me the great honour of keeping your gobs well and truly shut. Now, Neville, if you don't mind, I'd like to enjoy these sandwiches before I lose my appetite.'

Neville opened the door and, plate in hand, Bernard strode past him and marched off down the corridor, dragging his cherries with him.

'So do you think he fancied her or something?' said Neville, when Bernard was out of hearing.

No one answered.

'Great speech, mind. Must be the tobacco. Are we sure he didn't get it from Jamaica?'

'Poor Marge,' said Thelma, who stood up from her half-eaten bowl of soup and left the room, followed by Mo, who on the way past said to Neville, 'You know what you are, don't you? You're a *phenomenon.*'

She was followed a minute later by Neville himself, but not before he had pointed out that if Bernard thought he was filling in for Marjorie at court on Friday he could whistle for it.

Felix made a cup of tea for himself and Roy. Roy sat with his feet on the coffee table, trying to explain it to himself. The scar that ran diagonally across his brow appeared to be glowing with heat, as if a few moments of deep thinking had brought blood to his head.

'Weird, isn't it? Here's me with my background, and there's her, as sweet as they come and never hurt a fly, and it turns out she's the dodgy one. What do you reckon to that, man?'

'I think . . . I think we should have a collection,' said Felix. 'Send her some flowers.'

No one was in the mood for work that afternoon and Felix went home early. All this business with Marjorie had got him thinking about his own qualifications. Not whether he had any – he was pretty certain that the two years at college with a job as an ice-cream man every weekend wasn't just a dream, otherwise he would never have served Abbie that ninety-nine with raspberry sauce and they would never have met. But where were the certificates? He looked in the bottom of the drawer where he kept his passport and record of inoculations, but they weren't there. Neither were they in the bureau, or the lever-arch file with the insurance policies and television licence, and not in the bedside cabinet, although he did find a pair of binoculars he thought he'd left in a bird-hide in Cambridgeshire. He even looked in the shoebox under the bed where he kept the letters and the two little love gifts, and had just started to question his talent for never losing things when an image came to mind of pressing a faint crease along the middle of the certificates. And why? Because they wouldn't fit in the small, rectangular drawer beneath the side mirror of the dressing table without being folded in half. There they were, right on top, and beneath them a bunch of other papers he hadn't seen before, a couple of dozen sheets, some stapled together. When he opened them up he saw they were stories, or not stories so much as essays or articles on all sorts of strange but familiar themes. They had titles. Titles like *The Driving Range, The BBQ, The Stag Night* and

The Sperm Test. The pages were handwritten, and the writing was Abbie's.

It was Wednesday night. It was about half seven by the time they'd finished eating. Abbie was lying on the settee, watching telly. Felix sat down next to her and flicked through a couple of old magazines.

'I was looking for my social work certificates today.'

'Oh, yeah.'

'Found them in the dressing table.'

She nodded but wasn't really interested.

'In the little drawer under the mirror.'

Still no answer.

'The one like a secret compartment.'

No response.

'Where you might put something, if it were a secret.'

She still hadn't heard him, but must have sensed his eyes on her face, looking a little harder and a little longer than usual. And when she turned towards him, several seconds went by during which she replayed his comments in her head. Felix had noticed this in Abbie before, the ability to retrieve his words from her subconscious, even when she hadn't been listening. It led to some bewildering disagreements, the most famous of which was an argument over a birthday present in which she swore blind that Felix had asked for a suede jacket not a leather one, even though at the time she was totally engrossed in an episode of *Who Wants to be a Millionaire?* the night the posh woman from London scooped the jackpot. If truth be told, Abbie was probably right. He'd drunk a couple of bottles of Old Peculiar on an empty stomach and could easily have said suede by mistake, although it was obvious to anyone who knew him that he was not a suede jacket sort of person. Luckily she had kept the receipt. The shop was happy to make the exchange. The replacement item hung in the wardrobe for almost a year unworn, suggesting to both of them that Felix wasn't a leather jacket sort of person either. But it hadn't been an argument about coolness and fashion. It was an argument about communication. About who said what. As far as she was concerned, he was quiet to the point of mutism, never telling her what was going on in his head, so if he did venture an opinion once in a while she sure as hell wouldn't forget it. As far as he was concerned, what was the point in talking if she wasn't going to listen?

But she was listening now, all right, and with her full and undivided attention.

'Oh,' she said.

She stood up, walked over to the window and looked out towards the garden, even though it was black outside and in all probability she could see little more than her own reflection.

'So what did you think?' she asked, with her back to him.

'I don't know. What are they?'

'Just bits of writing,' said Abbie.

'But what are they for?'

'I don't know.'

They were avoiding the issue. Abbie continued to look towards the darkness outside.

'They're about me,' said Felix.

She didn't answer straight away. Then she said, 'They're about men. Aren't they?'

'But they're things that have happened to me, things that I . . .'

'Go on?'

He felt like he was walking into a trap. He could see the ground in front of him was nothing more than a thin layer of dry sticks camouflaged with leaves and grass, covering some enormous hole. But there was nowhere else to go other than forward.

'Things I never even told you,' he obliged.

'Exactly.'

There was a long and heavy pause, broken eventually by Abbie.

'The thing is, Felix, you talk in your sleep.'

'I do not,' he snapped. He didn't know why it should be such an insult, but his instinctive reaction was to deny it.

'OK, you don't. Not in the way that some people do. But there's this half an hour or so, just after you've dropped off, when I can

199

ask you questions, and even though you're asleep you tell me the answers.'

'What?' he said. This was ridiculous. It was an excuse. But where had she learned all those details, about the stag night and the driving range and . . . She must have been talking to Jed. Or Jed had been blabbing to Maxine, and Maxine had told Abbie.

'Don't you believe me?'

'No, I don't. It's rubbish.'

'I'll prove it, then.'

'How?'

Felix sat with his arms folded. He'd been told on one of his training courses that it was a defensive position to adopt. So what? He *was* on the defensive. He was under attack. Abbie on the other hand seemed to be moving to a point in the proceedings where she was actually enjoying herself. Her arms weren't folded. She perched on the windowsill with her hands on the radiator, tapping her fingernails on the hollow metal.

'What kind of week have you had at work so far?' she asked.

Felix shrugged his shoulders. 'Average.'

'Average?'

'Pretty much.'

'Apart from the thing with Marjorie?'

Felix stared at her. 'How did you know about that?'

'You told me.'

'When?'

'Last night in bed. I asked you what had been happening at work. And you told me.'

Felix was dumbstruck. Dumbstruck in the true sense of the word – astonished into a state of silence. And also dumbstruck in the cartoon, comic-strip sense – with his mouth falling slowly open and his eyes widening in their sockets. Dumbstruck and also gobsmacked. He talked in his sleep. And judging by the evidence, he told the truth. What else had he told her? What did she know?

She came to sit next to him on the settee. 'Don't be cross.'

He felt relieved. If she was asking him not to be cross, that meant she wasn't cross with him. And that was good, because that meant she didn't know about Jed and the sperm. She would have been cross about that. He shook his head. 'I'm not cross.'

'But you've got to admit it's a bit weird.'

'What is? What's weird?'

'Well, when you're awake you tell me nothing, but when you're asleep you tell me everything.'

'What do you mean everything?'

He had folded his arms again and tried to casually unfold them.

'Well, like someone getting sacked at work.'

Felix took a gulp of beer and kept hold of the glass and the bottle, to give his hands something to do. 'I suppose so. When you put it like that.'

'And the thing is, when you don't tell me things I start to wonder what's going on. What's going on in your life and what's going on in your head. Because, believe it or not, I love you and I'm very interested.'

Had he known it was a conversation about love, things might have got very strange and ended in a row. But having got all anxious and resistant, thinking it was a conversation about lying, suddenly they were holding hands on the settee.

Later, lying naked and huddled together, Abbie admitted that once, as he was falling asleep, she had asked him if there was anyone else. And with his eyes closed and his head on the pillow, he had answered, 'No, and there never will be,' and she'd realized at that moment they would always be together, no matter what happened.

The telly was still on, with the sound down. It was the only light. Its changing colours shimmered on the ceiling and the walls. Sometimes between programmes or between scenes the whole room went dark, but only for an instant, never long enough to believe in the blackness or feel that the evening had come to an end.

'But why did you write all this stuff down?' Felix asked quietly in her ear.

'I just felt like it. You tell me something in your sleep and it gets my imagination going. You know, seeing it from the man's point of view. I wanted to look at things from the other side. Do you think it's good writing?'

'Well, I only skimmed through, but . . .'

'Do you think I could get it published? Because I'm sick of standing in the precinct in my long johns and thermal gloves, asking men if they prefer roll-on or aerosol or how many times a minute they think about football. I send all the facts and figures off, and some halfwit in an office in London cobbles them together into an article. Why can't I do that? The pieces I've written, they're as good as anything in those magazines, aren't they? Felix?'

But Felix wasn't really listening. He was imagining hundreds of thousands of strangers reading about his golf handicap and his sex drive and his hopeless DIY. He thought of himself as a private person. But his wife interrogated him while he was unconscious, and not only that, she wanted to plaster the details of his personal life all over the shelves of WH Smith.

As part of a rather transparent and stomach-churning charm offensive Captain Roderick was doing the rounds, coming as close to an apology as he had probably come in his entire life. There were plenty of excuses for his commando-style storming of the school toilet, including his own high blood pressure on the day and his fear that Ruby 'might have being doing herself harm'.

'We are all very mindful for the girl's welfare,' he said, bringing both hands to rest on the handle of his umbrella, which was propped between his knees. 'If there's anything we can do?'

'No, nothing,' said Felix.

His voice was thin and cold. For the past two nights he had hardly slept, not daring to drift off before Abbie did, then lying awake well into the small hours, afraid of what he might say. On several occasions he had prodded Abbie in the back or whispered her name to check if she was sleeping. It appeared that she was, but who was to say she wouldn't wake up once he had drifted off?

It was an impossible situation, like guarding a lump of gold in the high mountains of the Sierra Madre. The minute his eyes were closed it would be stolen out from under his nose. Already he was seriously tired, not to mention irritable, and the more Captain Roderick slimed and slithered in front of him, the closer he came to losing his patience. Eventually, just as Rubberdick was expressing his concern for 'the girl's' health for the seventh or eighth time, Felix snapped.

'Is that nail varnish?'

'I beg your pardon?'

'I'm asking you if you're wearing nail varnish.'

The Captain extended the fingers of his right hand and examined the gleaming, translucent nails in the light from the window. The nail on the middle finger appeared to be broken or torn, a war wound from his battle with Ruby, and somewhere under the carapace was a dark blister of blood.

'Nail *polish*. As a matter of fact I am,' he replied.

'Why?'

'Excuse me?'

'I'm asking you why.'

The Captain looked again at his fingers, paying particular attention to the damaged nail, and grimacing slightly as pressed it against the desk, testing for pain.

'A protection,' he explained.

'Against what?'

'I have a calcium deficiency.'

'I see.'

'Besides which. This hand . . .' He dropped his voice to a low but serious hush. 'This hand has shaken the hand of the Queen of England. This hand has touched history. Preserved beneath those layers of polish are the actual molecules where contact occurred. Thus.' He leaned towards Felix, lifted his hand from where it rested on the mouse pad and, with what Felix took to be the authentic weight and control of a royal greeting – gentle, yet significant, and slightly menacing – he shook it.

'Wasn't she wearing gloves?' asked Felix.

The Captain dropped his hand. 'You can scoff. But we all need something to keep us going, some little sign or deed. She shook this hand because of the good it had done. And trapped beneath the polish is the will to go on doing it. It's what gives me the power, and the right.'

It was just about the weirdest thing Felix had ever heard. The man was clearly deranged. A maniac. And it suddenly flashed through Felix's mind that atoms of Her Majesty the Queen might not be the only things held in suspension beneath the see-through varnish. Captain Roderick was a teacher, wasn't he? And what do teachers grip between their fingers every day of their working life? Chalk. Just what they found on Ruby's knickers. Dusty white chalk. Somewhere within the layers of polish, specks of white powder were lurking, particles of the stuff that could be forensically identified then traced to a batch, a packet, an individual stick of chalk. Indisputable evidence. Suddenly everything was unmistakably obvious. The cause of Ruby Moffat's trauma was sitting no more than two feet from him, and the only mystery was why more of his students weren't barricading themselves in the toilets or jumping out of classroom windows. At least that's how it looked to Felix, through the fog of his exhaustion. In truth, though, the cause of Ruby Moffat's trauma was three or four miles away, and right at that moment was driving away from the Social Services children's home in a rusty dark-green van, with Ruby on the passenger seat next to him.

18

Felix was in and out of the surgery in no more than fifteen minutes. The waiting room was unusually quiet and only one ear needed to be syringed, despite the fact that the locum doctor had identified a blockage in both and for the past five days Felix had been dribbling extra-virgin olive oil into his auditory canals. When he left he noticed a definite improvement to his hearing and also to his balance, as if a valve had been opened and pressure released. Following one idea with another, he found himself thinking about a photograph he had once seen of a hole being drilled in the top of a man's head to relieve his headache. What he remembered most about the image was the drill itself – not a piece of surgical equipment or even a power tool, but a hand-operated thing with a wooden handle and what looked like a rusty bit. The patient didn't appear to be under any kind of anaesthetic or suffering any pain, although his eyes were wide and somewhat skew-whiff, looking in opposite directions. It was an expression not a million miles from the look on the face of Carlos, the duty officer at the children's home, as he ran towards Felix's car. PC Nottingham and PC Lily were also in the car park, talking into their radios.

'She's gone,' blurted Carlos.

'When did this happen?'

'About half an hour ago. Said she was going outside to play football with the others and she hasn't come back. Ben here saw her getting into a van.'

'A green 'un,' said a boy standing with his hands in his pockets.

'Are you sure she isn't at home? Maybe one of her brothers came for her?'

'No, I've spoken to the mother. Ruby's not at home and she's worried sick.'

PC Lily told Felix that they had several cars out looking for the van and even the police helicopter from Manchester making a sweep of the area. They searched through her room for any indication of where she might be and who might have taken her, but there was nothing. Felix told PC Lily he'd go up to the family house to try and reassure Mrs Moffat. Just then there was a squawk from the radio in the patrol car. Felix heard various code numbers being called out, followed by an address on the Lakeland Estate.

'We're on our way,' said PC Nottingham. He slid into the driving seat and started the engine, and PC Lily jumped in next to him.

'What shall I do?' Felix asked before they pulled off.

The two police officers spoke quickly to each other, then PC Lily wound down her window. 'Get in,' she told him.

With the siren going, they went through three sets of red lights and over the central reservation of the dual carriageway, but it still took a good twenty minutes to reach the estate. On the way, bits of information were relayed through the radio. Ruby had been spotted by one of her brothers being taken into a house not far from their own. He had barged his way in through the garage and there had been an altercation. The brother had been stabbed. A chase followed; a man had taken refuge in an old coach on Coleridge Avenue, where he was now holding Ruby as a hostage.

'The Big Blue One?' asked Felix from the back seat.

'Sounds like it,' said PC Lily.

That was as much as they were told. When they arrived on the estate there were already six other police vehicles at the scene, including two Black Marias and a dog van, and as PC Lily opened the back door of the car to let him out, Felix heard the drone of the helicopter as it hovered overhead. A small crowd had gathered, including the Moffat brothers, who were hurling stones and small chunks of broken paving stones at the coach. Eventually they were forced back by the dog handlers to a distance from where they could only reach it with insults and abuse. Teddy, the eldest, was standing on top of the metal container that housed the local betting office.

'You fucking pervert. You touch my sister and I'll fucking rip you apart. Can you hear me?'

In his coat and trousers, Felix looked and felt peculiar, standing among the group of police officers in their uniforms and polished buttons and boots.

'Who's this?' the officer in charge asked PC Lily.

'The girl's social worker.'

He didn't respond. He was trying to establish the order of events, the current situation and a plan of action. More police arrived. Two of them circled the coach with a spool of blue and white tape until the area was cordoned off. All bystanders were ushered outside the circumference.

'Anything on that address yet?' the officer asked one of his subordinates.

'Still waiting.'

Felix looked towards the houses to the left and could see an ambulance parked outside the garage and another policeman in front of the door.

'Is that the house of the man who's got Ruby?' he asked.

The officer scowled at him. 'Will someone escort this bleeding heart to the other side of the tape?'

'Come on.' PC Nottingham took him gently by the elbow to guide him away.

'But I know whose house that is,' said Felix. 'It's James Spotland's.'

Just as he spoke, the crowd to one side were suddenly running for cover, some of them screaming. Felix looked towards the Big Blue One and through one of the shattered windows saw the outline and then the features of the small bald man he had last seen carrying a pile of children's toys through the doors of the office. It was indeed Jimmy Spotland, and under his left arm he held a small, red-headed girl by her neck, and in his right hand he was holding a gun.

*

During the next two hours the entire street was sealed off and the houses surrounding it evacuated. What had seemed like a little local drama with an audience of residents had suddenly escalated into a tense and serious incident, with police marksmen taking up positions in neighbouring buildings and journalists and cameramen setting up camp in adjoining avenues. Felix had found Mr and Mrs Moffat in a large police vehicle like a mobile library parked three or four streets away. They were drinking tea from paper cups and watching a bank of closed-circuit television monitors, all of them showing the blue coach from various angles. The time codes rolled over in the bottom right-hand corner of the screens. Felix put his hand on Mrs Moffat's shoulder.

'I'm sure she'll be all right. I've known Jimmy a long time. He's not the type . . .'

Not the type to abduct a child, was he going to say? Not the type to carry a gun? What other types wasn't he? He changed tack.

'How's your son? Joey, was it?'

'He's OK. It was only a scratch,' said his mother.

In fact Felix had been told by PC Lily that the young man had been taken to hospital with two deep stab wounds, one in his fore-arm and one in his shoulder. But maybe in the life of a Moffat, or in comparison with your only daughter being held at gunpoint in an armoured coach, two penetrating blows to the flesh didn't really count. Neither parent had taken their eyes from the screens. Felix stepped back outside, feeling useless and with an unignorable sense of guilt growing minute by minute. He felt he should stay but had no idea what to do. The scowling officer and another important-looking policeman were walking towards him. Felix turned between two cars to avoid them. 'That's him,' he heard the officer saying.

'Is it Felix?' the other man called after him.

'Yes.'

'Spotland wants to talk to you.'

'To me?'

'Correct.'

'What, on the phone?'
'He hasn't got a phone. You'd better come with me.'

It was, as the officer in charge of the operation kept explaining, completely up to him. And yet before he had actually given his answer he was wearing a bulletproof vest and being walked towards the cordon. The words DO NOT ENTER were written on the tape in big letters. Things had been explained to him very clearly. Spotland had seen Felix from the bus window. He wouldn't talk to a policeman but he would talk to Felix. He trusted him. He wouldn't harm him. Felix was to walk slowly to the coach. Talk calmly to Jimmy. Find out what he wanted. Check that Ruby was OK. Then walk slowly away. Of course it was completely up to him, but even as he was told this for the eighth or ninth time, he saw a hand lifting the tape in front of him and felt a pat on the back. It was PC Lily, wishing him luck. The officer lifted a loudhailer to his mouth and in the direction of the Big Blue One shouted, 'He's on his way. Please acknowledge that he is free to approach the coach.'

There was a quick glimpse of Jimmy at the broken window and some sort of garbled reply.

The officer looked down at Felix. 'Whenever you're ready,' he said.

There were pellets of broken glass on the ground that crunched under his shoes. He purposefully crushed them into the tarmac, making as much noise as possible, and every two or three steps cleared his throat or coughed. Even though the officer had announced Felix's visit, he didn't want to risk any element of surprise. He wanted to be utterly conspicuous, as obvious as was humanly possible. But every step forward was a step towards loneliness, despite the dozens of people watching his progress and the cameras trained on the coach. He pictured himself on the surveillance screens, an isolated figure, walking away from safety. And at some stage, some mid-point between the loudhailer and the gun, he thought of Abbie, standing in the precinct with her clipboard, asking her questions. He should have phoned her to tell her where he was and what he was doing. He should have asked her permission – she would have said no. He thought of his mother also and glanced down at his watch. Whatever time it was, it didn't register. About ten feet away from the bus, in line with the broken window, he stopped and swallowed his breath.

'Jimmy, it's Felix.'

'I can see you,' said Jimmy's voice from inside.

Felix stood still, wondering whose turn it was to speak. After a while he said, 'I've been told to ask you . . .'

'Get on the coach,' shouted Jimmy.

'What?'

'Go to the door and get on the coach. NOW.'

There was a squeal from inside. Ruby, in pain.

'All right, all right. They told me to stay outside. Don't hurt her.'

Felix made his way towards the door, where several weeks ago he had been told by some anonymous and all-powerful presence inside the coach to fuck off. Now here he was, pulling on the handle and climbing up the metal steps, reluctant and afraid. He expected the sudden, amplified voice of the police officer telling him not to do it. But nothing came. Behind him was darkness, and silence. Inside the coach it was even darker. He reached out to steady himself and felt the ball at the top of the gear stick. Looking ahead, he could just make out the back window and the metal strips of the luggage racks on each side at head height. As his pupils widened, he could see that all the seats had been removed, and that boxes and crates were stacked at intervals along the length of the floor. It was from between two of the crates that a light suddenly flickered and glowed. Then out of the gap came Jimmy, on his knees, with a cigarette lighter flaring in his hand. He looked like some poor wretch who had been locked from birth in a cupboard or a shed. Like someone who'd never seen daylight or another human being in his life. His clothes were filthy and torn, and his movements were those of an animal, a wild animal cornered in its lair.

'Where's Ruby?' said Felix, his voice trembling in his throat.

Jimmy swung the lighter to the other side of the bus. Ruby was crouched on the floor with her head between her knees and her hair spilling down towards her ankles.

'Are you OK, Ruby?'

'Of course she's OK,' hissed Jimmy. 'Tell him you're OK.'

Outlined against the blackness, Felix could see the lifting and falling of her shoulders as she sobbed. She did not reply.

The lighter went out.

'Got any fags?' said Jimmy, from the darkness.

'No.'

'Listen, tell them I want fags. And some food, yeah? And something for her – a burger and a Coke.'

'I'll tell them. Just don't hurt her.'

'And listen, Felix, I need you to tell them about me. I'm a good character, right? And how the wife left me – you know all this stuff. This thing with Ruby – you've got to tell them what these Moffats are like. How they're liars and shit stirrers. You know 'em, Felix. You can tell the coppers what they're like. I'm just a small-timer. You know that, don't you, Felix?'

There was no conviction at all in his voice. It wasn't even a plea. Out of the silence that followed, the sound of crying finally emerged, and as Felix moved his head to listen, he realized they were not the tears of a young girl.

A loud and nasally voice came from outside. Through the megaphone the policeman boomed, 'We're just bringing up the lights. Nothing to be alarmed about.'

A generator started up in the distance and almost immediately a cool, silvery light pierced the windows of the coach from all sides and illuminated everything within it. Jimmy scurried back between the two packing cases. For a moment, Ruby looked towards Felix. Her face was dirty and creased. Strands of hair were plastered to her cheeks. Her eyes peered through the bedraggled red curtain of her fringe. Then came a loud pinging sound from the mesh on one of the windows. Like something had snapped.

'You fuckin' pervert. Touch our Ruby and I'll rip you up. You get out here, Spotland, and I'll fucking tear you to pieces.'

On top of the container again, this time in silhouette against the arc lights behind him, Teddy Moffat was trying to load a second pellet into an air gun broken across his knee. Felix could see him perfectly and could hear a policeman under the container shouting at him, telling him to get down. Teddy stood up and fired another slug in the direction of the coach. This time it entered through the smashed window and thudded into a cardboard box.

'I swear to God, Spotland, I'll savage your head.'

He broke the rifle to load it again. Felix had been hit with an air-gun pellet when he was a kid and it only bruised his thigh. But this was different. This was a man firing an air gun in the middle of a siege, with God knows how many marksmen with their fingers on the trigger and a desperate Jimmy Spotland holding a pistol in his sweaty hand. All hell could break loose, with Felix caught in the crossfire. He dropped down into the stairwell to shelter behind the door. Along the coach, he could hear Jimmy answering back, stuttering and muttering under his breath at first, then louder, sneering at Teddy's comments, shouting back that Teddy was Moffat scum and scum got what they deserved. Felix could hear that the police were now on top of the container, scuffling with Teddy, who sounded to be lashing out at anyone in his way. It was at this moment that Jimmy emerged from his hiding place between the cases, got to his feet and began walking down the coach. Crouched below the front seat, Felix could see him making his way forward, his bald head shining in the artificial light, the gun still visible in his hand.

'You Moffat scum, you're all gob,' he shouted through the window.

'Get out here, you dirty fucking monster,' yelled Teddy.

Jimmy laughed, leaning forward to get a better look at Teddy, sticking his bald, shiny head and then his upper body through the broken window, into the space where the most light fell. Into the one place where anyone outside, spying through the telescopic sight of a high-velocity rifle, would have a clear and uninterrupted view.

The fuse box at home was in the cubbyhole under the stairs. There was a problem with the wiring, a loose connection; every couple of weeks – usually when the outside light was switched on – a fuse would blow. It meant groping around in the dark for a torch, then trying to thread a length of invisibly thin fuse wire into the fuse box. And the light for the cubbyhole was on the same circuit, so it also meant Felix trying to hold the torch between his teeth and aim it at the problem. Three qualified electricians had not been able to trace the fault, but the last one had ripped out the old fuse board and fitted a bank of modern trip switches in its place. The outside light still caused an occasional overload, but now all that Felix needed to do was to find his way to the cubbyhole and throw the switch.

And the noise of the gunshot was very like that of an electrical short circuit. Close by there was a crack, coupled with an intense fizzing sound, and just a moment later came a crisp thwack, almost a pop, from somewhere in the distance. The blowing of a bulb and the tripping of a fuse. A marksman's single bullet outrunning the speed of sound, arriving milliseconds before the sound of the gun that fired it. Then another noise – a leaden thump – the sound and weight of a human being hitting the deck. Felix waited in his hiding place in the stairwell, but nothing happened. Peeping under the front seat he could see Jimmy on the floor, motionless. Still nothing happened. Eventually Felix pushed himself over the top of the steps and began crawling along the aisle of the coach. Jimmy had fallen backwards, with his legs underneath him, buckled at the knees. As if he had keeled over while praying. His arms lay open at each side, with the pistol held loosely in the hand furthest away.

'Jimmy? Jimmy?' Felix whispered.

Keeping as low as possible, he reached across Jimmy's chest, stretching as far as he could until his fingertips nudged against the handle of the revolver. He'd never held a weapon before and he hooked it into the palm of his hand, anticipating the heaviness and seriousness of cold steel. But the object he gripped was empty and light. It had none of the qualities of forged metal but all the properties of moulded plastic. It was a replica. A toy.

'Jimmy? Jimmy?'

The man beneath him was motionless. Inert. And lying there, Felix became aware of a growing heat between them. Not just body heat, but a true, tangible warmth, made of a substance, welling from somewhere close to Jimmy's heart and spreading through Felix's shirt and on to his skin. It was blood. He looked at Jimmy's face. His eyes were open. Metallic, unnatural light fell across his taut, razored scalp. From his brow to the crown of his head, pinpricks of sweat beaded the stubble and pores. As Felix stared, Jimmy's eyes rolled slightly to one side and his head followed, almost leisurely, until it came to rest on his shoulder, dragging his bottom lip sideways and pulling open his mouth. His top dentures had slipped forwards – he now had the mouth of a shark. Every perfect tooth glistened with saliva, and as his mouth gaped wider, something else glinted from the tip of his tongue. It was the piercing that Felix had noticed before. Except hadn't that been a small, silver stud? This was something far more elaborate and ornate. It was gold, apart from a precious red stone in the middle. And as Felix squinted at the finely worked jewellery only inches from his eyes, what finally came into focus were the eight golden legs and ruby-red body of an insect. A spider, in fact.

Felix was lying in bed with a pillow propped behind his back and the remote control in his hand. His eyes were half-closed, but he stirred when Abbie came into the bedroom and put a mug of tea on the bedside cabinet.

'Thank you.'

She had a quick shower before climbing into bed next to him.

'Tired?'

'Hm.'

Abbie took the remote from him and skipped through the channels. It was almost half past ten. The news finished with a couple of football results and a story about a dog being rescued from an abandoned mineshaft after three days. Then came the regional bulletin, with footage of a three-hour siege which had ended in the fatal shooting of a local man and the dramatic rescue of an eleven-year-old girl.

'Hey, isn't this your patch?' Abbie asked, nudging him with her elbow.

Half-asleep again, Felix grunted in reply.

Abbie watched as the incident unfolded. A cordon had been set up around a mobile shop on the notorious Lakeland Estate after a girl had been taken hostage by an armed man. Footage from the scene showed police snipers in doorways and windows with their weapons aimed at a dilapidated blue coach illuminated by floodlights. A senior police officer gave an account of events leading up to the incident and described how a 'trained negotiator from another agency' had entered the bus in the hope of bringing a peaceful end to the situation. Then came the climax of the story as the door of the coach opened and the girl – asleep or unconscious – was carried into the light in the arms of her rescuer. The next picture was a close-up of the man's face. His face was tense and streaked with sweat and dirt, or even blood. But still he was unmistakable. It was Felix. It was her husband.

Abbie screamed, 'FELIX.'

He pulled the cover back and sat up straight. 'What's happening?'

'I've just seen you on the telly.'

'Eh?'

'In a . . . coming out of a coach.'

'Huh?'

'With a girl in your arms. What's going on?'

Felix rubbed his eyes and looked at the television in the corner of the room, but the news had moved on to a different story, about speedway.

'Oh, that,' he said.

'What do you mean, "Oh, that"?' Abbie demanded. 'What's going on? FELIX?'

'It was Ruby Moffat. But she's OK.'

He could feel tiredness like a weight around his neck, pulling his head back to the pillow. The muscles in his face ached with weariness. Even breathing felt like a struggle, and when he spoke it was with a supreme effort and a miracle if what he said made any sense.

'That's all,' he muttered.

'But someone was killed. Felix, why didn't you tell me?'

'I'd been to have my ears syringed. I was tired.'

Abbie punched the remote control with her thumb, silencing the television. She kicked the duvet away with her legs and pulled the cord that hung from the ceiling. Brightness filled the room, stinging Felix at the back of his eyes. She wanted to talk. No, it was worse than that. She wanted Felix to talk. The whole story. From beginning to end. And when she said she wanted an explanation, she wasn't talking about why an armed man had taken a young girl hostage on a beaten-up coach. She was talking about the man she was married to. She was asking how the man lying next to her in bed could witness a fatal shooting but forget to mention it because earlier in the day he'd been through the trauma of having a wax build-up sluiced from his ears. She was flabbergasted. Absolutely bemused. She wanted a complete and utter analysis of everything, and she wanted it right here, right now. But through Felix's exhaustion came a sudden irritation. And from that irritation came an unusual surge of impatience, bordering on courage, bordering on strength. He said, 'Abbie, I'm fucked.'

She looked shocked, and mildly offended.

Then, with a forced, tuneless voice, he said, 'We can talk about this in the morning. Or if you'd prefer, you can wait until I'm fast asleep, when no doubt I'll tell you everything you want to hear. But if I don't close my eyes in five seconds, I'm going to pass out. So please, I'm really sorry, but if you don't mind . . .'

He didn't remember the light going out, but when he woke, no more than an hour later, it was pitch black. The sheet beneath him was sodden with sweat. Abbie was holding on to him tightly, with her arms around his shoulders and one of her legs twisted around his.

'You're shaking,' she whispered to him through the dark.

19

PC Lily beckoned Felix to duck beneath the counter at the front desk and follow her through the police station to an empty office at the back. The walls of the room were little more than partitions and screens, decorated with photographs and maps from a murder case that had made the headlines a couple of years ago.

'Ever catch anyone for that?' Felix asked.

'No.'

PC Nottingham poked his head around the door. 'Oh, aye. This is very cosy.'

'Why don't you do something useful and make us a brew?'

'Yeah, right, like I'm the tea boy all of a sudden.'

'Go on, Notts. And you can help yourself to one of my chocolate biscuits.'

He walked away, making a comment to the three or four other policemen sitting at their desks in the main office, of which 'debriefing' was the only audible word. A round of laughter followed.

'So how is she?'

Felix nodded. 'She'll be fine. She's back at home, and we've got lots of help lined up for her. When she's ready.'

'Counselling?'

'That kind of thing.'

'From you?'

'No. It'll be a woman. Anyhow, I've been given some time off. Compassionate leave. I'd just called at the office to tidy up some loose ends and got your message . . .'

'You were very brave.'

'I was very scared. And very stupid.'

'Well, for what it's worth you're a bit of a hero with the lads in there. They'd never say so, of course. They've even got a superhero nickname for you.'

'Go on.'

'Duffel Man.'

'Very good,' said Felix, and narrowly avoided twiddling one of the wooden toggles on his coat.

'But I'm going to call you the Corduroy Kid.'

'That's . . . very good as well.'

'Anyways,' she said.

'Hmm.'

From somewhere further away Felix could hear prisoners shouting in the holding cells, and the very occasional reply of the duty officer. Then another voice rang out in the distance, a voice that Felix thought he recognized. He ignored it, but a moment later heard it again, echoing around the bare-brick walls of a cell. 'Boss, I need a piss. Come on, boss, I'm fucking busting.'

It caused Felix to hold his breath and listen, because the last time he had heard that particular accent he was cowering in the stairwell of the Big Blue One, just seconds before Jimmy Spotland was shot dead.

'Isn't that . . .'

'Teddy Moffat.'

'Because of the air rifle?'

'Yes, technically speaking, but we're following up some other lines of inquiry.'

'Such as?'

PC Nottingham came in with two big mugs of coffee, but he didn't speak because his mouth was jammed with a whole chocolate biscuit, causing his bottom lip to stick out in a semicircle in front of his face. He winked and closed the door behind him.

'Did you ever go in Spotland's garage?' said PC Lily.

'I did, actually.'

'A right little Aladdin's cave. Anyhow, in and among the

knock-off tellies and DVDs we found a few dozen bags of powdered chalk.'

'I thought it was plaster.'

'He'd been supplying the Moffats with their kit. The stuff was everywhere.'

'Including Ruby's underwear.'

'I'm afraid so. But it seems like the odd packet of white powder that made its way into the Moffat house was a higher-calibre substance altogether. We've had our eye on Teddy Moffat for a while. We knew he was dealing but we didn't know where he was getting it from. He's not told us much but we think him and Spotland fell out over a batch that went missing. All that shouting and bawling on the roof of the bookie's – it wasn't just about Ruby. It was about cocaine as well. And money.'

'But the rest of the family weren't involved?'

'We don't think so. Except poor Ruby. Spotland told her that her brother was buying drugs and he'd have him sent to prison unless she came to visit him in his . . .'

'Web?'

'Web. Precisely.'

Felix nodded, satisfied with his choice of word.

Then she said, 'They had a job pulling that thing out of his tongue, once he'd stiffened up. It's sitting in a pot on my desk – exhibit A. Do you want a look?'

'No. I can . . . still see it pretty clearly,' said Felix. 'But thanks for the offer.'

PC Lily folded her arms across her chest and leaned back in her chair.

'Any time.'

It was Friday. Late afternoon. The end of one hell of a week – and it wasn't over yet. From the secure car park at the rear of the police station, Felix rattled over the metal plates beneath the exit barrier and turned left on to the dual carriageway. Almost instantly he was part of a traffic jam that extended into the distance, and twenty

minutes later he was still crawling along in first towards the temporary traffic lights – a big metal sign with the word 'Stop' written
against a red background. Felix yanked on the handbrake and was
fiddling with the cassette player when there was a tap on the
window. It was the traffic light operator, one of the Moffat boys.
He grinned and gave Felix the thumbs-up. Felix lifted his hand to
acknowledge the compliment, and saw the boy, Gerry was it, or
maybe Connor, speaking into a walkie-talkie in his fist, radioing
ahead. After the stream of traffic had passed in the other direction,
the sign was swivelled around and Felix made his way through the
red and white cones across a section of scarified tarmac and along
the opposite carriageway. The contraflow extended as far as the
roundabout at the far end, but halfway along Felix was confronted
with an apparition almost biblical in appearance. An old man with
wild grey hair stood in the middle of the road, prophet-like in the
fading light of the evening, demanding with the palm of his hand
that Felix should halt. In his other hand he carried fire. As he
approached the vehicle, Felix recognized the mystical figure as Mr
Moffat senior, his face illuminated by a flaming gas jet that only
moments ago had looked like a burning staff. He didn't speak. But
when Felix wound the window down the old man reached into the
car and took him by the hand. It wasn't a handshake as such,
because there was no movement involved, just a prolonged and
meaningful grip, accompanied by a long, hard stare and a slight
nod of the head.

'How are things?' Felix asked.

He nodded again.

'Ruby OK? Good. That's good.'

A car in the queue behind sounded its horn, which caused a
wave of honking from other cars further back in the line. Mr
Moffat's eyes were not deflected and his grasp of Felix's hand didn't
soften.

'I'm sorry about Teddy.'

He nodded again.

'And listen. It's none of my business, but if there's anything at the house . . . anything you don't recognize . . . I'd get rid of it if I were you. For Teddy's sake.'

There was yet another nod of the head but with it came a smile. Mr Moffat stepped back from the car and held the fire-torch out towards the centre of the road. Felix didn't know what the gesture meant at first, but as he followed the direction of Mr Moffat's outstretched hand, he suddenly got the message. Beyond him, a brilliant white line extended unbroken from where he stood to some vanishing point in the dark. Wet and freshly painted, the line shone and glimmered in the reflection of headlights and the shimmer of late, wintry sun. And its whiteness had a quality that was quite brilliant, luminous almost, the product no doubt of some very rare and very expensive . . . stuff. Now it was Felix's turn to nod, and Mr Moffat's turn to laugh. Then, with the sound of car horns growing longer and more frequent, he turned away and waved Felix on. At the far end of the roadworks, two more of the Moffat clan had dipped long, bitumen-coated sticks into a brazier. They raised them, making a gateway of fire through which the honoured stranger, the saviour of their sister, must pass.

Still buzzing with pride, Felix turned into the car park of Prospect House and made his way up the back steps. The door was bolted from the inside, which meant the office was empty. Everyone had gone home and the place was locked up for the weekend. He skipped back down, went in at the front door and jogged up the main staircase. As soon as the door was unlocked he made straight for the reception hatch, intending to slide his hand through the glass shutter and punch the code into the keypad. But the usual stream of high-pitched beeping never came. The alarm hadn't been set. And even though it wasn't his job to secure the premises at the end of the working week, Felix felt another wave of self-importance. One day without him and the whole operation started to creak. He tutted loudly, then vaulted over the desk and made his way inside. It was properly dark by now, and although the glow of street-lamps outside would not normally have been enough to guide him along the corridor, they were enhanced by a row of fairy lights on the huge crane standing in the Strawberry Field, its arm running parallel to the corridor. Decorated for Christmas, it looked like a sign of peace. But in the weeks to come it would swing into action, hoisting machinery and materials on to the town's last few acres of common ground. The people had lost. The developers had won. Soon, the view from the office would be the roof of a supermarket. A superstore. The Strawberry Field Shopping Centre. Whatever. There would be no more grass or mud. No more talk of ancient grazing rights, the Domesday Book and rare butterflies. No more bulls.

Reaching his office, he opened the door with a speedy, two-handed manoeuvre, pushing down on the handle with his left and reaching for the light switch with his right. His entrance was met with a terrifying shriek. It came from somewhere in front of him, on the floor, and even though his first reaction was to turn and scarper, his momentum carried him into the room and almost on top of the two half-naked bodies scurrying for the safety of their clothes. Even under the instant glare of the bare bulb it took several seconds of standing and staring before Felix could comprehend what was going on. Several long, illuminating seconds. By which time, Felix had seen enough. Or rather he had seen too much.

'I'm just going to the loo,' he said.

He turned, closed the door and, as an afterthought, switched off the light. In the toilets he washed his hands until they were pink, then held them under the dryer until every last drop of moisture had vaporized. But that only took two minutes. In the staffroom he washed a bowlful of dirty cups, wiped them with the tea towel and put them in the cupboard. He then rearranged the newspapers and magazines on the coffee table according to publication date, then boiled the kettle and made a drink from the only available ingredient – Bovril. A total of seven and three-quarter minutes had now passed since his untimely entrance. Judging this to be an appropriate interval, and armed with his steaming mug of hot beef drink, he set off in the direction of his office again, clearing his throat dramatically before opening the door. The window had been opened. It was quite cold. Both people were now fully dressed. The man, Neville, sat behind the desk, with his hand covering his mouth and his eyes. The woman, Mo, sat on the chair in front of the desk with her legs crossed and her arms folded. She looked at the floor.

'Sorry,' they said in unison, which produced a strange, three-way harmony of voices, given that at exactly the same moment Felix had chosen to say exactly the same word. He sipped at his drink. The heat of it bit into his mouth. The taste offended his tongue.

'I . . . we thought you were on leave,' said Neville, with a further note of apology in his voice.

'I've just come in to collect a few things.'

He turned to the set of filing cabinets and bundled various papers, books and other oddments into a bag. He had to squeeze past Neville to retrieve his diary from the top drawer of his desk.

'Right, then,' said Felix. He waited for a moment, before turning and going out through the door.

Neville caught up with him in the corridor and walked him down the stairs.

'I'm really sorry, Felix. That shouldn't have happened.'

'Not a problem.'

'You won't say anything, will you?'

'No.'

'It's not allowed. We'd get relocated, and, you know, it's going really well.'

'I thought you hated each other.'

'We did. Then all of a sudden we didn't. But we kept all the aggro going as a kind of cover. Do you think it worked?'

'Fooled me.'

They were on the third floor by now. Neville took hold of Felix by the elbow and brought him to a halt. 'Guess you've had a bit of a funny old week. Seeing that Spotland guy getting popped and then . . . this.'

They stood next to each other, leaning on the banister rail and looking down the stairwell for a minute or so.

'It's fine,' said Felix eventually. Then he smiled. 'I'm happy for you.'

Neville smiled in return. 'Thanks, mate, thanks,' and he touched Felix on the elbow again, more gently this time, as an act of gratitude and a sign of understanding.

Felix scratched his head. 'But why here? You've both got homes to go to, and it's not like you're married or anything. Are you?'

'Mo shares a flat with an ex-boyfriend. Bit complicated. And I've got my dad with me at the moment. Angina. All that wheezing and spluttering, kind of takes the romance out of it.'

'I see.'

'We've been going to the Travelodge at the motorway exit, but it's fifty quid a throw.'

'That's reasonable, isn't it? For a night?'

'It's not bad, but it doesn't include breakfast.'

'Oh.'

'So this was the last resort. I mean, we're not kinky. We haven't been doing it on the photocopier or anything like that.'

In the lobby on the ground floor Neville held open the door as Felix buttoned his coat against the cold wind outside. Before he went out he said, 'Will you tell Mo . . .'

'What?'

'That I didn't see anything.'

'What?'

'Will you tell her?'

Neville chuckled. 'You know what you are, don't you, Felix?'

'What am I?'

'You're a sweetheart.'

From the edge of the moor the giant crane on the Strawberry Field looked like a slightly lopsided cross. It was interesting that the town's one and only Christmas decoration should be a company-owned, crudely lit mechanical device, poised to obliterate the last remaining patch of nature. But maybe there was a sort of justice involved. Last year the council had erected a tree in the precinct, a towering, swaying Norway spruce imported at great expense and strung with coloured bulbs. In the days that followed, the local paper carried dozens of letters from disgusted citizens, comparing the cost of the tree with scanning machines and other much needed items of hospital equipment. Then all the bulbs were stolen, followed by most of the lower branches and finally the whole tree. That Christmas, every living room on the Lakeland Estate glowed with a different colour, and the air in that part of town was mentholated with the smoke of pine needles and unseasoned wood. Or so it was said.

20

Being in the house with nothing to do was hard work. It reminded Felix of the days he had feigned illness to avoid going to school, those mornings when he'd simulated some well-judged ailment – one that did not require the attendance of a doctor but could still secure a day at home. A bout of vomiting noises behind the bathroom door usually did the trick, or something undetectable like a stomach cramp or headache. But by lunchtime a true sickness had set in – boredom. It was often compounded by hunger, given that his mother's reaction to most forms of ill-health was to restrict the patient to hot water, or at the very most diluted chicken soup. As a medicine it worked, because by next morning Felix was invariably 'cured' and ready to face the education system once again.

Bernard had insisted that Felix should not return until after New Year at the very earliest. On Wednesday he sat down with his lunch and for the first time in his life watched daytime telly. It was astonishing. Celebrities he'd never heard of making three-course meals with whatever they'd found at the bottom of their fridge. Neighbours decorating each other's houses with loud colours and chipboard. Quiz shows. Antiques. It made Felix realize why a great many of his clients were in trouble with the law. Faced with so much artificiality eight hours a day, wouldn't even the mildest person end up throttling someone, just for an honest reaction? Faced with so much cheerful banality five days of the week, crime was the only credible alternative. Felix wasn't a client or a criminal, though. He was a practical man. He turned the television off manually by removing the plug from the socket and went upstairs

to shelve the paperback novels in the spare bedroom in alphabetical
order. It took two hours. That done, he spooled through the dozen
or so camcorder tapes lying in a heap on the windowsill, making
notes as he went along, arranging them chronologically, writing
the year on the spine of the case and a brief description of its subject
on the inside flap. Through the viewfinder he watched an excited
group of parents and children lining the playground of Sconford
and Tilden School, Norfolk, waiting for the festivities to begin.
Inside the building, former May Queens of different ages chatted
nervously with each other among the cocktail sausages and cheese
straws, ready for the parade.

'Didn't you put that chicken in? Felix?'

Abbie was standing in the hall in her coat, having returned from
work expecting to be met by the smell of chicken casserole in white
wine sauce and new potatoes.

'Come and look at this,' he shouted in reply. Still in her coat, she
followed his voice upstairs to the back bedroom, dragged an old
wicker chair next to him and sat down.

He leaned over and kissed her on her cheek. 'Hi.'

The cold had come in with her, trapped in the folds of her
clothing, clinging to her hair.

'Hi. What?'

'Look.'

He set the tape running through the computer.

'Oh, God, I'd forgotten you'd filmed this. How funny.'

She watched the children streaming through the school doors
and chuckled at their homemade spacesuits and rockets. And she
spoke the name of the first two May Queens as they appeared on
the screen, and smiled and blushed as she heard Mr Fellows, the
headmaster, announcing her own name, and watched him peck her
on the cheek before guiding her to her seat on the podium. Then
she roared with laughter as the other women and girls entered
the parade, some filmed in sepia tone, some in slow motion,
black-and-white, split-screen, soft-focus and so on. It only lasted

five or six minutes, because Felix had edited out all the crap bits, but judging by Abbie's face it was a success.

'I love it,' she said. 'Come on, let's eat. We can watch it again later.'

'Actually that isn't what I wanted to show you,' he said.

Rewinding the tape, he paused on a shot of little Eliza Hardison, this year's May Queen, taking her seat on the throne. He moved the film on, frame by frame, freezing the shot as Eliza lifted the posy of flowers in her right hand and turned her face to the left. Then he reached for a photograph in a silver frame – the one he'd given Abbie for her birthday – and propped it up next to the screen. Taken thirty years ago, it captured her on exactly the same throne, in an almost identical position – flowers held aloft in the right hand, head turned slightly to the left.

'What do you think?' he said expectantly.

'Amazing,' said Abbie. 'It's the same chair, the same sash, even the same tiara. You'd think they could have run to a new tiara. Cheapskates.'

'No, I'm not talking about all that regalia. Look.'

With the mouse, he highlighted part of the image – Eliza's face – and enlarged it. Felix lifted the photograph of Abbie and held it next to the screen, pointing at one face, then the other.

'Don't you see?'

'What?'

'The likeness.'

Abbie's eyes moved from left to right, from the photograph of herself age ten to the image of Eliza Hardison, then right to left, then back again. 'Do you think so?'

'You're the spitting image. Look at the bridge of the nose. And that curve under the lip. She's even got the same teeth.'

Felix traced the profile of the two girls with his finger, emphasizing his point. To him it was so obvious. It was literally staring her in the face. After a while she shook her head and stood up. 'Let's get some food. I'm starving.'

They ordered a takeaway and ate in front of the TV. It was too late to think about going out, so Felix went into the kitchen and found a bottle of red wine at the back of the cupboard, something unheard of and unpronounceable that Jed and Maxine had brought round about a year ago during the great Trivial Pursuits wars. It smelt musty but tasted OK, besides which there was no other alcohol in the house apart from a three-pack of novelty ales (another donation from next door) and a bottle of advocaat with a yellow crust around the cap. Abbie had gone upstairs, for a shower maybe, but after half an hour still hadn't returned. When Felix found her, she was in the back bedroom, staring at the screen.

'Do you see it now?' he asked her.

'So what are you suggesting?'

Felix sat down beside her and pushed a glass of wine into her hand.

'A family connection?'

'But she's got blonde hair. And blue eyes.'

'She's also got that funny smile. The thing you do with your lip when someone takes your picture.'

'What funny thing?'

'That,' said Felix, picking up the photograph and outlining the tight wrinkles of skin around the corner of her mouth. 'That,' he said again, turning to the screen and pointing out an identical sneer to the same side of Eliza Hardison's lips.

'It's coincidence.'

Felix drained the wine and stared at the trail of crimson dregs on the inside of the glass. Then, tasting the fumes at the back of his throat and imagining the boozy, red grapes entering his bloodstream, he said, 'Why don't we give them a call?'

'What? Who?'

'That family. The Harmisons.'

'Hardisons.'

'Yes. Them.'

'Don't be stupid.'

'Why not?'

'You're drunk.'

'Not much.'

'And we don't have the number.'

'It's on a sheet in the drawer. Everyone at the parade wrote down their name and address.'

He felt a powerful physical sensation, a sort of adrenalin rush. Felix was one of life's helpers. That was his nature. If Abbie wanted a baby, he assisted in every way possible. If she wanted to find her family, he gave her his time and his experience. He applied for documents, shovelled earth from graves, drove to the East Midlands, held her hand – that kind of thing. But now he was taking the lead. *Pushing the envelope* – was that the phrase? Here he was, standing in front of her with an idea – *a blue-sky idea* – that was all his own. Admittedly it was a crazy theory, with odds of hundreds of thousands to one, and it involved phoning a complete stranger 200 miles away at ten o'clock on a Friday night. But it was hope. And, like all hope, it required trust.

'I don't know. All right.'

Felix left her in the back bedroom. He went downstairs to use the telephone, via the bottle of wine. He made the call.

She would have heard him upstairs, the humming of his voice, but not the words themselves – she wouldn't know what had been said. And she would have guessed from the length of time he was gone – a good five minutes – that a conversation had taken place, something more than a polite hello and a courteous goodbye. But not the meaning. The significance. The weight and worth of every turn of phrase. He was back upstairs now, standing behind her as she peered into the screen.

'Who did you speak to?'

'Eliza's mum.'

'What did she say?'

'She said she's been expecting a call. She said she was surprised it had taken you so long.'

Felix was locking up when he saw Jed in the back garden, throwing a ball for Smutty, drinking from a can and smoking a roll-up. The episode with the sperm had made things difficult, but now it was time to have a beer and a joke over the garden fence. Leave all that nonsense behind. He turned the key and flicked the switch for the outside light. There was a fizz and a bang. The bulb popped, and in the cubbyhole under the stairs the tripswitch blew with a clean, hard crack. Like a gun. Felix swivelled on his heels and dived to the floor, then rolled away from the glass-panelled door and behind the barricade of the breakfast bar. He curled in a tight ball, like a baby. And he raised his open hand towards the noise, as if the palm of a hand could parry a bullet from its target. As if the flesh and bones of the hand could catch a bullet in mid-flight, pull it out of the air, save a life. After a minute or so staring at the collection of lost pens, old coins, dehydrated peas and balls of fluff under the fridge, he stood up, dusted himself down, helped himself to a bottle of Becks and went outside to see his friend.

21

As they pulled up on the grass verge in front of the house, a hand waved from the kitchen window, then a moment later Mrs Hardison opened the door and waited for Abbie and Felix as they made their way up the garden path, which was laid with crazy paving and lined at each side with old bricks. Mrs Hardison had been baking. With her fingers coated with cake mix, she raised her arms to avoid shaking hands, and they pushed past her into the house. It was a tight squeeze. She was massively pregnant and the cooking apron tied around her middle only accentuated her bump.

The teapot was covered in a hand-knitted tea cosy. A stove burned quietly in the corner. It was a scene of apparent domestic bliss, although Felix was no more than a couple of strides into the room when he detected a smell that didn't quite tally with the aroma of freshly baked pastry. It came from a cigarette balanced on the edge of the wooden chopping board. Abbie noticed it too, and Felix watched as her eyes flitted from the cigarette itself towards the ashtray on the dresser containing at least half a dozen stubs. Abbie had once said that she felt genuine indignation when she drove past those parking bays at the supermarket reserved for mothers with babies. Wasn't it enough that they already had children – what other privileges could they possibly need? If she felt as strongly as that about car-parking, thought Felix, what must she feel about women who jeopardize the miracle of procreation with nicotine poisoning?

'Well, rest your arses,' said Mrs Hardison.

'Mum!' tutted Eliza, in mock disapproval.

'Er, when is it due?' asked Abbie.

'Last week. Look like I'm going to pop, don't I?'

'You must be exhausted.'

'That one was early. Little ferret. Couldn't wait, could you?' she said, tipping her head in the direction of Eliza, who was sitting at the table grating a lemon. Eliza smirked in agreement. Mrs Hardison lifted the cigarette to her lips and drew the smoke into her throat.

'But this one isn't in a hurry.'

She sat down on a stool and straightened her back, kneading her spine with her fingers and leaving sticky handprints on her woolly cardigan. Her hair was light, like a faded version of her daughter's, and she had a redness in her cheeks, maybe from the heat in the room, or maybe from carrying the weight of her unborn child. Or maybe from smoking while pregnant.

'How about a drink?'

'Let me,' said Abbie. As Mrs Hardison untied her apron and wiped her hands on a cloth, Abbie filled the kettle from the tap and took down three mugs hanging from hooks over the fireplace.

'I was thinking of something a bit stronger actually,' said Mrs Hardison.

'Oh,' said Abbie. 'Are you sure?'

'There's a Guinness in the fridge. Shouldn't really, but you've got to keep your strength up.'

Felix looked for Abbie's disapproval, but with her back to him she dutifully collected the can and cracked the ring pull. Mrs Hardison pointed to a pint glass on the sink, empty apart from a thin layer of dark liquid at the bottom and streaked with white froth. Abbie poured the drink and carried it to the table. Felix perched on the arm of a large, threadbare chair next to the stove so as not to disturb the big, mean-looking tomcat asleep on the cushion.

'Liza, why don't you run up to the shop? I need a packet of raisins and fetch me twenty Benson while you're at it.'

'Aw, Mum.'

'Go on. There's money in my purse. And you can get something for yourself.'

Through the window Felix followed the bobbing blue hood of Eliza's winter coat as she made her way down the garden path and around the corner. The kitchen became quiet, except for the long, circular breathing of the gas burners in the stove. The two women sat either side of the table. When the kettle boiled Abbie made tea for herself and Felix, and set her cup down on a coaster next to the glass of black beer.

'It's good of you to see me.'

Mrs Hardison nodded. The cat stood up on the chair, stretched its legs and arched its spine, then snuggled back into position on the cushion and closed its eyes.

'It was Felix who spotted the resemblance. I hadn't noticed myself.'

'Sometimes takes an outsider to see these things.'

There was quietness again, before both of them tried to speak at the same time.

'Go on.'

'No, it's OK. You first.'

'What were you going to say?'

Their words died out, prompting Felix to make a comment. 'Abbie's been looking for her family, but we had some bad news this summer. We found her mother's grave. And that was the end of the trail really, until I called you.'

Mrs Hardison said, 'Why don't I tell you everything I know? Save a lot of fannying around.'

Abbie looked taken aback but nodded gratefully.

Mrs Hardison took a gulp of beer. 'Your mother – Maria, wasn't it? – she came here to the village from Spain. She met your father at a dance. She got pregnant, which was a scandal in those days. *Big* scandal. But this couple in the village – the Lawrences, was it? – they wanted a child. Wanted one badly. So they took you on. Are they still alive?'

'They moved to the coast. They're fine.'

'And Maria died, didn't she?'

'In '88. How do you know all this?'

Mrs Hardison sucked at the cigarette. 'Your father told me.'

'My father . . . and Eliza's father . . .'

'Same man.'

'So Eliza is . . .'

'Your half-sister. Correct.'

Abbie lifted the inside of her index finger to her face to blot the tiny droplet of brine forming on the rim of her eye.

'I'm really sorry. I've come crashing in here. I don't mean to cause trouble.'

Mrs Hardison waved her hand in the air, indicating that it wasn't a problem. Specks of ash floated down towards the stone floor. Abbie sniffed back the tears. 'You see, your little girl, she's the first person . . . the only relative I've ever seen . . . the only one I've got.'

Mrs Hardison laughed. In fact it was less of a laugh and more of a cackle.

'Except your father.'

Abbie looked up from under her hair. 'You mean he's still alive?'

'Alive?' She cackled again, louder this time, and ran her hands over the thin wool of her cardigan that was stretched to the point of transparency across the globe of her stomach. 'I'll say he bloody well is.'

Abbie's jaw opened to full stretch. 'Never.'

'There might be snow on the roof but there's fire in the front room. Know what I'm saying?'

'But he must be . . .'

'Sixty-five.'

'Oh, my God.'

Then they both cackled, a raw, exultant noise that caused both Felix and the ginger tom to turn their heads.

'Does he . . . know about me?' she asked, swallowing the last part of the sentence so the final word was just a shape made by her mouth.

'Oh, for sure.'

Abbie was nudging forward with each question. 'Does he want to meet me?'

Mrs Hardison grinned, an enormous grin which gave a momentary impression of smugness. She took another slurp of the Guinness and licked the froth from her top lip. 'I'm sure he'd love to see you again.'

'He saw me when I was a baby, did he?'

'He saw you seven months ago.'

'What?'

'Gave you a little peck, right there,' she said, poking her finger into the soft flesh of Abbie's face.

Felix was now convinced that Mrs Hardison was enjoying her part in the proceedings, and rather than holding back the truth to spare Abbie any sudden shock was actually cranking up the drama. And by her reaction, Abbie was enjoying it too. She put her own finger to the dimple in her cheek. In fact it was more than enjoyment – she was captivated. Enthralled. She gazed back at the woman in front of her, the woman whose every utterance was a step closer to home.

'Let's say he kept an eye on you. Just like he kept an eye on Eliza.'

Now she was hosting a guessing game. Abbie gazed and gazed. Mrs Hardison fed her the next clue.

'And if a father can't make his own little girls Queen of the May, then who can?'

Abbie's mouth began to form a word, but even if she was on the very brink of saying her father's name, she was beaten to it by her husband. Her husband who had been replaying the last seven months of Abbie's life through his mind, and at that very moment had reached the scene when the man in question bent forward and put his lips against Abbie's cheek. A tall man of retirement age. In a playground. Kissing his very own, long-lost Queen of the May. Felix knew the answer.

'THE HEADMASTER!' he blurted out. 'Mr . . . what's-his-name.'

The cat shot from the cushion and out through the cat flap, chased by the clattering metal tankard that Felix had head-butted from its hook.

'Mr Fellows,' said Abbie, speaking his name on her breath. 'Mr Fellows?'

Mrs Hardison's head moved up and down in agreement and satisfaction. 'William,' she said. Then, in a puff of smoke, 'Bill.'

They had more things to say to each other. Leaving them to it, Felix went outside with the kettle to top up the water in the windscreen-washer. Eliza was suddenly next to him, peering into the engine. 'Are they talking?'

'Yes.'

'Can I check the oil for you?'

'It's filthy. You might get your coat dirty.'

Eliza put the shopping bag on the floor, rolled up her sleeve and drew out the long, dirty oil gauge, until it dithered in front of her face. She squinted at the half-inch of smoky, slow liquid on the end and pushed it under Felix's nose. 'It's fine,' she told him, before inserting it back in the hole.

'Who told you about cars?'

'My dad.'

'William?'

'People don't know he's my dad but they do really.'

'Where does he live?'

'Over there,' she said, pointing in no particular direction.

'And does your mum see a lot of him?'

Eliza shrugged her shoulders. 'Not really. They're just shagging each other.'

Felix lowered the bonnet, then pushed down hard with both hands to snap it closed. To wash off the grease he plunged his hands into a water butt under the sawn-off fall-pipe at the corner of the greenhouse. A rainbow-coloured film spread across the surface.

'Is she my sister?'

'Who, Abbie?'

'Her in there.'

'Half-sister.'

'Mum's having a boy. You could see his willie on the scan.'

'It'll be nice to have a brother, won't it?'

'Mum says he was an accident. She was going to have an extermination, but Bill talked her out of it. I was listening through the floor.'

Eliza showed Felix around the garden and they made a lap of the house before going back inside. The two women were still hunched over the table, Abbie with a handful of tissues, Mrs Hardison with a cigarette between her fingers. Another one. She got slowly to her feet and waddled towards a large mixing bowl on the worktop.

'Got any kids yourself?' she asked Abbie.

Abbie looked at her feet. 'No. We're still trying, though. Aren't we, Felix?'

From over in the corner Felix nodded his agreement.

Mrs Hardison said, 'We've got a superstition down here about Christmas cake. It's good luck if everyone has a stir.'

From the drawer next to the sink she pulled out a wooden spoon and offered it to Abbie. 'Everyone in the family. That's what I mean.'

For Abbie it was a triumph. A connection had been made. A transaction had taken place. A lifeline had been offered and she had taken hold of it without hesitation. And for one, photographic moment, Mrs Hardison and her daughter and Abbie were joined together in one common task, their six hands interlocked around the one wooden spoon.

For Felix, though, over by the stove, witnessing the spectacle, there came a second wave of discomfort. Like a mild nausea. Something like labyrinthitis. He'd felt it earlier in the conversation, with Mrs Hardison's remark about how it takes 'an outsider' to recognize these things. And now he felt it again, but stronger this time, a kind of lurch in his senses. 'Everyone in the family,' she had said. This new family, she meant, the one forming in front of his eyes, these people connected by genes and DNA and complex physical bonds. There they were, huddled around the mixing bowl, celebrating their coming together, commemorating their new kinship. 'An outsider,' was how she put it. 'Everyone in the family,' was what she had said.

So where did that leave him?

The Father

'I loved Maria and I thought she loved me.'

His hat hangs on a hook behind the door. The hat of an older man. Velvet. Banded. Black. On another hook behind the same door hangs the hat of a younger woman. Lilac. Stylish. It was left several months ago on a platform after a May Day parade. The older man had lifted it. Covered his face. Inhaled air from the dark, scented hollow. He had taken it home. Hung it next to his.

'I still take flowers to the grave.'

His fingers are slender and scrubbed clean. Teacher's hands. They have turned pages, explained ideas in the air. Now they handle a china cup and a jug of milk. He wears no rings. His watch is analogue, everyday, worn with a crumbling leather strap. The skin on the back of his hands is tight, stretched, and a patch that runs from the underside of his thumb to the outside of his wrist is skewbald with freckles or liver spots. Or an old burn. Or a birthmark. His white cuffs shoot now and again below the sleeve of his dark-blue jacket. His blue tie trails in the plate of biscuits as he leans to pour the tea. He hooks it aside.

'But she loved God. She was ashamed. She said we had sinned.'

When he sits he crosses his legs, so a band of pale flesh shows above a hoop of black, elasticated sock. He wears brown suede shoes laced with a double knot. Comfortable. Old. Suede should never be polished or scrubbed, only brushed or sponged down with a damp cloth.

'For me to have kept you . . . a single man . . . a teacher . . . in those days . . .'

The room is a bachelor's room of mementoes and souvenirs. The mantelpiece carries trophies and cups for cricket and golf. Elsewhere, a pair of book ends. A cut-glass paperweight. An ornate cigar box. An *art-deco reading lamp. A gallon whisky bottle full of copper coins. Nothing seems bought – only given or won. There is no organizing principle or overriding sense of style – just the random accumulation of material goods over time. There is evidence of a companion – hairs on the carpet, a bowl of water and a rubber bone. Man's best friend.*

'The Lawrences were desperate for a child. It meant I could watch over you. It seemed perfect. At the time.'

The woman has heard him speak on many occasions. Years ago. In assembly, reading the notices, calling out the names of star pupils or troublesome kids. In front of the blackboard inscribing letters and numbers, turning to ask a question, choosing the girl with her hand stretched high in the air, the girl with the right answer and the long black hair. At sports day, his confident announcements compressed and amplified through the PA system, his orders and instructions echoing around the playground, rippling out across the football field and the park. And singing once, stood next to her at the carol concert in the school hall, the only man on stage, his true bass voice bringing home the third and emphatic, 'Oh, come let us adore him,' after the boys and girls had floated their own weightless syllables into the ether. Never words like these, though. She came here for facts and detail – she didn't expect to hear feelings and thoughts. She came for a description of the past. A lesson in history. But when he looks away, towards the window and the clear, winter sky, and says, 'Forgive me,' it is all about the here and now, the present moment, and whatever she replies will determine not just the minutes or hours that lie immediately ahead but the days and years beyond. And the hazy blueness he gazes towards, waiting for her answer, isn't a place she expected to go. She can't meet him there yet. Which is why she doesn't answer or speak.

The LPs in the cabinet look like classical or jazz. The record player on the sideboard has a wicker handle and beige fabric cover. An umbrella is propped against the radiator. A fishing rod stands in a wellington boot. Through the kitchen door, a rusty bike leans against a whitewashed wall gouged and grazed by pedals and brakes and handlebar grips. The archaeology of habit and routine. Maybe tomorrow she can join him in the future, but not yet. Which is why she does not reach out, touch him on the shoulder, close her hand around his wrist when he pushes his fingers beneath his glasses and holds them there against his eyes.

Her husband is waiting in the car. Before she leaves he hands her a gift. Something he prepared. Something he wants her to have. She opens it on her knee. Unwraps the paper. Unties the string. Inside, upside-down, is a wooden frame. A photograph frame. She turns it around. It is a face she has never seen before. A woman with long, dark hair, brushed until it shines. She is wearing a pretty lace blouse. She is wearing eyeshadow, lipstick and a small silver cross around her neck. She is nineteen. Twenty, perhaps. She stares unblinkingly into the lens. Abbie stares back. Meets her eyes. She is seeing her mother for the first time. A stranger, half her own age, gazing at her across the years.

IN THE END

22

When the doorbell went, Felix had just prised the top from a bottle of Waggledance. The bubbles rushed up and over the lip of the glass as he poured and he had to slide the Christmas edition of the *Radio Times* underneath to stop the sticky liquid marking the coffee table. Abbie was at the door for half an hour, maybe more. After a while, Felix could feel the cold air from outside seeping into the living room. The flames of the gas fire burned thin and blue. He pulled a settee cushion over his lap and put his feet on the windowsill above the radiator. On the telly, the world's strongest man was pulling a caravan along a length of running track with his bare hands. He thought of his parents. That holiday in Windermere. Even though it was against the law, his father had allowed him to travel to Cumbria in the caravan itself, on the proviso that he kept out of sight and didn't use the toilet. They'd chatted to each other via a toy walkie-talkie, until Felix had grown tired and clambered up into the narrow bed in the bulkhead. It was the best journey ever, that's how he remembered it. The greatest form of travel. There he was in something like a house with its rooms and doors, its tables and chairs, its photographs on the wall, its fixed dimensions, its measured and contained space, its undisturbed air. Something like a home. Yet outside, through the orange Perspex skylight, the world went by. Pylons, tree tops, the underside of bridges, cloud formations. Then empty sky, then the upper reaches of pine forests, then bare hills and escarpments and ridges, then rocky peaks and then the steep-sided, snow-topped mountains.

The back door closed. When a car started up in the yard outside,

Felix hooked back the curtain with his toe and saw Eliza Hardison waving from the passenger seat, and her mother at the wheel, steering away from the house. Abbie came into the room.

'Why didn't you invite them in?'

'They couldn't stop,' she said. 'They were dropping off a present.'

'They could have said hello. Norfolk's a long way to drive and not stop for a cuppa.'

'Felix, look.'

When he glanced up, Abbie was holding what looked like a bundle of washing in her arms. As she lowered it towards him, he saw a doll's face in the middle of the bundle, the face of a doll, except the skin was too fleshy, and the eyes too alive, and the lips too wet, and the murmur it made as she ran her finger across its eyebrows and cheeks was altogether too real.

Bewildered, Felix waited for the explanation.

'I don't get it,' he said eventually.

'This is Gabriel.'

'Gabriel?'

'Gabriel.'

'And who is he?'

'He's ours.'

'What do you mean?'

'This is our baby.'

'We haven't got a baby, Abbie.'

'A gift.'

'A what?'

'A gift.'

'A gift from who?'

'From Eliza and her mum. And from my dad.'

'Abbie, what are you talking about?'

She was thoughtful. Then she spoke to Felix but never took her eyes from the child. 'He's my baby. To keep. Now, I'm going upstairs to give him a bath and make up a cot, and when I come down I want this house warm and tidy, and I want the Christmas tree in the corner instead of your golf clubs, and I want all the lights working and the angel on top.' She said all that very calmly. Then she said, 'And not another word.'

Lots of objects had been deposited in the porch. A baby chair. Various mats and covers. A car seat. A buggy. A carrier bag full of bottles and teats. And a smell he didn't recognize. A smell that didn't belong to him. Pulling the plastic tree out of the garden shed, Felix looked up at the bathroom, and listened to the crying and splashing coming from the open window.

Gabriel?

He plugged the Christmas lights into the socket in the kitchen. They didn't come on. He trailed them on to the patio, sat down on the step and, one at a time, began meddling with the bulbs, twisting and tweaking them as hard as he dared without crushing the glass in his fingers. Thrown from the bedroom window above him, Abbie's shadow was suddenly thick and black on the concrete slabs and the square of lawn, until the curtains were pulled. Then it started to snow. It was cold and dark and snowing, and Felix was outside, trying to get a string of dead stars to come alive in his hands.